EVERY TIME
WITH A
HIGHLANDER

GWYN
CREADY

sourcebooks
casablanca

Published by Sourcebooks Casablanca, an imprint of Sourcebooks,
Inc.
P.O. Box 4410, Naperville, Illinois 60567-4410
(630) 961-3900
Fax: (630) 961-2168
www.sourcebooks.com

Printed and bound in Canada.
MBP 10 9 8 7 6 5 4 3 2 1

For Carol Scott Cready and James W. Cready.
Thank you for three gifts I treasure deeply—
intelligence, curiosity, and humor.

One

Peering from the shade of the massive copper beech on the banks of the sparkling Tweed, Lord Bridgewater's feast set out on long, low tables under the shade of the nearby elms, Undine looked from guest to guest and lover to lover. She was, they said, a fortune-teller, and it was little challenge to read the thoughts on the faces of those she called her friends at the party—Abby Kerr, chieftess of Clan Kerr, and Abby's steward, Duncan MacHarg, standing at opposite ends of the makeshift quoits court, hiding their infatuation about as well as a peacock hides its plumage, and soon-to-be shipowner Serafina Innes and her new husband, Gerard, innocently playing whist, though any careful observer could tell by the gleam in their eyes the prize at stake was far from innocent.

Hidden truths and visible lies. The world would be a very dangerous place if one believed in appearance.

"Sherry, ma'am?" the servant asked.

"Thank you. I believe I'll stay with my ginger water."

A sleek, tortoiseshell cat stole her way back into the party after being shooed away not once but twice by one of the estate's fastidious servants. The cat added to her list of crimes by neatly snagging a half-eaten quail from the plate of Bishop Rothwell, the archbishop's chief catch fart, who was speaking animatedly—and at yawn-inducing length—to those seated on the lawn near him of the plans to replace the draperies at his estate.

The brazen thief made her way, quail in mouth, under several tables to the copper beech, where she gave Undine an impatient look.

"I'm not moving," Undine said firmly.

The cat stared, undeterred.

"Is there no other place to feast upon that?"

The answer, it appeared, was no. The cat placed the carcass on the ground, and Undine shifted a few inches on the blanket to give the creature room to enjoy her prize.

Rothwell's injured gasp cut through the buzz of the crowd. Stripped plate in hand, he looked left and right. The servant, instantly gleaning the nature of the transgression, wheeled around, scanning the grounds with murder in his eyes.

Undine obscured the transgressor with a lift of her knee.

"You will put my poor servant in his grave," said Colonel Lord Bridgewater, sinking onto the blanket opposite Undine. Without looking, she felt the collective stiffening of her friends, and she sent them an unspoken wave of reassurance.

Handsome, blond, cruel, and powerful, Bridgewater was the most feared man on either side of the border, though the soldiers in the English army grudgingly admired his political and battlefield skills as much as they chafed under his stringent command. This was his parkland, his party, and his house, leased only, as his ancestral home was ensconced in a far more civilized part of England, not straddling the bloody divide between the country he loved and the one he would drive to its knees unless someone stopped him.

That someone was Undine, and she, as it had come to pass, was his fiancée.

"Who's this?" he asked, eyeing the cat, who continued her noisy evisceration of the quail.

"An admirer of your cook's talents, it seems." Undine looked across the patchwork fields of green and gold and the scattering of buildings in the small town across the Tweed to the east. Over the town rose the ruins of the ancient priory gate, which once held the severed heads of traitors to England. The land did not make distinctions between countries. The river curled and stretched its way through both places, favoring neither one nor the other. If nature didn't, why did men have to? It brought them such misery.

"John, do you think it odd that, without conscious thought, I situate myself facing the Scottish hills and you the English vale?"

He chuckled, and the sound had only the tiniest edge to it. "I don't think our differences over this war will be a barrier to our happiness. 'Tis why I took this house, you know—for you. To demonstrate compromise is possible."

The potion he'd swallowed, created by Undine for another pair of lovers, bound the heart of the swallower to the first person he saw for whom his regard had already begun to warm. But someone had stolen the potion from her, and it had fallen into Bridgewater's contriving hands. Driven as always by a reckless and unrelenting sense of entitlement, he'd drunk it thinking it was an aid to carnality. That part hadn't surprised her. But what had surprised her was that the person with whom he had fallen in love was her. She'd been shocked by the revelation he had feelings for her. He was a man of many repulsive appetites who used his power to take what he wanted. He had once beaten Undine nearly to death for the secrets she held, and he'd blackmailed Abby and attempted to rape Serafina, among many other crimes. Undine had no sympathy for the involuntary transformation he'd undergone. A man who took a potion—especially one of Undine's potions—not knowing what it was got exactly what he deserved. And though the potion had been strong enough to render him almost docile, she knew its power would eventually weaken and the true Bridgewater would reemerge. When it did, he would unleash his fury on her and anyone else he thought was responsible for his humiliating transformation to a mere thrall to a woman working to defeat him.

If she were wise, she would run. But while she would ensure her friends stayed beyond his reach, she was too dedicated a spy to pass up the opportunity afforded by agreeing to his offer of marriage, no matter how close to harm it may bring her.

She gave him a smile. "And that's what you're doing? Demonstrating compromise?"

"It is. 'Tis the only house I know which is half in England and half in Scotland. I know the mission of the English army seems unkind to you, but I believe in my heart that uniting Scotland and England is the best way to bring the Scots security and peace. 'Tis something I truly hope for. In that, at least, I think we are the same."

He stroked her arm, and in his touch, Undine could still feel the cold steel of command.

"Besides," he added with a wolfish smile, "I've dedicated myself to winning you over. I've won your hand. Now I wish to win the rest of you. And the day you forget the border there," he said, tilting his head toward the river, "is the day the border between us will fall as well."

"You're a cunning strategist."

"You're a prize worth winning."

He took her hand in his, and her skin prickled into gooseflesh. She reminded herself that the real prize was gaining access to the secret plans of the army, plans the rebels she worked with might use to forestall Scotland's forced marriage to England, plans that might, at this very moment, be sitting on Bridgewater's desk. The trick was to keep Bridgewater simmering without boiling over long enough to find out what she needed to know. There wasn't an inch of room for error. Spies discovered in flagrante delicto, even those affianced to British officers, would find their heads mounted on the priory gate for all to see.

"Are you chilled?" He smoothed her flesh with his carefully groomed thumb.

"Aye, a bit," she said and adjusted the wrap over her shoulders.

"I have a proposal for you. Do you see that part of my house?"

The "house," an enormous demi-castle built by Henry VIII as a hunting lodge, gray and implacable, stretched halfway across the lawn, piercing the sky with a very un-lodge-like crenellated tower. Henry, it seemed, had few friends here in Northumberland. Bridgewater pointed to the delicate, redbrick wing added two centuries later, grafted to the side like a rose on an oak.

"Aye," she said.

"I want you to move in there." He held up his hands to stop her protest. "Bring your friends. I have no intention of locking you up or encroaching on your privacy. I only wish to have you nearby and share more in your daily habits. In a few months, when you find yourself more acclimated to the idea of marrying, we'll have established a deep and abiding friendship."

Even knowing how powerful the potion had been—and she had ground every last bit of the lovage and lady's bedstraw herself—to hear such a plaintive lover's wish come from the lips of John Bridgewater and be directed at *her* was astonishing. She'd always taken care to remind those who came to her for herbs or a glimpse of their futures that the outcome could be startling. However, it was one thing to say it and another to experience it so vividly.

She shifted. His offer was a prize beyond compare. As a guest in his house, she would have access to the most intimate reaches of Bridgewater's life. And yet the risk…

"You're thinking about it," he said, blue eyes shining. "I can tell by the look on your face."

"I am inclined to say aye."

He brought her wrist to his lips and kissed it. "You've pleased me more than you can know."

The afternoon sun caught the silver tip of the priory gate and shone in her eyes as if to remind her what she risked. She held up a hand to block the ray. "And you me."

Abby and Duncan were drawing toward them, and she straightened.

"Go tell your friends," Bridgewater said, smiling. "Let them rejoice in our happiness."

I doubt joy will be their reaction.

Undine made her way down the rise, debating how she'd break the news. Her last vision of Bridgewater before the beech's trunk obscured him was of him booting the cat away and tossing the poor creature's dinner in the Tweed.

Two

"ARE YOU OUT OF YOUR *MIND*?" ABBY STARED AT Undine, aghast. "Move in *there*? With *him*? 'Tis dangerous enough to be within pistol-shot distance of the man, let alone living with the wee fiend."

Undine put a finger to her lips to remind them of the party going on around them and led the group to the shelter of a hedgerow of firethorn and honeysuckle.

"'Tis only till I find the proof I've been looking for," Undine said.

"Proof?" Serafina's eyes narrowed. She knew what Bridgewater was capable of as well as any of them.

"Someone is planning an attack in Scotland. We've heard rumblings for weeks. Yet none of my sources in the army can confirm it. I think Bridgewater knows something, and to be honest, I wonder if the bishop is involved as well, but I need proof. When I get it, I'll disappear into the Cheviot Hills faster than a hare."

Duncan gave her a hard look. "You ken that's impossible. For the information to be useful, Bridgewater will have to be confident no one's discovered it, and if ye leave, he'll know the truth. You'll have to stay here, as his fiancée, until the attack has been foiled—and even after that because if that blackguard thinks ye had anything to do with the information being acted upon…"

The memory of the acts Bridgewater had demonstrated himself capable of settled over the group.

"I'll join you," Abby said. "You'll need a chaperone. I can—"

"*No*," Undine said flatly. "There's little danger. And in any case," she said, adding to the lie, "Bridgewater would never allow it."

"*Little danger?*" As chieftess, Abby was used to having her suggestions obeyed, and her words grew sharper. "Lie to us if you wish, but assure me you're not lying to yourself. The man blackmailed me and nearly forced himself on Serafina. His scurrilousness knows no bounds."

"I know he's a danger," Undine admitted, fingering the honeysuckle to avoid meeting her friend's eyes. "But I'll be cautious. You needn't worry."

Serafina, ever the peacemaker, said, "We know how powerful Undine's spells are. I'm certain she has nothing to fear."

"How long will the spell last?" Abby said.

"I don't know," Undine said. "The couple has usually fallen in love by the time the spell wears off, so I never noticed."

"Are we certain that won't happen?" Abby asked.

Gerard bit back a laugh. "I mean, the man *is* quite handsome, right, Undine? What's a rape attempt or two between friends?"

Serafina elbowed her new husband and looked at her shoes.

Duncan, who had once run an office of fifty clerks perennially in crisis, stepped forward. Though he didn't exercise it often, he had a presence that commanded a room. The group fell silent. "What happens if it does wear off? Bridgewater will know he was drugged."

"The man stole the potion and drank it willingly," Undine said. "I accept no blame in that."

"That's not what I mean," Duncan said. "He'll ken well enough you wouldn't accept an offer of marriage from him because ye love him. He'll know you took advantage of his drugged state to spy on him."

Something pricked Undine's finger and she jerked. She'd mistaken a branch of firethorn for its fragrant neighbor, and a tiny globe of crimson appeared on her flesh. "Then I'd better be done and away before that happens."

Three

MICHAEL KENT RUBBED HIS EYES, SIGHED, AND OPENED them again. No luck. Eve, the stage manager, was still clutching her headset, her eye twitching in time to the iambic pentameter being reeled off on the other side of the National Rose's back curtain.

"Are you kidding me?" he asked. The last act of the last matinee of the last play he would ever have to direct, and one of his idiot actors had left the theater to register for a kickball league? "Where's Jasper? Can't he step in?"

"He's already subbing for Stuart. Pink eye."

"Jesus Christ. It's like a bloody fucking preschool in here."

"Language, Michael. *Really*."

Lady Velopar, ancient patroness of the National Rose Theater and Michael's own personal guide through the circles of fund-raising hell, had appeared in a puff of Harvey Nichols perfume, along with her equally irritating companion, Lady Louise Balmaine.

"I beg your pardon, your ladyship." He bowed.

"I was hoping you'd take Louise on a tour," she

said. "You know how people love those little insights of yours."

"I would adore it. However—and I do hesitate even to mention it—you may have noticed we're in the midst of a performance…" He tilted his head politely toward the booming voices beyond the curtain.

Lady Louise clapped her hands. "Oh, how delightful! Is it *Lion King*?"

"Shakespeare," Michael said.

"A shame," the noblewoman said, her spirit pierced but not conquered. "I do like the spectacle."

"I'd be honored to take you around," Michael said, "but as we're in the midst of a performance as well as a small technical crisis, if you would be so good as to take a seat in the backstage lounge…" He forced a smile.

"What's on?" Lady Velopar asked, peering around the curtains with interest.

"*Romeo and Juliet*—your request, I believe." Before she'd fallen pregnant by the heir to the Velopar Biscuit fortune, Constance Velopar had been an actress. Bonny Connie Bells, the Fort William Firecracker. He'd heard she'd played Beatrice to John Barrymore's Benedick—or had it been John Wilkes Booth's?

"Ah, Juliet, our fair, doomed Capulet." Lady Velopar drew herself to full thespian readiness as if turning over an Austin 10 that hadn't been started since before the war. "'Come, vial,'" she said, sweeping her arm through the air. "'What if this mixture do not work at all?'" After a pause so long that Michael worried she'd suffered a stroke, Lady Velopar shook off her dramatic fugue and clapped her gloves into her palm. "An unhappy ending all around, this one is."

"Actually," Michael said, "if I can't find someone to play Friar Laurence and give Juliet the poison, we may have the first *Romeo and Juliet* that ends with a happily married couple on our hands."

As if on cue, the actress playing Juliet flounced off the stage and came to a stop in front of Michael. "'Thus from my lips, by yours, my sin is purged,'" she said in a fair imitation of her leading man. "Yeah, well, tell that jackass if I have to purge the taste of bloody lamb vindaloo from my lips one more time, I'm going to bite off his leathery old tongue." She swiped at her mouth and added, "Isn't Romeo supposed to be *under* forty?"

"His Oscar is the reason we're packing them in like cordwood, you know," Michael said politely as she stomped off. "Best Ingenue, York Regional Theatre, doesn't draw like you'd think it might."

"Friar Laurence," Eve reminded him forcefully.

Michael sighed.

"Is there liquor in the lounge?" Lady Velopar asked.

"God, I hope so."

"We'll wait for you there then." The women floated off like mist on the Thames.

"Joy." He turned to Eve. "Any chance *you* know the lines?"

"I know all the lines," she said, then lowered her voice to a whisper and pointed beyond the curtain. "I just can't say them in front of *the audience*."

A stage manager with stage fright. Perfect. "How bad is it?"

"Random jabbering followed by hyperventilation, dry heaving, and tears."

"Wow. And you're sure you're not an actress?" He patted her shoulder. "Don't worry. We shan't throw you to the wolves. You're the only sane one left." He was glad he'd recommended her for the role of managing director. She was a dependable island of calm in an ever-stormy sea. His only regret was he wouldn't be there to see her surprise when she heard the news.

"Mr. Kent, I don't want to rush you, but we have"—she held up a finger to hear the lines onstage—"exactly two minutes and fifteen seconds before Friar Laurence makes his entrance." She looked at the ball of burlap in her arms, then back at him with a hopeful smile.

Oh Christ.

"You *were* an actor," she said.

He took the priest's habit and unfurled it. "A thousand years ago."

"You played Romeo. You won an Olivier for it."

"I played Mercutio too. And Benvolio," he said. "And the nurse once in sixth form. But that was all before I realized I hated acting and actors, and became a director so I could kick their bloody arses."

"*Michael*," snarled his Juliet, who'd returned even angrier. "There are two old harridans in my dressing room drinking the last of my gin. You *know* how I look forward to my gin."

"Take Stuart's dressing room," he said, tearing his shirt buttons loose and kicking off his loafers. "And one of those old harridans pays your salary. So button your lip and drown yourself in cheap whiskey like the rest of us."

She stormed off.

"Do you know the lines?" Eve asked.

"Of course I bloody know the lines." He threw the shirt under the soundboard and pulled off his socks. "I could do the thing in my sleep—if I ever sleep again."

He slipped the friar's habit over his head, and she handed him the sandals and cincture.

"I can't believe you're retiring," she said. "You've been such a savior to the Rose. Bankrupt, down at the heels, no artistic point of view—until you stepped in and lifted her from the gutter."

"And it only took twelve years and fifty-odd pints of blood." He took the stage beard from her hands, fumbled with it a minute, realized he wouldn't have time to put it on properly, and shoved it in the pocket of his cassock.

"Don't joke. You did so much."

"Yes. From artistic director and fund-raiser to nanny, tour guide, and supporting player. My trajectory has been meteoric—if you think of a meteor on its way to crash into the earth. If I stay any longer, I'll be cleaning the loo."

"People love you. The queen called you a national treasure."

A national treasure but no knighthood. Apparently, they're saving those for telecommunication billionaires. "One always loves the people who'll work for glory. Cheaper than a pension."

He rolled up his pant legs and slipped his feet in the sandals, which were two sizes too small and cut into his instep like a garrote.

Get on with it, Michael. In another week, you'll be sitting in a pub in Barcelona, sipping Sangria and reading David Copperfield.

"Michael? Yoo-hoo?" Lady Velopar's call cut through the afternoon like a dagger. "There's no tonic."

"Tonic," Eve said, handing him the bottle of stage potion. "I'm on it."

He was no longer surprised Genesius was the patron saint of actors, clowns, and torture victims. He only wished the man were the patron saint of spontaneous human combustion as well. What he wouldn't give to be lifted bodily from the place and spit out somewhere he'd never see an actor or patroness or corporate sponsor again.

"Why oh why," he said, looking at the bottle, "can't this be real poison?"

Four

UNDINE WOULD RELINQUISH NEITHER THE SMALL satchel of clothes nor the much larger case of herbs, already propped open on the chest of drawers, to the young, doe-eyed lady's maid assigned her.

"I shall manage on my own," Undine said, observing the ornate bedchamber without much enthusiasm. "Pray, don't trouble yourself."

"'Tis no trouble, Lady Bridgewa—Miss Bridgewater—I mean, milady. Oh dear, I'm afraid I don't know what to call you." A bright pink crossed her cheeks. The girl shifted the linens in her arms and looked as if she may cry.

"Any of your choices is fine," Undine said, "though I'm not Lady Bridgewater yet. Could you call me Undine, do you think?"

The girl stiffened. "I should be whipped for it, milady."

"By whom?" Undine inquired casually, gazing at her case. A fortnight of flux ought to break the spirit of even the most hardened villain.

"Mrs. Janus. She's the housekeeper."

"We shan't upset Mrs. Janus then. You may call me Mistress Douglas."

The girl's jaw fell. "You *have* a surname?"

Undine laughed. Witches, she supposed, were born without fathers. Naiads, unfortunately, weren't. "I do, though few have ever heard it. But I shouldn't like to see you get in trouble."

The girl bobbed her head. "Thank you, ma—er, Mistress Douglas."

Undine smiled. "And you? Might I be honored with the gift of *your* name?"

The girl's color rose higher. "Ardith." She curtsied. "Very pleased to make your acquaintance."

"Well, Ardith, I shall require a great deal of privacy. The bed may be made and the fire drawn, but you are not to touch or move any of my things. There are herbs in that case that will scale your skin and turn your eyes a bright shade of orange."

The girl took a step back. "In truth?"

"Ardith, we're going to have to work on your credulity, aye? I need you to be sharp-eyed and skeptical. 'Tis the only way to make your way in this world."

"Aye, ma'am."

"How long have you been part of the lodge's household?" she asked lightly, hoping Ardith was familiar with Bridgewater's habits.

"Not long. A few weeks. His lordship wishes to know if you'd like him to bring in a dressmaker?"

"Does his lordship not care for my taste?" Undine peered at the simple but exceedingly flattering silk gown that shimmered blue and chartreuse in the candle's glow. The snug bodice required no boning, the elbow sleeves permitted ease of movement, and a half-dozen hidden pockets meant she was never far from the tools of her trade.

"I think he thought only of the size of your satchel." She added in a small voice, "And he is quite in love with you. I believe he longs to give you whatever you will accept from him."

Undine sighed. "I am in need of a sturdy pair of boots."

"I'll let him know."

The door opened without a knock. "Undine," Bridgewater said, "may I have a word?"

Oh, this will become tiresome quickly. "Of course. Enter."

Bridgewater's gaze cut to Ardith and flicked her away as if she were a trifling bug. She put down the linens and ran.

"How happy I am to see you settled here," he said.

Undine ducked a curtsy in agreement.

"Is the girl to your liking?" he asked. "The housekeeper has some questions."

"She'll do nicely. Thank you."

"Good. Very good." He glanced briefly over his shoulder at the hall, and Undine had an uncomfortable sense Ardith should have stayed. "The bishop has surprised me," he said. "I'm expecting a man from my solicitor's office tomorrow from London to work out some matters regarding my estate and will. 'Tis a long distance, aye, but the matters are important. There'll be additional papers for them to draw up after we marry, which will entail another journey."

Undine felt an odd tingle up her spine. "Oh? And how has the bishop surprised you?"

"He's offered to forgo the banns and marry us tonight."

Undine swallowed her shock. "*Tonight?*"

"'Tis only for the paperwork, my dear. Nothing will change between us till you're ready. The bishop's offer is kind, and I need his support—*we* need his support—if we are to bring this eternal fighting to an end. In any case," he added with a gentle smile, "if anything were to happen to me, I'd want you to have the protection and benefit of my name."

She looked in the sharp blue of those eyes. *Does he even remember the beating he gave me?*

"No," she said firmly. "I can't marry at a moment's notice. I've barely unpacked my things here. Give me a few weeks. Please."

"The bishop is near to insisting. 'Twill make no difference in our lives." He took her hand in his and the blue turned as deep as a loch's. "You swore your troth to me, even if you said you needed time. You have not made me so happy only to break my heart, have you? Your affection was real, was it not? Not false or…or…" His gaze caught the case of herbs, and he hesitated.

"No, of course not," she said firmly. "My heart is unchanged. Of that you can be certain. I just… Tonight?" She blew out a puff of air and gave him a weak smile.

"Aye, my love, tonight."

The joy in his eyes was unsettling. "But my friends…"

"We shall throw a real party when you're ready and do it all again. Your friends will be here then, I promise. No one needs to know about tonight's vows unless you tell them. Except the bishop, of course, and my solicitor."

And the servants. And by tomorrow, the news will have reached every man, woman, and child between Carlisle and Edinburgh.

"I'll need a dress," she said. "Surely you don't want me to become Lady Bridgewater in this old thing."

"You look lovely in everything. But you needn't worry. I took the liberty of having a gown—several, actually—made for you. Have you not looked in your wardrobe?"

She shook her head. He crossed to the painted ebony piece and opened the door. The most spectacular gown of pale pink and seed pearls hung at the front. It would befit a queen on her coronation.

So why was the queen that emerged in her head Anne Boleyn?

"It makes me almost breathless," she said, sinking into the chair.

"Truly?"

"Oh, aye. Give me a few moments to marshal my reserves and I shall…join you."

"Marshal your reserves?" He laughed. "You make our wedding sound like an army tactic."

And I have been ambushed.

When he disappeared, still chuckling, she sunk into a chair and considered. She could run, she could marry, or she could delay. The risk of delay was elevating his suspicion. Through the cloud of the spell he had, for an instant, considered the relevance of her herbs to his love. She had pushed him from the edge of realization with a quick affirmation of her affection, but she might not be around when the next moment of clarity descended.

The risk of running was discovery. If a slight hesitation was enough to arouse suspicion, her disappearance would end the game. On one hand, she'd be safe, though Bridgewater would pursue her to the four corners of the earth to exact his revenge. On the other, she'd know no more of England's plans than she did now.

She forbore to consider the risk of marrying. Having to submit to the will of any man, let alone that ruthless prick… She might as well be hung.

Undine unfolded herself and stood before her jars and pots—wormwood, yarrow, elf's wort, ashweed. What had the versatility? The immediacy? The impact? She rubbed her neck to soothe her jangling nerves. She needed something to happen right now that would convince Bridgewater to put off the wedding. But she'd seen the way he ran the lives of the people around him. It would take an act of God to—

An act of God?

She straightened as the realization washed over her. *That's exactly what I need.*

Five

MICHAEL HURRIED TOWARD THE STAGE, BUMPING INTO his Romeo in the wings.

"Hang on, mate," Michael said, catching him by the arm. "The tongue thing—it's against Equity rules, not to mention vulgar and abusive. Knock it off, or I'm filing a complaint with the union. Got it?"

The idiot looked as if someone had jerked his lolly away. *Buck up, my friend. A little tough love will do you well.*

Juliet hit the "Go, Counselor" moment, insisting on her right to die rather than being married off to Paris. The lights went down, and Michael stepped onto the boards for the first time in fifteen years.

He had forgotten the thrum of the darkness, like a charge in the air, in those seconds before the lights rose, the shifting of a thousand bodies as they strained for the next sound. It was different in the wings, in the cyclone of cues and props and gin and whispers. The magic played like fireworks on a thirteen-inch TV there. But here…

"The potion," a woman's voice whispered, stage left. "Is it strong enough?"

It wasn't Juliet. Was it Eve? It didn't sound like Eve either, but it had to be.

"What do you mean strong enough?" he said under his breath. He pulled the vial from his pocket. Was she standing near him? His eyes hadn't adjusted to the dark, and it was like trying to pull a void into focus.

"I don't know how to judge," she said, desperate. "Not for this. And it must work."

"Do you need me to check it?" It should be water. Had yet another screwup happened? Would Juliet be downing the infamous gin or something worse? They had seconds left. Eve, if that's who the voice belonged to, needed to get off the stage.

"Hurry," the voice said urgently. "I need to be sure."

He extracted the cork with a huff and lifted to the bottle to his lips.

Someone's getting their bloody arse kicked tonight.

Six

THE BLINDING LIGHTS WERE ON, HE THOUGHT, BLINKING, but he was no longer sure how long he'd been onstage. Seconds? The set had changed—he'd have to speak to Eve, though he felt rather woozy, as if he'd left her a few hours ago and been drinking ever since. What was the stained glass doing in the back? Who'd authorized such an expense?

Someone cleared his throat, and Michael wheeled around, searching for his line.

But it wasn't Paris nor Romeo nor even Juliet or Eve. It was an actor in a tawny frock coat with a waterfall of lace at his neck—he must speak to the costume manager as well—and the theater was empty.

Well, another theater perhaps, not the National Rose. One with hand-carved pews and an enormous painting of Henry VIII beyond its door.

The spiking adrenaline of missed cues and forgotten lines had nothing on finding oneself sucked out of a play into an unknown room with an unknown man. Sweat began to form on Michael's back, and his mouth moved in an incoherent attempt to speak.

"I beg your pardon," the man said, mildly incensed. "I asked you where Bishop Rothwell went."

"I told you, John," said a woman Michael hadn't noticed. "He was called away."

She stood apart from the man, arms crossed, in a gown of ethereal pink. Her words had been accompanied by a laser look at Michael that would have reduced the Greenland ice cap to a large cup of steaming tea.

Why were these people dressed for Shakespeare—or Congreve, really—yet nothing from their mouths rung of any play he'd ever seen? His gut began to tighten.

"Called away?" the man she'd called John said. "For what?"

"An emergency in the bishopric." The "-pric" lingered on the woman's tongue a second longer than necessary, though this time the look that accompanied it was for her companion.

She was beautiful—stunning, really—with hair like wet gold and eyes that shone an emerald green, but everything about her carriage and voice carried the expectation of being obeyed. In the instant Michael could spare to process the players rather than his own uncertain circumstances, he could see John might be an overbearing prig but the woman was flat-out trouble.

"And this…cleric?" John looked at Michael's habit with poorly concealed distaste.

"The bishop's colleague," she said. "An ascetic, it seems."

The two clearly weren't actors—though they were nearly as irritating—and this wasn't a set. Somehow, between stepping onstage and the lights going up, Michael had lost the National Rose. What had happened? The closest he'd ever gotten to feeling what he felt now was playing Jack in *The Importance of Being Earnest*, when the actor playing Algernon jumped twenty-seven pages ahead, leaving Michael thrust unexpectedly into Act Three's happy engagement to Gwendolen with all the play's loose ends resolved, hoping in earnest for the curtain. At least Michael had known what theater he'd been in then—and what play.

"Is he capable of marrying us?" John asked, dubious.

"I should think so," she said. "It's woven into the burlap."

In a remote place in his head, at a distance from the panic that had seized control of his cerebellum, the amusement in her words cut him. He may not be the most rehearsed Friar Laurence who ever walked the stage, but that was certainly no reason to impugn the character's inner nobility.

"Then let him do it." John's exasperation was growing. "You're still willing, aren't you, my love? Even without a proper bishop?"

"Most willing." She smiled sweetly, but Michael saw the falsehood even if her fiancé did not. "Are we not in need of witnesses, though?" she added.

John growled. "They were behind me a moment ago. Let me find them. I'll be but a moment." He strode out.

Perhaps this was a dream—a dream conflating all the Shakespeare and Farquhar and Marlowe that Michael had ever done—with a generous helping of

Wicked thrown in for good measure. Then it came to him. *The potion*.

He willed his fingers open and looked at his quaking palm.

A hand snatched the empty bottle away.

"*Wake up*," the woman said in a razor-sharp whisper, and *now* he realized the voice he'd heard had been hers. "Listen carefully. I called you here for one reason. Keep that blackguard from marrying me or I shall shrivel your man parts like dates in the Barbary sun." She stashed the bottle in her bodice and turned, smiling, to greet her fiancé as he returned with two footmen straight out of Molière.

Michael felt as if a blast furnace had scorched him from brows to sandals. He also felt his indignation grow. *No one* threatened Michael's man parts, certainly not in a theater—even if this wasn't exactly a theater or a play...or even a space he remotely recognized.

"Are you ready?" John said.

Michael held up a finger. "Actually, I'm not."

He felt rather than heard the woman's exhale of relief.

"Your fiancée was just telling me how truly eager she is to begin life as your wife," Michael said. "However, she has made me aware of a few, well, shall we say blemishes upon her conscience, and I know she wishes to unburden herself before the happy marriage is consummated."

John blinked. "Undine...my fiancée...wishes to *confess*?"

Undine, was it? Like the water fairy in Giraudoux's play? More like Ursula in *The Little Mermaid*.

"I most certainly do not," she said, eyes flashing.

"No?" Michael shrugged. "Well then, let us proceed apace with the ceremony. Good sir, do you have the Book of Common Prayer?"

"Wait," Undine said.

Michael turned, triumphant. "Aye?"

"I might have something to confess after all," she said with an iron glare.

"Ahh," Michael said, hand over his heart, "the heart wishes to forget, but the soul demands its redemption. Aye, let us retreat to a private place, where you can unburden yourself of everything—*everything*—that I and the Lord need to know."

Seven

"Where *am* I, and what the hell am I doing here?"

Undine stood arrow straight against the closed door, hands behind her on the knob, unmoved by his demand. "Keep your voice down," she said in a heated whisper.

"Keep my voice down?! I'm trying to keep my lunch down."

"He's just outside the door."

"Good, because if you try anything else, I'll want help. What *is* this? Where am I?"

She sighed. "You're in the home of Colonel Lord Bridgewater."

"Colonel Lord Bridgewater?" For an instant, a potential explanation appeared in his head. "So this is a costume party?"

"A masque?" She chuckled. "No, but the metaphor is apt. No one here is who they truly seem."

"Do you mind telling me what I'm doing here?"

"I've told you," she said. "You are here to prevent him from marrying me."

"Have you considered just saying no?"

"Aye," she said archly. "I have."

The woman was infuriating. "*And?*"

She shifted. "This is what needs to be done."

"Oh, well, if this is what needs to be done, then by all means, make use of me however you see fit. Your wish is my command."

"Sarcasm is not an attractive quality in a priest."

"How's anger?"

"You have nothing to be angry about," she said. "You'll perform your duty to me, which is to say *not* performing your duty at the altar, and you shall be returned unscathed."

"I have already been 'scathed,' madam. What was in the potion?"

"'Tis of no concern to you, and I warn you not to repeat the word."

"You're quite the taskmaster. I think I like my odds with the cravat guy better." He reached past her for the knob.

She jerked backward, trapping his hand against a captivating bottom.

They stood eye to eye. "I suggest," she said, unblinking, "you move that."

He considered several responses—verbal and isometric—before tugging his arm free. He adjusted the burlap of his sleeve. "You do realize, I hope, I am entirely capable of moving you from the door."

"The Barbary sun is a hot one."

A knock sounded, and she started. If it was Bridgewater, she didn't just dislike the man. She was afraid of him.

"Undine," a voice called. It was Bridgewater.

She looked at Michael, and neither replied.

"How long does he think a confession takes?" Michael said under his breath. "Sixty seconds?"

"I'm sure the only times he's confessed, it's been a lie."

"Undine?" Bridgewater repeated. "Are you there? Undine?"

"Jesus," Michael said, "*what* is his problem?"

Undine rolled her eyes. "Love."

"Undine." The knob rattled harder. "*Answer me.*"

"Oh, for Christ's sake." Michael lifted her by the waist and placed her to the side. Then he opened the door, blocking Bridgewater's entry with his body. "The walls of the confessional may not be breached, sir," he said hotly. "What do you want?"

Bridgewater looked as if he'd been slapped. Michael wished the man felt as if he'd been slapped as well.

"I beg your pardon." Splotches of indignation appeared above his lordship's cravat.

"'Tis not my pardon you must beg but the Lord's! We are deep in the work of unblackening her soul. Pray give us the time we require." Michael shut the door with a *bang*.

"Well done," she said when the footsteps faded. "Though 'unblackening' was a bit much."

"Says the woman threatening Barbary dehydration. I could have invited him in."

"There's no need to be rude."

"*Rude?* You think *I'm* being rude? I have no idea where I am or why I'm here."

"Are you a bit slow?" she said. "We've covered this ground before."

"Yes, I know I'm somehow supposed to keep you from your fiancé, though why, I have no idea. And I know you drugged me with the"—she gave him a piercing look—"liquid. But I don't know why you picked me for this or where we are or—most important—why I should put up with any of it."

"Father, this will no doubt violate every belief you have about the world, but I offer no apology for upending those narrow-minded views. I am a naiad—to the simpleminded, a witch—though if you repeat that to anyone, you'll regret it."

Michael needed to sit, but his legs wouldn't bend. His only experience with witches was with the perennially overacted ones in *Macbeth* and the hay fever–suffering Corelza in *Trevor Quince, Boy Wizard*, the movie franchise which had funded his early retirement. None of them looked like a Greek fury crossed with Grace Kelly.

He rubbed his forehead. "A *witch*?"

"Naiad, if you please. And you are in 1706."

He felt as if he were standing on a spinning carousel with no pole to cling to. The world spun with stomach-churning speed, and no matter how he turned, he couldn't find a way to get his feet under him. *1706?* 1706 was Congreve and Queen Anne, garters and frock coats—

Oh God, I am in 1706.

He looked at the burnished desk and gilded wallpaper and rococo plasterwork. The house meant nothing. There were homes that could pass for 1706 all over England. But not that gown. And not her in that gown. If twenty-five years in the theater had taught him anything, it was that, no matter how accomplished a costume designer was, it was impossible to fully capture the look of clothes from another period. The fabric was different, the thread was different, the trim was different, even the way seamstresses held needles was different. All of it added up to a costume that might be award winning but would never be mistaken for a real gown of the time.

He looked at Undine in that resplendent silk—the intricate pleats, the tiny pearls, the understated color—nothing like the oversaturated synthetic dyes used today.

Not today. Today—the "today" he woke up in—was three hundred and some years from the year in which he found himself now.

And even more than the gown was Undine herself. No one in any land would ever mistake that smoldering-eyed, alabaster-skinned, unyielding seraph for a woman of the twenty-first century. Was she even a woman of this earth?

"Then this is London…in 1706?"

"Coldstream," she corrected. "In a lodge house by the Tweed that straddles the bloody border."

Coldstream, Scotland? Home of black-faced sheep and palace guards? His eyes went to the horizon beyond the windows, where a band of azure water snaked through the patchwork fields. He'd gone from the National Rose in London to the borderlands in the blink of an eye. His father would have called it a step in the right direction.

"Where's your parish, Father?"

Still reeling, he gazed at her blankly. Then it dawned on him. The woman, the naiad—Good Lord, was he really saying that?—actually believed he *was* a priest. She'd brought him here with the potion but apparently didn't know the specifics of the time or place he'd come from—or really anything about him if she thought he was a priest. Had she simply tossed a line into the sea of time and reeled in whatever bit? Not the most flattering way to snare an acting gig.

"Father?"

"Oh, yes, er…Bankside. My parish is in Bankside." Well, the National Rose was, and that was about as close to a parish as he was going to get.

She screwed up her face. "'Tis rather a tawdry place, isn't it? Full of cutpurses and actors, isn't it?"

"You get used to the cutpurses."

"Well, you needn't worry about your bishop. I promise you, he'll be fine."

"You have a pretty high regard for clerics, madam, if you think we spend much time worrying about our bishops."

A curve rose at the corner of her mouth. "I'm heartened to see you becoming acclimated to your circumstances. Shall I explain what you need to do for me in order to earn your return to Bankside?"

He brushed his palms as if removing the detritus of his situation. "No."

She cocked her head. "No?"

"No. I have no interest in serving as your unwitting slave. If you'd like my help, you may convince me to do it, as a reasonable person might."

"I'm not sure what you mean."

"Two words: beg me! Otherwise, you can—and I hope you'll excuse my language—pound salt."

Her mouth fell open. "Have you forgotten the Barbary sun?"

"You threatened me at the door a moment ago. I picked you up." He made a magician's flourish in the area of his midsection. "Balls still here." There were a few things he'd learned playing Orlando Brashnettle, senior wizard, in the *Trevor Quince* movies, and a convincing flourish was one of them.

Her eyes narrowed into gamma-ray slits.

He began to sway his hips, humming and doing a hula as he turned in a circle. "Not a care in the world. Like a pair of monkeys swinging through the jungle."

"Father."

"I can't hear you…"

"*Father.*"

He wheeled around.

Bridgewater was standing in the open doorway, lips white with anger. "I see the confession is over. Perhaps we can adjourn to the chapel now."

Eight

TWO WORDS, WAS IT? UNDINE SNORTED. SHE COULD think of two particularly Anglo-Saxon words she could offer him.

She could hear the *swish* of the priest's habit behind her as they walked. She kept her gaze forward, on Bridgewater's proud back, refusing to dignify the smugness in the priest's eyes. She considered herself nearly fearless—she'd faced the wrath of men who'd heard fortunes that did not sit well with their egos, and the risk of death when gathering intelligence for the rebels—but she'd face all of it ten times over rather than bear the utter horror of having Bridgewater think of her as his wife. Damn the man—damn both of them.

The priest had surprised her. Her experience of churchmen did not allow for a man of such…well, full-bloodedness. Those she'd known had either been prigs, as in the case of the bishop; vainglorious maneu-verers, as in the case of the archbishop; or kindhearted fools. Provocative dancing aside, there was something about the man himself that seemed unorthodox.

Perhaps it was the piercing blue eyes or the touches of gray at his temples or the finely cut profile. He carried himself like a man of the world, which was not what she'd expected when she'd conjured a cleric unlicensed to perform a ceremony.

"What on earth was going on in there?" Bridgewater said under his breath, having slowed enough to allow her to reach him.

She stole a glance at the priest, who, despite Bridgewater's best efforts at subterfuge—which, admittedly, had not been particularly good—had overheard the question and was giving her a smile.

"I believe he has a suppurating testicle," she said loudly. "Possibly two."

Bridgewater winced and looked back himself. "He *told* you that?"

"One hardly needs to be told. Just look at the man."

Bridgewater turned again, and on cue, the priest began to walk with a bowlegged gait worthy of one of the actors from his Bankside home.

Bridgewater shook his head. "He came with a message, did you say?"

"Aye. And when he gave it to the bishop, the bishop looked quite overcome."

In Bridgewater's eyes, a silent calculation took place. "Bad news, do you think?" he asked after a beat.

"He didn't say." Undine could now add the archbishop to the list of men Bridgewater was suspicious of, in league with, or both.

Bridgewater fell into a distracted silence. When they reached the doors of the chapel, he stopped. "Father…" He hesitated, hunting for a surname. "Er,

I beg your pardon. I do not believe I have been given the honor of your name."

"Father Kent." The cleric made an abbreviated bow.

"Father Kent, I believe I too would like a few moments to cleanse my soul."

Undine would've laughed had not the motivation behind Bridgewater's request been so transparent: he wanted to question the priest about the contents of the note he'd delivered to the bishop—a note that only existed in Undine's imagination—and he was willing to put off the wedding he'd been so eager for only a moment earlier to do it. She gave Kent a look in which she tried to convey a warning about the danger he'd be stepping into. She'd brought him here to help her, not to put the man in harm's way.

"John, I hardly think he is the man to hear you," she said. "I mean no insult to you, Father," she added with a small curtsy before turning back to Bridgewater. "You should wait for the return of the bishop, or even the archbishop. They would be the appropriate vessels for the confession of a nobleman, not this man."

Bridgewater cupped her hand and kissed it. "Do you think the man who heard the confession of my beloved fiancée would not be appropriate for me? The man is an ascetic, aye, but that doesn't mean he can't help my contrition reach God. 'Blessed are the poor, for theirs is the kingdom of Heaven,' aye?"

"John, he is not quite—"

"I will hear you, sir," Kent said flatly. "Let us adjourn to a quiet room to give you the privacy you need."

She looked at Kent. *Don't do it. You don't know what you're getting into.*

He blinked once, owl-like, acknowledging—and dismissing—her concern.

"Follow me," Bridgewater said to the man and strode down the twisting hall.

Kent bowed to her, a deep-kneed bend as graceful as Undine had ever seen, and followed his host. Just before he disappeared from view, Kent did a quick turn, hips undulating, and gave Undine a nod.

Nine

MICHAEL NOTICED BRIDGEWATER'S OFFICE HAD ONLY one chair, the overstuffed one that sat behind the desk. Bridgewater immediately took possession of it. The man had little interest in indulging those who came to him on business, it seemed. And if Michael had any hope of finding evidence that refuted Undine's assertion that he was in the early eighteenth century, he didn't see it here. There were no power outlets, laptops, air-conditioning vents, or phones, and the only thing approaching a light fixture stunk of singed oil.

Bridgewater pushed aside a horn mug filled with quills, the only items on the desk save a silver-tooled knife and ink pot, and looked at Michael. "You'll pardon me, I hope, for telling you I have no desire to confess."

Michael nodded, unmoved. "Most men feel that way."

"No, what I mean is that I will not confess."

Michael, who'd known exactly what Bridgewater had meant, said, "I see." He fixed the nobleman with a look reserved for misbehaving actors. "Your feelings have changed in the last two minutes?"

"My feelings are unchanged. I brought you here because I require a tête-à-tête."

"As you wish. The act of contrition comes in many forms."

"I am not contrite," Bridgewater said, voice rising. "I will not be confessing. I intend to ask *you* a few questions."

"Ahhh." Michael ducked his head knowingly and gave Bridgewater an embarrassed and slightly condescending smile.

"'Ahhh'? What do you mean by 'Ahhh'?"

"There are things that a man wonders about before his wedding night," Michael replied.

Bridgewater's eyes bulged so far out of his head, Michael thought they might burst like water balloons.

"I would hardly be asking *you* if that were the case," Bridgewater said.

"Why not?"

"You are unmarried, sir," Bridgewater said hotly. "'Twould stretch the bounds of credulity to imagine you live as an ascetic *and* support a wife."

Michael shifted. "I admit you're correct, though in fact I was married once and am, therefore, fully equipped to answer your questions. Do you love her?"

He'd surprised Bridgewater with the question.

"I-I...do."

Michael found this disappointing, though he couldn't say why. He had no idea why he'd even asked the question. "I'm glad to hear it. She's an exemplary woman—and worthy of the title you'll bestow on her." And she was. He might not like the imperiousness with which Bridgewater's fiancée conducted her business, but there was something eminently fitting about a woman like Undine being given a title, even if it was only Bridgewater's.

Bridgewater dug at the base of the mug with his thumb. "Did she…say anything about me?"

"She did. She was hesitant to say too much, of course, as befits a proper gentlewoman, but 'tis clear she admires you ardently."

Bridgewater flushed, clearly pleased, the fool. He busied himself with the proper placement of the ink pot for a moment. "Then you really are a priest?"

"Oh, aye. What else would I be?"

"And you're an associate of Bishop Rothwell?"

Now we get down to business. "I could hardly be a priest, sir, and not be His Grace's associate."

"I understand he was…upset by the note you delivered."

"I would not say 'upset.' 'Disconcerted' is perhaps a better description." Michael hoped Rothwell didn't show up to prove him wrong.

Bridgewater tapped the desk. "'Twas personal then?"

"I was not privy to the contents."

Bridgewater's flush deepened. "I only meant—"

"But if I were to guess," Michael added with a conspiratorial wink, "I would say the matter was not entirely diocesan. You know the bishop."

And this was where things got sticky. Michael didn't know what sort of subterfuge Bridgewater was a part of, or if the bishop, Michael's supposed boss, was in on it as well. Bridgewater might be hoping to discover something incriminating about the bishop because he and the bishop held opposing objectives and Bridgewater wanted to stop him. Or he might be hoping to discover something incriminating about the bishop because he and the bishop shared the *same* objective but Bridgewater questioned his loyalty to the cause.

"Whores?" Bridgewater suggested.

Michael shrugged coyly.

"Church funds?" Bridgewater lifted a prurient brow. "Not opium again?"

"All I can say is the note was delivered to me by a young urchin with a limp and it smelled heavily of perfume."

Bridgewater savored this information like a child with a sweet. "I do hope the issue resolves itself satisfactorily for the bishop," he said, "whatever it might be."

"I do as well."

"Well…" Bridgewater placed his palms on the desktop and stood. "I suppose we need to see about this wedding."

Michael, who had only threatened to perform the ceremony as a reaction to Undine's infuriating demands, now had to consider what he was actually going to do. He couldn't *legally* marry the couple. Directors had godlike powers, it was true, but as far as he knew, they didn't extend to granting Church of England sacraments. On the other hand, it would serve Undine right to be bound for life to this egomaniacal asshole. She had no business plucking innocent people out of their lives whenever the mood suited her.

"There's no need to mention our conversation to my fiancée," Bridgewater said. "Women are ill equipped to handle the subtleties of intrigue, and this one especially is too interested in the secrets of others for her own good."

Michael frowned. "She's a spirited woman. There's no doubt about that."

"I suspect a few applications of the back of my hand will free her of the affliction. One mustn't shrink from setting boundaries at the start of a marriage. It helps a wife find her footing."

Michael ground to a halt. "No."

"What do you mean, 'No'?"

"I mean I can't perform the ceremony—at least not at the present. I have a few concerns and require time to reflect upon them."

"What concerns?"

"Nothing I can share with you at present."

"Is it about Undine?" Bridgewater had the grace to look truly concerned, though it didn't soften Michael's heart to him much.

"It is. I want more time with her. I have some questions."

Bridgewater was clearly unused to men beneath him making such demands, and his face betrayed his reluctance to accede. Michael wondered for an instant if he might find himself thrown into the nearest dungeon in chains—that is, if anything in Coldstream in 1706 would be grand enough to have a dungeon—or chains.

Looking grave, Bridgewater said, "It isn't because of, well, her past, is it? I mean if she's confessed, can she not be forgiven?"

Did he mean the fact of her being a witch? If so, Michael wanted to inform him that the status was certainly not limited to her past. But the look of embarrassment on the man's face suggested a condition less fear-inducing than mortifying.

"Aye, she can be forgiven," Michael said. "And already has."

Bridgewater's shoulders relaxed, and Michael smiled. How satisfying to wield the power of a god. Apparently he was rather good at it.

"I can grant you more time with her," Bridgewater said, "but I must be able to marry her before morning."

"Why is that?"

Bridgewater must have heard something unclerical in Michael's voice because his eyes instantly narrowed. Michael tried to look as uncunning as possible, which wasn't particularly hard for him as a man three centuries out of his time.

After a long moment, Bridgewater shook off whatever suspicion had come to him and said, "Because I care for her, of course. And I fear she'll change her mind. My solicitor is coming tomorrow, and it would be convenient for us to be able to get a few things signed and settled relative to the marriage as long as he's here, which I can't do if Undine is not my wife. But I admit that isn't the reason I sent for him. He must serve as a messenger for me on another matter."

Michael bowed. "I will endeavor to keep my discussion with your fiancée short, and I would expect—"

A knock interrupted them, and Bridgewater made an irritated noise. "Aye?"

"'Tis Bishop Rothwell, sir," a voice called, and Michael fought every instinct to pitch himself immediately out the window.

"What about him?" Bridgewater said warily.

"They've found his clothes at the edge of the woods, but there's no sign of him."

Bridgewater met Michael's eyes. "I knew it."

Ten

MICHAEL TOOK ADVANTAGE OF THE GENERAL ALARM being raised to break away unnoticed and return to the chapel. When he got there, the place was empty and he paused to think. He hadn't done much of that in the last few minutes. It had been easier to jump into the role of priest than live even for a moment as a man who'd been transported in time.

1706.

He blew air from his cheeks. It was impossible to believe and yet equally impossible to deny.

Outside the stained glass windows, he could hear the sounds of horses being called for and search parties being raised. The mere ordinariness of the moment's details—the flatness of the groom's vowels, the chip missing from a stone framing the window, the distant scent of baking bread—seemed to confirm this was real, not a fantasy.

Not even my *dreams are this boring.*

He began a slow walk around the perimeter of the chapel, partly to look for a hidden door that might take him back to the National Rose, partly to calm his rising panic. He never thought he'd be able to say he missed the actors there, but right then, he'd have happily given half his life savings to be forced to preside over a dispute about dressing room sizes or lead the hunt for a missing tin of throat lozenges.

How long had he been here? A quarter of an hour? A half? Did each extra minute reduce the chances of him finding his way home? Was the play continuing without him? Would he return to find no time had passed, that Paris was still onstage, waiting for his cue? Hell, would he be able to return at all?

Between the dizzying jolt of arriving in another time, Undine's demands, and trying to navigate Bridgewater's game of cat and mouse, he hadn't had time to contemplate the full extent of his plight. But now, in the silent chapel, he felt alone—very alone.

What did he even know about the eighteenth century? Let's see, there was Richard Brinsley Sheridan and his *The School for Scandal*, and Oliver Goldsmith and *She Stoops to Conquer*. Wait. No. Those were from the far more sophisticated end of the eighteenth century, the one that butted up to Jane Austen and Alexandre Dumas. Here, in 1706, they were barely past doublets and jerkins. In fact, in 1706 in Coldstream, they were barely past running each other through with swords. If he recalled his history properly, the last pitched battle between the English army and the Scottish clans didn't take place until 1746. And Coldstream, as Undine so picturesquely put it, straddled the bloody border.

A shiver went through him.

There's no point getting lost in the terrifyingly broad canvas of history, Michael. Concentrate on what you do know.

Which is?

He considered. Undine: witch or naiad; blond and irritatingly beautiful caster of spells; woman with a past who wants no part of her fiancé, nobleman John Bridgewater. Bridgewater: imperious, self-centered, backward-thinking nobleman and army officer, whose only weak spot appeared to be—

Michael paused.

The bastard does seem to love her. Whatever she may think of him, he seems to love her.

He wanted to hate the man, but he found he couldn't. He actually felt a bit sorry for him. How was it that Bridgewater loved Undine when she so clearly didn't love him? Why, if she didn't want to marry him, had she accepted his proposal of marriage? And how on earth did a man like that ever come to court a woman like Undine?

Michael slouched against the cool stone of the wall. His tour had not uncovered a single hidden door, genie bottle, or DeLorean. If he was able to return, it wasn't going to be as easy as coming. And since he had no intention of living the rest of his life as an ascetic in the already-far-too-ascetic-for-his-taste eighteenth century, he needed to find the witch.

As he began toward the door, an odd shape on the side of the lectern caught his eye. He wouldn't have noticed it if he hadn't been looking for a secret door. He drew closer and saw it was two ovoid pieces of wood connected by twine hanging from a nail—rather like, well, a pair of testicles—a pair of testicles with a piece of paper wrapped around the top of one of them. When he picked them up, he saw that each piece had been painted to look like a monkey.

Don't we think we're funny?
He pulled it free and read it.

Come to the pump house. I need your help. Hurry.

Eleven

MICHAEL SPOTTED THE PUMP HOUSE IMMEDIATELY through the arrow slits that lined the curving stairwell. He exited in unsettling awe past a musket-armed guard standing outside the door at the bottom of the steps, hurried by a dank-smelling well from which a bonneted maid pulled a bucket, and nearly ran into a man with a cleft lip hammering a wheel onto the front of a carriage.

Every image sent another stab of uneasiness through him, and the more seemingly "normal" the image, the sharper the stab of unease. He felt like Hamlet, stumbling unhappily through his haunted dreams. Now that he figured out how he'd gotten here (whether or not his brain could accept it as fact), he needed to figure out how to get back, and there was only one person who could help him with that.

The pump house was no minor outbuilding. Perched on the banks of the river, with a gabled roof and an astounding array of wheels and valves visible through its tracery windows, the pump house was an engineering marvel, and Michael might have spent a moment or two imagining the work necessary to put such a thing together had not the other marvel in view commanded his attention.

Undine stood at the edge of the beech-lined court-yard adjacent to the pump house. Despite her note, she appeared in no urgent need of help. She stood with her back to him, gazing happily at the Tweed, her skirts licked by the breeze.

She hadn't noticed him, and he watched her without making a sound for as long as decency would allow.

"Look at them," she said without turning. "See them dance."

He flushed, realizing she must have known he'd been watching, and looked in the direction of her gaze.

There, just past a bend in the river, scores of fish were leaping in the air and wriggling in the warmth before returning to the churning blue with a splash.

"Salmon, yes?"

"Aye," she said. "Cuddies and glowers too. But salmon mostly."

The energetic exercise, like a tiny display of maritime fireworks, seemed to enchant her. He found himself wishing he could elicit the same response.

"There was a huge rain yesterday," she said. "The fish always come out after that. They like the current. It massages the stiffness from them."

She'd said the last with such empathetic certainty Michael didn't quite know how to respond. "It sounds as if you'd like to be in there swimming with them."

"I would."

He had come to a stop a little behind her, enjoying

the graceful curve of her neck as much as the view. She reached absently under the thick knot of blond at her nape to rub a muscle. Without thinking, he lifted his hands toward her shoulders and recovered himself with a start.

Good Lord, you hardly know the woman.

Undine chose that moment to turn, and he shoved his hands in his pockets, mortified.

"How was my fiancé's confession?"

"I'm afraid I can't tell you," he said, remaining true to his supposed office.

"I very much doubt he said anything."

He shrugged, apologetic. "Confidentiality. It's woven into the cloth."

"But you're not a real priest."

He lifted a brow. What could she mean? He knew she believed him to be a priest. She'd called him "Father" and asked about the location of his parish.

"Am I not?"

She pinkened. "No. I wouldn't have called you if you were. I'm sorry. I don't say it to embarrass you. I thought at first when I mixed the potion you would be an acolyte, but you're too old for that."

He coughed. "How flattering."

The pink deepened to red, though she didn't apologize.

"I assume you've been defrocked then?" she said. "Or suspended from service in some way?"

"In the corner in a dunce cap? That's how you see me?" She seemed to have no knowledge of his having traveled three centuries to serve her. She certainly had no idea he was a theater director. The gaps in her knowledge were large. Perhaps the gaps would prove useful.

"You needn't be ashamed," she said. "I'm sure you're a competent man. Everyone makes mistakes—and in this case, your failing will serve some good."

"Whom exactly will my failing serve—other than you, of course?"

She shifted. "That's complicated."

"I assumed it would be."

"The people who long for peace in the borderlands, which too often doesn't include the English."

He laughed out loud. "Oh God, you're a Scot." Her accent was northern English not Lowland Scots, but he knew well enough one can hide anything with the right training.

Her brow rose. "I am neither a Scot nor an Englishwoman."

"And how is that? Has a new principality been established along the border? A sort of Andorra of Northumberland? Oh, wait. You're a fairy. I forgot. Fairies don't have nationalities."

"I am a naiad, sir," she said, furious. "Half-naiad, in any case."

"And the other half? No, let me guess. Unicorn? House elf? Monarch butterfly?"

She didn't reply, but he caught a flicker of something in her eyes, something beneath the fury, something she wanted neither to talk nor think about.

"Well, I'm sorry to report my paperwork is fully up-to-date," he said. "Your wedding, should I perform it, will stand the test of time. Which is why you should send me back. Now. Before my hand starts to shake and I accidentally sign the license even without a ceremony."

Her jaw flexed. The seeds of doubt had been planted. "'Tis not possible," she said.

"Isn't it? Have your spells never gone awry?"

She opened her mouth and closed it again.

"I'm willing to help you," he said, "but I want your word you'll get me back—today. I have no desire to spend the rest of my days in godforsaken Coldstream."

"You are a very unpleasant man."

"Is that your way of saying yes?"

If her eyes had been bolts of lightning, he'd have been nothing more than a large puff of burlap dust. She gave him a derisive nod of agreement.

"If you don't mind," he said, "I should like your word—spoken, please—and a handshake."

"Naiads don't shake hands."

"Of course they don't. Do we touch elbows? Meet at a circle of stones at midnight?" He hid his disappointment. He'd been looking forward to holding that slim, capable hand.

"I give you my word."

"I'm assuming I can count on it?"

"Once a naiad gives her word, she cannot withdraw it, ignore it, or undermine it."

She made the pronouncement with such certainty, he could hardly doubt it. He bowed. "Thank you. There's a lot I need to learn about naiads, I guess."

She snorted.

He turned at the sound of hoofbeats. Bridgewater appeared over the rise on a bay stallion and rode directly for them.

"Have you seen the bishop?" he said, pulling his horse to a stop.

"I haven't," Michael said, "but—" He turned to suggest Undine might have, only to find Undine was no longer in sight. "But I was just about to check the, er, pump house."

"Which you think he might have chosen to explore after having the clothes savagely torn from him a mile from here?"

"He has a great curiosity regarding mechanics."

Bridgewater viewed Michael with hopeless disgust. "Well, I shall leave it to you to investigate the entire catalog of machines here. Do let me know the instant you find anything. Have you seen Undine?"

Michael shook his head.

"If you do, tell her I insist she return immediately to the house. If a madman is on the loose, I don't want her in harm's way."

"I will tell her."

He geed his horse to a gallop and disappeared. Michael peered down the gentle slope that led to the river and walked around the entire length of the beeches. Undine was nowhere to be seen.

"You nearly got us found out," she said.

He wheeled around. She stood at the far end of the courtyard, arms crossed, by a mass of overgrown roses in front of the pump house. With her face hidden by the pump house's tiny buttress and her dress barely distinguishable against the pink of the flowers, she'd been nearly invisible—or completely. Who knew how naiads' powers worked?

"Found out?" he said. "What do you mean?"

She pointed to the fountain. In it lay a motion-less and exceedingly naked man. Michael jumped back. "*Jesus.*"

"All we needed was for Bridgewater to decide to investigate the pump house. He'd have had to walk right by him."

"Is he *dead*?" Michael said. Sending someone through time for your own purpose was one thing. Killing a man for it was something else entirely.

The man rolled from his back to his side, letting out an enthusiastic fart. He drew up a knee, resettled himself on his granite bed, and began to snore.

Michael's own back began to stiffen just looking at it. "The bishop?"

"Could you tell by the ecclesiastical ring?"

"What happened to him?"

"He was about to marry us," she said, hinting in her tone that there was more misfortune to be had for those who thought to cross her.

"Well, you're a nondiscriminatory drugger, I'll give you that. Same potion?"

She gave him a narrow look. "Hardly."

"What happened to his clothes?"

"I needed to divert Bridgewater and his men away from here."

"So you drugged him, stripped him, and—wait. How did you get him here?" Undine looked capable of a lot but not carrying a hundred-and-fifty-pound man the length of the estate grounds.

"Oh, my *skies*." She rolled her eyes. "You don't incapacitate a man and *then* bring him to the place you want him. You incapacitate him on-site."

"Pardon me. I'm new to the assault-and-kidnapping game."

"Are you?" she said, lifting a theatrical brow. "I'm astonished."

"Why did you want me here?"

"I've *told* you—"

"No, *here*," he said, gesturing to the courtyard. "Why did you want me *here*."

"Oh." She straightened. "To help hide him. The man will wake in a few hours, and we need to get him to a place where coming to naked with one's head thumping and no memory of the night before won't arouse suspicions—one's own or anyone else's—which of course means—"

"Oh Christ, no."

"—a whorehouse."

The sound of men's voices rose in the distance.

"And how might we accomplish that?" he asked.

"I have an idea," she said, "but we'll have to hurry."

Twelve

THE CART BUMPED ALONG THE PATH TO THE TOWN, and the farmer driving it whistled "Tam Lin" loudly. Undine could feel Father Kent's annoyance with her, and she adjusted the cloak over his shoulders as a means of appeasement.

"A hunchback?" he said. "Really?" He made an exasperated growl as the cart hit a particularly large rut.

"'Tis the only way to move what needs to be moved without being seen."

One of the bishop's hands flopped out, and Undine shoved it back under the fabric.

Kent wiped his forehead with his sleeve. "There's nothing like wearing a wool cloak over a sweaty bishop on the most humid day in eternity while getting one's teeth rattled out of one's head to make one really long for the pleasures of Bankside."

"We shall have you home soon enough."

"Oh, we are *miles* past soon enough."

After she'd explained her plan, Kent had lifted the bishop from the fountain onto his back like a summer pig and directed her to fetch rope to secure him and a cloak to hide him. She thought of the ease with which Kent had managed the effort. For a man of the church, he had the forearms of a blacksmith and the dexterity of an acrobat—not to mention the high-handedness of a sultan.

"Where did you get your training?" she said.

"I beg your pardon?"

"Your ecclesiastical studies. Where did you do them?"

He shrugged. "You know. Here and there. One picks up what one can."

There was something about the way the corner of his mouth curved when he spoke that made everything he said feel like the start of an improper joke. She found herself wanting to smile even in the silences, which was very unlike her.

"But you studied under a rector or bishop, did you not?"

"Oh, that." He waved a hand. "Yes, of course."

"Where?"

"In, er, Basingstoke."

"Basingstoke? The miller here is from Basingstoke. Perhaps the two of you—"

"Though I was only there for a short while," he added hurriedly. "Bit of a kerfuffle with the chief patroness. Had to move on."

She gave him an interested smile. "Does kerfuffle mean what I think it does?"

"Bite your tongue," he said, horrified, and she laughed. "If you knew the patroness, you would apologize at once. She's eighty if she's a day—though in reality, I think she's been dipped in amber. She's been haunting young clerics for the last several centuries at least."

And the wit of a courtier.

"Please accept my apology." She bent in a make-shift curtsy.

The farmer slowed enough to make it over a squat stone in the path without tipping his passengers onto the ground, though she slid rather indelicately into Kent's side.

"How long do we have until your fiancé raises the alarm over your absence?" he asked, helping her regain her former position.

"I can only guess." The warmth of Kent's hand lingered on her arm. "He wouldn't want to be seen as a man whose lover had fled, that is certain. He'd take matters into his own hands rather than enlist help."

"And *are* you his lover?"

The curve of his mouth was gone, replaced by curiosity and something closer to concern. "I can't stand the man."

"It's none of my business, of course, but that's not quite what I asked."

"No," she said. "I'm not."

Did she imagine his shoulders relaxing?

"Yet you accepted his proposal of marriage?" he said.

The farmer, peeved by a flock of passing sheep, stopped his whistling and began to wave his stick. A necessary silence fell over the cart's occupants. Undine adjusted her skirts, feeling Kent's probing gaze. After a beat or two, the cart started up again, and so did "Tam Lin."

"It has nothing to do with desire," she said under her breath.

"Money then? Or position? You'd be Lady Bridgewater, after all."

He said it without judgment, just interest.

"Believe when I tell you that receiving the wifely honorific of an English title—*that* English title in particular—would offer me no pleasure."

"So not for love, lust, wealth, or title. What then?"

What could Kent know of the struggles for peace? Of men who wish that the bows and pistols in their hands would never rest? Of sons cut down at twenty or sixteen or twelve? Of the noblemen on both sides of the border who treated the centuries-old struggle like a game of cards, a pastime only for those who could afford the stakes? Nothing.

Or could he?

She saw compassion in those eyes as well as a desire to help, and she found herself tempted to tell him the truth.

In a farmer's cart? To a man you hardly know? Fool.

"For satisfaction," she said. "Mine."

He turned, full face, to appraise her. For a long moment, he didn't say anything, and Undine wondered if she'd offended him.

"Revenge can be a powerful motivator," he said at last, adding more wistfully, "I doubt you'll find it very satisfying, though."

She nearly laughed. Kent thought Bridgewater was a former lover who'd slighted her. She wished to tell him it wasn't true, that Bridgewater would be the last man in the universe she'd ever choose as a lover, but her training would not allow it. Besides, the less Kent knew, the more secure she could be in his safety.

The wagon bumped to a halt at the corner of the town's square, and Undine hopped down. Kent scooted to the edge, an exercise that should have been made ungainly by his deadweight companion, but he unfolded himself with surprising grace.

In any case, more grace than one would expect from a hunchback.

Undine gave the farmer a wave of thanks, and when she turned back, she started. Bent and twisted now, Kent had transformed from a man in his prime to a weary, limping cripple who looked ten years older and half a dozen inches shorter.

"Father," she said, speechless.

"Hunchback you said, and hunchback it is. Are you familiar with the play *Richard III*?"

His voice too had changed, sounding flatter with a faint rasp, and his cadence had slowed. When he stepped from the roadbed to the footway, she nearly offered him her arm.

She smiled. "The play and the king, both. Aye, I am."

"'And thus I clothe my naked villainy, with odd old ends stol'n out of holy writ, and seem a saint when most I play the devil.'"

Now the voice had turned a rich, fluid baritone, and the restrained malevolence in the words made her hairs stand on end.

"You're *very* good," she said.

He made a small bow. "One can hardly be a priest without a bit of the actor in one's blood." He attempted to hike the bishop's limp body higher and managed only to move the center of the mass to the level of his armpit. "Carrying a ten-stone hump certainly adds to the realism."

She leaned in to help but, being rather scrupulous when it came to naked bishops, used a shoulder rather than her hands to shove the man's arse high enough to get his head back over Kent's shoulder.

"Where are we going with him?" Kent said. "Please don't say far."

"Do you see the building with the black shutters?"

He cocked his head. "Yes."

"I have a friend there—a woman. She knows Rothwell's coming. I sent a note earlier. There's a door around the back, and you should—"

"Undine," called a man from across the road.

She recognized the voice and groaned.

"Who is it?" Kent asked.

"Go," she said. "I'll take care of it."

Thirteen

"Go" was easier said than done, and Michael trudged toward the house with black shutters with the bishop, who had begun to murmur. If he had to carry the guy much longer, he wouldn't have to pretend he had a limp.

Before he slipped into the alley behind the house, he stole a glance over his shoulder—well, over the bishop's head—at Undine. The man who'd called out to her wore a blue brocade frock coat with gold rope at the sleeve and finely polished boots. She didn't look especially pleased to be talking to him. On the other hand, in Michael's experience—which admittedly was limited to the last two hours—she hadn't yet looked especially pleased to be talking to anyone. He'd decided it was part of her unusual charm.

The bishop lifted his head, and Michael froze. If the man woke up, how would he explain the fact of him being bound, naked, strapped to a stranger's back, and on his way to a whorehouse? The only thing worse that could happen would be someone spotting this limping beast with two heads.

The bishop laid his head back down and sighed. Michael relaxed. The man's hot breath gathered like summer humidity on Michael's neck. His back hurt; his sandals pinched; he had a man's balls pressed against his back. A friar in the eighteenth century was not stacking up to be the role of his dreams.

Michael reached the passageway behind the building, which couldn't be called a proper alley, as it was barely wide enough to accommodate a man on horseback, let alone a cart or carriage, and gazed at the building's dirty daub exterior.

The place didn't look like a whorehouse—not that Michael had a clear idea of what a whorehouse should look like, other than the petticoat-filled bordellos above whiskey bars in the American Westerns his great-aunt Morag used to watch. It looked more like a tea shop, he thought, and then an odd frisson ran down his spine. He turned his gaze to the river, visible down the street, and back to the building.

Jesus, it is a tea shop! Or at least it will be in a few hundred years. This was the shop Auntie Morag had taken him to on that miserable visit to Coldstream so many years ago. They'd driven down from Peebles, boring enough in its own right, in her ancient Morris to visit the Coldstream Historical Museum. He'd sat in the front window of this very building; he remembered the view of the water clearly. They'd eaten blackberry jam biscuits and lukewarm tea with no sugar ("Bad for your teeth, Mikey. Might as well floss with licorice whips."), while he'd squirmed on the uncomfortable chair listening to her describe the afternoon of "fun" they'd be having at Coldstream's biggest attraction.

Christ, he could hardly be still now thinking about the place. Bloody boring bits of pottery and faded pictures of farmers with plows that had seemed to him from the Pleistocene Epoch. He'd actually looked for James IV in the photos, hoping to catch sight of his bloody, fifteenth-century battlefield death at nearby Flodden Field, the only thing that would have made the interminable visit worthwhile.

Well, he thought with some amusement, wouldn't Auntie Morag have been surprised to find out they'd been sitting in what had probably been the parlor at Coldstream's favorite whorehouse.

Ha.

"The door's open, you ken," said a plump, middle-aged woman with graying hair standing behind him in the alley. She held a large basket of green and purple cabbages. "Ye need no' be shy."

"Are you, er—"

"Aye. Come in, come in."

She gave his habit a quick up-and-down and shook her head. "I guess nothing should surprise me anymore," she said, and put the basket on a table in what was clearly the kitchen. A variety of pots hung by the unlit hearth, and the scent of cheap, flowery perfume hung in the air. A bright-red handbell stood on a shelf.

"Do you have a preference, Father?" she said. "Fat? Thin? Gold hair? Brown? We even have a girl with six fingers, but she's extra."

"Oh God, no," Michael said, horrified.

The woman shrugged. "The men like her because she can—"

"Thank you, no," he said firmly. Why wasn't Undine

here to navigate this medieval house of horrors? "I'm waiting for someone. A woman," he added helpfully.

She turned and crossed her arms. "Father, I ken ye must be new to this, but ye canna bring your own woman here. You must use one of ours."

He shook his head. "Sorry. I know this is confusing, but I'm here"—he lowered his voice—"with a *delivery. The* delivery."

She offered no sign of recognition.

He jabbed a thumb toward his hump. "Rothwell. He needs a room."

"He has a *name*?" She moved her hand closer to the bell.

"Of course he has a name. What do you mean?"

"What do *you* mean?"

The bishop farted, and the woman glared at Michael. "It wasn't *me*!"

A younger woman in a close-fitting leather coat stepped in and looked at Michael. "Are you Kent?"

Before he could answer, the sounds of an argument came in from the street. Michael stepped to a window. The man who had stopped Undine had a hand on her sleeve, and even at this distance, Michael could see Undine was irritated. Michael jerked the ropes under his cloak loose, and Rothwell toppled to the floor.

"I hope you can—"

"Go," the woman in leather said. "We'll take care of him."

Michael sprinted down the street before remembering his former "afflictions." He slowed to the pace of a speed walker—a speed walker with a limp.

The look in Undine's eyes warned him away, and

he stopped, but he wasn't willing to leave entirely so remained at a slight distance.

"You're the one who told me she'd abandoned me," the man said loudly. "It's your duty to tell me how to win her back."

The man was drunk. Michael could see that now. And a few of the inhabitants of Coldstream were slowing to watch. The man's grip on Undine's arm was tightening into a lock hold. Michael looked for a sign from Undine.

"Give me a potion," the man begged. "Tell me what she's thinking."

Undine had remained silent until this point, though the unexpurgated disdain in her eyes would have cut Michael's ego to shreds had it been aimed at him.

"You want to know what she's thinking, do you?"

Though he'd known Undine only a short time, Michael knew the answer to that question should be a resounding no.

"Aye, I do," the man said, "ye white-fanged witch."

Her gaze traveled to the man's hand on her arm. The onlookers fell silent. Two beats, three beats, four. The man loosened his grip and released her.

"She thinks of you often," Undine said, brushing the remains of his touch from her person.

"Does she?"

"Oh, aye. You gave her a bracelet. Emeralds, perhaps?"

The man nodded.

"She rarely removes it. Her husband can't quite place it. He thinks he might have given it to her before their marriage."

A buzz ran through the crowd. "An adulterer,"

someone whispered. The man licked his lips, mildly unnerved to have his secrets aired on the streets of Coldstream, but the onlookers were his inferiors and thus invisible to him. He stood straighter.

"She wears it even in bed," Undine said.

An older man in the crowd grabbed his wife and hurried away.

"'Tis there she thinks of you most."

The man stood rapt. His breath quickened. If Undine had been paid to tell the man the story he most wanted to hear, Michael thought, she couldn't have picked a better one.

"What does she think?" he said in a choked whisper. "Tell me."

"If I were you, I would take what I've told you and treasure it till the end of your days. She won't leave her husband for you. That you already know, and I told you as much the first time you came to me."

"Tell me," the man demanded. "Who are you to decide what I should and shouldn't hear?"

"I'm the person who makes it possible for you to know anything, sir."

"Tell me, you bloody witch."

Undine grew stock-still. "She thinks if you'd been half the lover her husband is, she'd have stayed with you long enough to allow you to drape her neck and ears in emeralds as well."

The women in the crowd tittered. Cold fury filled the man's face.

Michael stepped into his line of sight. He hoped the presence of a man of God, or at least of one who appeared to be of God, would cool the man's temper.

"You lying *bitch*."

No luck. The man reared back, but Michael moved faster. He caught the man's arm before it delivered its slap and swung him off his feet.

"Seriously?" Michael said, dropping a knee into the man's solar plexus. "Did your mother not teach you manners?"

The man's eyes bulged. "What happened to your hump?"

"Would you like to try an apology?"

"What sort of a cleric are you? Who is your bishop?"

Michael felt the touch of Undine's finger on his shoulder, but when he turned, she had faded into the crowd, watching the melee as if she were one of the onlookers. He hopped to his feet, brushed off his habit, and offered his hand to the man on his back, who shook his head.

"I will *not*."

Michael shrugged and slipped through the gaping crowd, remembering to bend and limp only after he was halfway across the road.

"I'll find you, you poxed blackguard!" the man shouted.

"Nicely done," Undine said as she hurried ahead of him down a side street. "You've assaulted Berwickshire's highest-ranking judge and now half of Coldstream can identify you."

"Oh, you think *I* caused this? You're the one who dressed me in a hump! And I was most certainly *not* the person casting aspersions on the man's bedroom prowess."

"Like all men, he places far too much importance

on the mechanics and not nearly enough on the moments leading up to them."

"*All* men? Your certainty extends that far? Not a single rice farmer in China? A bureaucrat in some Moscow bank? A reindeer herder in Nordic Jutland?"

"There are, perhaps, a handful of men in Great Britain who could be called tender lovers."

"Oh, a *handful*! Well, I suppose we should be grateful there are any of us at all"—he heard her snort at his use of "us"—"and such a delightful concentration right here in the British Isles! You Englishwomen must be celebrating your luck."

"I'm not an Englishwoman."

"Right. Nor a Scot. Tell me, how are the lovers in Fairyland?"

She gave him a devastating sidelong look. "English prig."

"Is that what I am? What if I told you I wasn't English?"

She stutter-stepped.

That's right. Maybe you don't have everything down pat.

"I'd say you were probably lying."

Probably. The promotion from flat-out liar buoyed him.

Somehow, they'd arrived at another door in another dreary Coldstream passageway. The whole town couldn't have held more than fifteen buildings, and yet Undine's twists and turns had made it seem like they were traversing half of London. She knocked twice, paused, knocked again and opened the door.

The woman in the leather coat stood at a counter, her back to them, in a heavily curtained room that smelled of strong perfume and burned oatmeal, and Michael realized that even though they'd entered through a different door, they were in the same whorehouse/tea shop he'd been in before.

The woman waved them on without turning, and Undine slipped through a hidden door, pulling Michael behind her. They descended a set of thickly carpeted stairs and a moment later the other woman joined them.

"Is he…one of yours?" the woman asked. She was a Scot with dark hair and an imperious gaze—even more imperious than Undine's.

"One of her what?" Michael said.

"Colleagues. We use this place as a base. My friend is helping," Undine said, adding to the woman, "Aye, unfortunately. He's been recognized."

"In that?" She tilted her head toward the habit. "I'm not surprised."

"I didn't dress him."

"Dressed myself," Michael said, holding up his hands proudly. "Have been doing it since I was a lad."

"Has the bishop been secured?" Undine said.

"Aye. Snoring like a polecat."

"Bridgewater is making arrangements for a confidential delivery. We don't know what it is or who it's for. Someone from his solicitor's office will serve as the go-between. He's arriving from London tomorrow."

"Not if he's going through Wooler," the brunette said. "The river's overrun the banks there, and the ferry's out. He'll have to wait there or travel west all the way around to Jedburgh. Either way, it'll take him at least two more days."

"Bridgewater will not be pleased," Undine said with a grim smile.

"Aye. 'Tis a shame."

"In case anyone cares," said Michael, who was growing tired of them talking around him, "I was the one who made the discovery regarding the confidential delivery."

The brunette pursed her lips and gave him a once-over. "He's a bit older than your usual."

"An unfortunate necessity," Undine said. "He's entirely untested. I make no claims regarding his abilities."

"Actually," Michael said affably, "I'm quite well tested. In fact—"

"He needs a disguise, though," Undine said. "He caused us some trouble in the street."

"*I* caused trouble?"

The brunette snagged a shirt hanging on a peg and handed it to Undine. "Will a sark and plaid do?"

"Can you contrive a Scots accent?" Undine asked, finally addressing him directly.

Michael quoted from Robert Burns in his best burr, "'A prince can mak a belted knight, A marquise, duke, an' a' that; But an honest man's abon his might, Gude faith, he maunna fa' that!'"

Undine looked horrified. "Silence, then. And no, no plaid."

"I'll have you know my accent is extremely good."

The brunette grabbed the knot at his waist and began to loosen the rope, and Undine reached for his wrist. He knew what it was like to have backstage dressers yanking and pulling on his clothes, but not a woman he'd barely met. And definitely not a woman he'd barely met alongside a woman who felt it within her right to pass judgment on the sexual abilities of the entire male world. God knows what she'd make of his—

"Too short," Undine said definitively, looking at the sark. She lifted Michael's arm and stretched it across her chest. "We need something longer in the arm and broader in the shoulders."

His elbow rested in the soft valley between her breasts. He could feel the warmth of her skin. Any words of protest he might have mustered died on his lips.

"Odd," Undine said, peering into his eyes. "You don't look that tall."

He wanted to say he didn't look that tall because Friar Laurence—*his* Friar Laurence, at least—was a plump man built close to the ground, and the way he'd walked and stood and gestured were meant subtly to communicate that, but only another actor would understand.

"Stand up straight," she commanded. "Full height."

He shook off the role and allowed his body to expand into its usual space.

Her eyes widened, and as they did, her grip slackened. The elegant hand still holding his fell, pulling his arm unconsciously—and torturously—across the plump flesh and rigid nipples. Propriety demanded he separate his arm from her, which he did, but no force on earth would have been able to convince him to release her hand.

"You *are* quite tall," she said shocked. The grayish green in her eyes was like fog rolling off a Scottish hill.

She could say she wasn't a Scot all she wanted, but he could see the fiery independence there, that I'll-have-you-or-not-as-I-choose that resided in the eyes of all Scotswomen. It was nothing like the cool appraisal of an Englishwoman.

"Take off your habit," she said. "Quickly."

Reluctantly, he released her hand. She touched the burlap, and he stripped it off, remembering too late he'd left his shirt backstage.

He'd spent most of the summer rebuilding an ancient stone wall on his property, and the ropiness of his arms and brown of his skin showed it.

She seemed to realize she'd been staring and busied herself with the habit, which she'd been clutching.

"You seem to have forgotten your hair shirt, sir," she said with a mocking smile.

The hair he wished to feel brushing his chest was not from a shirt but twisted tightly in a blond knot at her nape.

"Undine," the brunette said, trying to catch her friend's attention.

"I thought even Bankside clerics could afford a sark."

"*Undine.*"

That broke the spell. Undine cast her gaze in the direction the brunette was looking, and so did he.

His trousers.

Not breeks. Not trewes. Not even Elizabethan cannions. He was wearing bespoke trousers from a tailor in Savile Row. He'd never had a woman, let alone two, more entranced by the real estate below his belt. It would have been less uncomfortable if he'd been naked.

The brunette shook her head. "Oh, Undine…"

Speechless, Undine looked at the habit and back at his trousers.

"He's not…from here," the brunette said in a tone laden with a meaning Michael couldn't quite unpack.

"I can see that."

"He's from—"

"*Aye*. I can see that too, Abby."

"How does this keep *happening*?"

Undine's eyes cut to his. "You told me you were from Bankside." The fiery independence had turned into flat-out fire.

"I am from Bankside," he said.

"You're a *liar*."

Gah. Downgraded. "I didn't lie. I am from Bankside. You presumed I was from Bankside in *your time*. Your presumptions are not my responsibility. Your presumptions are—"

"Be quiet," she said. "I need to think."

The door at the top of the stairs opened, and a man called down softly, "*Mo chridhe*, there's a man up here looking for a priest."

"He's here," Undine said, adding to Michael, "Take off your breeks."

The man on the stairs said, "I beg your pardon. Did you just say, 'Take off your breeks'? To whom are you speaking? Should I be coming down?"

"Try to send our visitor away," Undine called.

Michael strained for a view of the man, who closed the door, grumbling. "*Mo chridhe*" meant "my heart," and Michael wondered who would be calling Undine that. He kicked off his sandals and unbuttoned his trousers. "Was that…your brother?" he asked.

The brunette chuckled and Undine silenced her with a look.

"Find him shoes, breeks, and a bigger sark, would you?" Undine said, and Abby scampered off.

"You need to leave here as soon as possible," Undine said. "The judge is an acquaintance of Bridgewater's. Go to the Leaping Stag," she said. "There'll be a couple there—brown hair and red, deeply in love— it's quite stomach turning, believe me—and tell them you're my colleague. They'll hide you until I can gather the herbs you'll need to leave and get them to Abby in Coldstream, probably tomorrow."

Michael extracted himself from his trousers reluctantly. He understood the need to get into a different disguise, but he would have preferred if one of the steps in the transition hadn't included him standing in front of the naiad in his bright-red Arsenal trunks.

She frowned, a mixture of shock and fascination on her face. "Is that a cannon?"

"Yes. It's their symbol—the team's, I mean. Arsenal. They're a football team." He found it hard to clarify his thoughts while she examined the design with such intensity.

"Foot...*ball*?"

"It's not... It doesn't have to do with those balls. It's a sport. The players use a leather ball filled with air. You kick it, you know, with your foot." He demonstrated a slow-motion kick, but her attention remained undiverted.

"It's quite large, isn't it? And red?"

It felt very, very small from Michael's perspective.

"Tell me," she said, "do all the men in your time

wear drawings of weapons on, er, the coverings for their cocks?"

"No, and we call them trunks."

"You call your cocks 'trunks'?" she said, dubious. "Like an elephant's?"

"*No*. We call the coverings trunks."

"Ah. Well, that makes more sense."

He shifted, trying without success to remove his cannon from the heat of the spotlight. "Maybe I've been reading the wrong books, but aren't women of the eighteenth century supposed to be a little more, well, demure when it comes to cocks—you know, heart pitter-pattering, smelling salts, that sort of thing?"

Undine snorted. "Cocks are like snakes," she said. "If you don't learn how to spot the bad ones and immobilize them, you're not going to last very long in the borderlands."

"You immobilize snakes, do you?"

"I avoid them entirely." She gave him an unapologetic look. "Best strategy."

Abby, returning with an armload of clothes and boots, skidded to a halt when she saw Michael. "Verra eye-catching."

He tugged the trousers from the articles in her hands and thrust his foot into a leg. The fabric was roughly woven, not nearly as nice as the trousers he'd given up. "It's a symbol," he said primly.

"It certainly is." She turned to Undine. "Remind me to find out more from Duncan."

"Who's Duncan?" Michael asked curtly. "Or you, for that matter?"

The brunette's head rose, and her shoulders went

back like the wings of Winged Victory. The room seemed to shrink to half its size.

Undine cleared her throat. "Lady Kerr, please allow me to offer you the acquaintance of Father Kent of Bankside. Father Kent, this is Lady Kerr, chieftess of Clan Kerr."

His eyes nearly popped out of his head. A clan *chieftess*? Hell, a *clan* anything. Clan chiefs had people *forsworn* to them. They were like gods on earth. Queen Elizabeth in her pink coat and purse had nothing on a Scottish clan chief. He tried to process the different layers of his shock and was still working on a suitable response when he realized Lady Kerr was waiting expectantly.

Sheepishly, he dropped into another bow and immediately realized half of his trousers were still hanging from his hand. Nonetheless, he managed a very courtly flourish.

"Verra bonny, Father. Would you mind telling me how you happened to make Undine's acquaintance?"

He hopped into the rest of the trousers. "Certainly. It seems she needed a priest to—"

"Try to get Bridgewater to confess," Undine finished, and gave Michael an iron look.

"Indeed?" said the chieftess. "And were you successful?"

"Yes. No. Well, partly," Michael said, returning Undine's look. "There's a lot more to uncover. A *lot* more." Undine didn't want her friend to know about the wedding. *Interesting.*

Lady Kerr studied Undine closely, clearly not believing she'd been given the whole story.

"You appear to be a man of action," Lady Kerr said to Michael. "I would be most appreciative if you were to keep a close eye on my friend. Her fiancé isn't to be trusted, and she has made the unfortunate decision to take up residence in his home, despite the strenuous objections of her dearest friends."

Michael felt the tension between the women, but it was the discomfort on Undine's face that struck him most. "I doubt she wishes to disappoint those who care for her," he said. "But she has an obligation to do what she thinks she must. I feel certain you, as a clan chieftess, would have some sympathy for that."

"You've been made privy to her plan?" Lady Kerr looked surprised.

"I have not. Well, not all of it."

"Yet you're willing to defend it?"

"Let's just say I know enough of Undine in my short time with her to be sure that while one might question her means, one could never question her objective."

Lady Kerr looked at Undine. "Well, you certainly have him bamboozled."

Michael's face must have shown his surprise because the chieftess grinned.

"You like 'bamboozled,' do you?" she said. "Duncan—the man on the stairs—taught me that. I'm glad to have someone to use it on."

"Duncan, is it?" Michael straightened. "And he's your…?"

Lady Kerr's eyes twinkled. "Fiancé. Aye, he is mine. No one else's."

Michael held up his hands. "I didn't mean—"

"No, of course you didn't. And I can count on you to watch Undine?"

"Absolutely."

"Though I long desperately to fulfill everyone's wishes regarding my safety," Undine said, "I'm sorry to report Father Kent will not be returning to the house with me."

"Why?" asked Lady Kerr, and he wondered the same.

"First, because he has been identified as a man with a hump. Second, because he has been identified by the same gentleman as a man without a hump. Third, because the gentleman who now knows Kent in both his humped and humpless forms also happens to be the gentleman Kent punched as well as an ally of Bridgewater's. Fourth—"

"I didn't punch him," Michael said, pulling the threadbare sark over his head. "I guided him to the ground with my arm and put my knee on his chest." He stuffed his feet into the muddy boots Lady Kerr had brought.

"*Ooh*," said the chieftess, impressed.

Undine handed him a handkerchief.

The linen had a *U* embroidered on it as well as a several colorful fish. "What's this for?"

"Your cheek to begin with. You've got mud on your hands from the boot and now it's on your face. Fourth," she said, returning to her list, "because he has made his desire to leave clear."

"Bridgewater?" Lady Kerr asked, with hope writ large.

"No," Undine said dryly. "Kent."

"Oh dear. Is that true, Father?"

"Well, yes," he said, wiping his face. "I mean eventually. But I think I can be of further service to Undine here."

"I'm afraid your usefulness has been exhausted," Undine said to Michael, "and I…" Her voice trailed off.

"What?" Michael said.

"And I can't guarantee your safety," she said with a touch of honest sadness. "You have to see that. You don't know Bridgewater as I do, but if word of our doings today reaches him…"

"You will be equally at risk then," Michael said. "And I can guarantee my own safety."

"I believe that," she said, and Lady Kerr made an impressed *Hmm*. "However, putting outsiders at risk is not in the code I follow." She extended her hand.

She was cutting him out of whatever this was, and while he had every reason to want to return to the comforts of the twenty-first century, he found himself wanting to do it only *after* he'd ensured Undine's safety. He had one piece of leverage.

"Perhaps if your friends knew more about your intentions with Bridgewater, I'd feel better about leaving…"

Whoa! Wrong tack. The regret in Undine's eyes was replaced by fury, and she withdrew her hand. "Father," Undine said, "you are—"

"Quite mistaken," Michael said instantly. He cursed himself for his cravenness, but her hand was so close, and he couldn't bring himself to give up the chance to hold it, just once.

The fury left as quickly as it had arrived, and Undine extended her hand again.

Michael took it. Her skin was warm and alive. Then he remembered. "I thought you said naiads don't shake hands."

"I am only half naiad, sir, and besides, you do, and I am not so set in my ways to pass up the opportunity to meet a friend halfway."

At this, Lady Kerr snorted aloud, but Michael didn't care. He had received a naiadan honor and would treasure it always. He lifted Undine's hand and brushed his lips over her delicate, long fingers. She made a graceful curtsy and met his eyes.

He searched for an appropriate parting sentiment for the woman who had brought him out of his unremarkable life in the twenty-first century and thrust him into intrigues of the borderlands but found nothing suitable in his vocabulary.

"Good-bye, my friend," he said at last. "Good luck."

An instant later, Lady Kerr was rushing him down a dark hall, through a low door, and out into the light of the afternoon. The clouds seemed pregnant with rain, but none had fallen yet. He imagined a naiad would enjoy a rain shower. "How will Undine get back to the house?" he asked. "What if Bridgewater still insists on—" He caught himself before he said "marrying her."

"Insists on what?" Lady Kerr said, eyes narrowed.

"Seeing the priest."

She looked at him thoughtfully. "Undine is verra resourceful. If I were you, I'd spend my worrying on looking out for myself. This world can be a treacherous place for a man not used to it."

"Thank you. I'll try."

He turned toward the door, then turned back. "Lady Kerr?"

She'd started for the door. "Aye?"

"I think I should stay. For her safety, you see."

"Of course," Lady Kerr said. "Well, I certainly canna suggest you defy Undine's orders. What sort of friend would I be?" She'd said it with conviction, though the look of amusement in her eyes didn't seem to gibe with her tone.

"Is she in danger, do you think?" Michael wished he could tell her about the marriage Bridgewater was trying to engineer, but he felt he'd made an unspoken promise to Undine to remain silent and wouldn't break his vow.

"She is certainly in danger," Lady Kerr said, "and while I don't think it's of being attacked by Bridgewater, she may find it to be something equally startling."

The amusement on her face grew, and Michael was even more confused.

"'Tis very kind of Undine to offer to return with the herbs tomorrow to ensure you can get home. I have seen others wait considerably longer for their release," she added. "However, twenty-four hours is a long time to spend with nothing to do. I trust you'll find a way to fill the time."

There was no more to be said. Michael bowed and she nodded her good-bye.

He considered his choices. The nerve endings in his palm still vibrated with the memory of Undine's touch and his lips with the sweetness of her fingers. He lifted his hand to his nose and searched for traces of her clean scent.

"Father Kent?"

He started, having thought Lady Kerr gone.

"The Leaping Stag, aye?" she said. "A couple, brown-haired and red, deeply in love?"

"I remember," he said. "I remember it all."

"I'm certain you do."

Fourteen

UNDINE PICKED UP THE TROUSERS AND FOLDED THEM carefully. They'd have to be hidden so no one would ever find them again.

She thought of the man who'd worn them—the insightful eyes flecked with gray, the sharp wit, the ability to keep his head in circumstances that would undo a lesser man—features most admirable and too rarely found in the opposite sex. Of course, there was also his infuriating and complete refusal to be cowed by her.

She smiled.

In truth, she rather liked that. She'd lived her entire adult life as a feared outsider. Men sought her out, of course, for her wisdom and her ability to see their futures—as if any man's future wasn't written plainly on his face. And they paid her well for it. She owned a cottage in Cumbria, had money in the bank, and could live as she chose.

But apart from Abby, Duncan, and their new acquaintances, Gerard and Serafina, she did not have friends. One didn't befriend a person who knew his or her most uncomfortable secrets and held the power of exposing what one wished to hide. One villainized her—privately, of course, and out of the hearing of the woman who held the secrets. It was the only way to equalize the power. Undine had long ago accepted that and, at times, even used it to her advantage.

But it was still quite nice to have a man—a colleague—who regarded you as a friend.

She'd been absently caressing the wool and stilled her hand. As dark as a night sky, with a weave as smooth and gleaming as silk, the touch of the fabric filled her not just with a sense of him, but also with an unexpected longing for a time now lost to her. Perhaps her mother had had a dress or a jacket of similar material. But that was a secret she'd shared with no one.

"Are you cradling his breeks now?" Abby stood in the doorway.

"Don't be ridiculous," Undine said and stuffed the trousers haphazardly under her elbow. "But we must remember to keep them out of sight."

"Burn them and be done with it," Abby said, reaching for them.

Undine stepped back. "There's no need to *destroy* them. He might need them tomorrow."

"I see." Abby crossed her arms.

"Stop looking at me that way."

"Tell me, my friend, do you have any idea how, if you wanted a priest from our time to confess Bridgewater, you ended up with a man clearly *not* a priest from the future?"

"You don't think he's a priest?" Undine asked, surprised.

"You *do*?"

"Well, aye—I mean, what makes you think he isn't?"

"Oh, Undine, I can't *imagine* what is blinding you on this particular point, but the man is most definitely not a priest. He has a beautiful head of hair, for one thing. No priest in a habit would allow himself to cultivate such a thing."

"Perhaps priests in the future disdain shaving."

"Aye, perhaps. And perhaps they dress themselves in wool luxurious enough to swaddle a royal baby, as well as breechcloths that could stop a ship at three leagues."

Undine bit her lip. "I admit they were most gaily colored."

"But more than anything, 'twas the way he looked at you that made me certain."

Undine scoffed. "As if priests do not desire women."

"So you dinna quibble with the lusting, only with me concluding that it means he's not a priest?"

Heat raced up Undine's neck. "Men lust for anything in a skirt. 'Tis nothing remarkable."

"No, 'tis nothing remarkable, I admit. But what *is* remarkable is the way you hem and haw and paw at his breeks." Abby grinned.

"You're crossing a dangerous line. Perhaps a little hawthorn in your evening wine will dampen your tongue."

"And perhaps a little opium in yours will loosen your chemise."

Undine gasped. "You are quite…inappropriate."

"Aye, I am. Though I have a verra clear recollection of you stripping me of any thought of denying my desire for Duncan. All I'd wanted was a strong arm.

You're the one who insisted I pursue him. Consider the favor returned."

"You *said* all you wanted was a strong arm, but that's not how the herbs work. The herbs I gave you work in accordance with one's desires and—" Undine stopped midsentence, horrified.

"Aha! You asked for a priest, but you got a very nonpriestly paramour. My dear friend, dinna look so downhearted. I'm sure even naiads occasionally lose control of their hearts."

"You are… You are…"

"Right? Is that the word you're searching for?"

"Infuriating," Undine said.

"And before you return tomorrow—and, no, you may not send the herbs with a messenger—I want you to loosen that knot of hair—"

"What's wrong with my hair?" Undine looked in the ancient mirror.

"—and find a pretty gown—something with ruffles."

"*Ruffles?*"

"Aye, and in a brighter color. We need to move ye from pales and darks to something with color. Do ye have anything in emerald or gold?"

"No," Undine said with honest fright. "Wait. Bridgewater had gowns made for me—"

"There we go. We can appease him and put you in the eye of Mr. Kent at the same time."

Undine touched the smooth, pale-blond locks she saw in the mirror, feeling self-conscious for the first time in her life. "What's wrong with my hair?"

Abby threw her arms around her and hugged her tightly. "There's nothing *wrong* with your hair. Your hair is gorgeous. Breathtaking. But ye have to offer men a wee bit of hope of actually touching it. A loose curl. A fat braid with a silky tail. Right now, that spun gold is locked up tighter than the Tolbooth."

Undine's throat seemed to be narrowing, and she struggled to fill her lungs. She felt as if the mill's ancient grinding stone had been laid atop her chest. She couldn't breathe or think. *Curls? Ruffles?*

"No," she said. "'Twould be outlandish. I am quite comfortable in the gowns I have. And right now I have more important things to concern myself with."

Abby clasped her friend's cheek. "I have erred in rushing you. I can see that. Let us take this in smaller steps. Could I convince you to start with a pair of earbobs?"

"Well…"

Abby pulled the ones she wore from her ears.

"I have no holes," Undine said warily.

"I refrain from comment." Abby threaded Undine's lobe into the tightly-looped spring wire to which the tiny gold front was attached.

"It moves," Undine said, horrified, as she explored the piece with her finger.

"Aye. 'Tis shocking, I know. Good thing the world already thinks you're a whore. Consider it part of the disguise. The main part there on your ear is a thistle. The blue gem hanging from it is called a water sapphire."

"It is?" Undine gazed more closely at the mirror. "Why?"

"I'm told by Serafina, who as you know is the final word in all things maritime, that Viking sailors relied on them to determine the direction of the sun on over-cast days. Something about the stone's structure. See?"

Abby removed the other earbob and held it up to the room's small, grimy window. When she turned it one way, the stone looked full blue. When she turned it a quarter turn, the stone turned almost transparent.

"I'll be damned," Undine said.

"I have no doubt," Abby said, putting it on her friend's ear, "though I suspect it won't be for wearing earbobs."

Undine shook her head. The stones gave a sultry wriggle. "I don't know…"

"Pretend they're not there," Abby said, pulling Undine's questing hands away, "you know, as you do with most people."

Undine took a deep breath. "For you, I will try."

"Not for me. For Mr. Kent."

Mr. Kent. Was he really not a priest? And if so, why had he persisted in letting her believe he was? The man might have worthy breeks and handsome eyes, but if he thought he would have a fling at her with his burlap and rope and godly ways, he would find himself one very sorry gentleman.

"Oh, dear," Abby said, looking into her eyes. "The fear has just barely subsided, and now we've moved full force into anger."

"Why would he lie to me?"

"Indeed, why?" Abby said. "Does he not know your fiendish ways with hawthorn and twinflower? 'Tis something you must investigate, to be sure. I'm only sorry I willna be here to see it unfold."

Undine frowned. "Where will you be?"

"I've been asked to call on Chieftain Hay in Jedburgh. Duncan and I will be leaving tonight. I've asked Rosston to join us there."

"What is it, Abby?" Rosston was the leader of a former sept of Clan Kerr, and in an uneasy peace, he and Abby had agreed to lead their joined forces as co-commanders. Rosston had wanted Abby to join him in a marriage as well. But Abby, who'd had no intention of giving up her power completely, resisted, and Duncan's arrival had made the question moot. For Abby to have willingly invited Rosston to any meeting with another clan chief was a sign the meeting was unusual.

Abby made an uncertain noise. "Nothing yet. I dinna wish to concern you. If it comes to anything, I'll tell ye what I can. I promise."

Abby's responsibilities lay with her clan; Undine's, with those who desired peace. At various times, the two friends had found themselves on opposite ends of a fight, which meant neither could be as open with the other as she wished. And though Abby worked almost as hard as Undine to ensure the families of the borderlands could live their lives free from conflict, Undine knew a time might come when she'd have to stand against Abby if the two sides were ever thrust into a full-on war.

Undine squeezed her friend's hand, and Abby pulled her into a close embrace.

"Be safe."

"You too, my dear."

Undine straightened and smoothed her gown. Then she remembered what would come next, and her happiness faded. She dreaded returning to Bridgewater, who had probably sent out search parties to look for her. Though with no priest and no bishop at hand, there could be no wedding ceremony—at least not for the next day or so, or however long it took him to summon someone else from the bishopric.

But there was no point in taking comfort in that fact. Bridgewater would come upon some other way to try her patience. About that, she had no doubt.

Fifteen

MICHAEL KEPT THE CAP PULLED LOW AND STUMBLED past the parcel-laden shoppers. A tipsy laborer, even during the day, was sure to be an uneventful occurrence in a small, rural town, especially one as small and rural as this. The disparate buildings looked so inconsequential in comparison to the miles of verdant hills that surrounded them, it was almost as if the town might be swallowed up by nature and disappear completely at any moment.

He was supposed to be looking for the Leaping Stag, and he was but with only half his attention. The other half was struggling with the unexpected end to his brief time with Undine.

He realized the hands thrust deep in his pockets were curled into balls. Part of the reason why was an actor's instinct, to summon the concentrated carefulness of a man trying to appear less drunk than he actually was, but part of it was an effort to preserve the sense of her touch.

Embarrassed, he stretched his fingers.

He hadn't asked to be whisked three centuries back

in time, and he'd certainly had no desire to be a private in Undine's one-man army. He'd spent the last decade and a half bowing to Lady Velopar's every wish. But he still felt as if the curtain here had come down too soon on the drama with Undine. He wasn't exactly sure what the second or third act would have wrought, but he wished he'd have gotten a chance to at least page through the rest of the story.

A towering red-haired man leaned against the front of the whorehouse/tea shop, eyeing him. Michael made a small belch and passed.

"Hey," the man said, and Michael kept up his lumbering pace, hoping the man was talking to someone else.

A green carriage with polished fittings and a pair of white horses barreled toward a large, muddy puddle near him, and Michael squeezed closer to the shop front, but he wasn't able to evade the entire splash, and mud splattered his trousers and shirt.

Bloody bastard.

The bastard, it turned out, was Bridgewater. He leapt from the carriage in a state of some agitation. "Stay here," he ordered his driver and footman. Michael stepped out of sight.

Bridgewater looked up and down the street. He took a step toward the whorehouse and hesitated. The lanky man was gone, which was good. Undine had said the bishop would wake tomorrow without remembering anything, so even if Bridgewater was heading there and found him, it shouldn't be a risk for Undine. However, if Bridgewater found Undine there, that would be a different story.

But Bridgewater turned on his heel and headed in the opposite direction—directly toward Michael.

Michael knew from his training that people were not particularly observant. Ask five witnesses at a car accident what happened, and you'll get five different stories. People were better with faces, but not faces they'd seen only once or twice, and especially not faces they were seeing in an entirely new context. The nurse who helped your mum in the hospital is a complete cipher to you when you run into her by the tomato bins in Sainsbury's. The theory was your brain builds its understanding of a person over time. Nonetheless, Michael preferred not to test the theory's validity. He did an about-face and found that the red-haired man had simply moved to the opposite side of the street. It dawned on him that the man was watching him watch Bridgewater. Michael began to walk faster.

There's a certain snobbery one brings to matters of the past, he thought, a sense that everything one knows and understands is superior to the poor, benighted people of earlier times—not unlike visiting one's cousin in Lower Pilsley. But Michael's snobbery was quickly evaporating. Without Undine, he had no one to ensure he navigated the odd practices of 1706 correctly, and now men—large, angry men—appeared to be hunting him down. He had no idea what sort of law enforcement existed here. He imagined resolving conflict boiled down to whoever held the biggest weapon. He could wind up dead and thrown in some damp Coldstream ravine before Undine even had a chance to miss him.

Did she miss him? It was a thought he wished he had more time to explore, but Bridgewater was coming up behind him at a clip.

Michael braced himself but felt only the brush of the man's frock coat as he hurried by. At this point, Michael knew he should exit quickly. He took one last look back on the off chance of seeing Undine again and ran directly into Bridgewater, who had reversed course.

"I beg your pardon, sir," Michael said—in a *perfect* Scots accent—before tugging his cap and hurrying on.

"Wait!"

Michael sighed and stopped. There was no point in delaying the inevitable. "Aye?" He turned around.

"You dropped something." Bridgewater snagged a flash of white off the ground, and Michael realized with a sickening lurch it was the handkerchief Undine had given him. He didn't know which would be worse—to have to explain why Father Kent was in laborer's clothes and talking in a Scots accent, or to be found in possession of the handkerchief belonging to Lord Bridgewater's fiancée. Scratch that. He knew exactly which would be worse.

Michael waited, fists clenched, for the man to come to one realization or the other.

"That's the trouble with a long summer," Bridgewater said, gesturing absently with the handkerchief. "When it doesn't rain, you have dust everywhere. But when it does and you drop something, especially something fine…" He shook his head sadly, looking down at the linen. "And yours is remarkably—"

"Verra kind of you, milord," Michael said, snatching

it away and stuffing it in his pocket. The man rubbed the corner of his mouth contemplatively, and Michael's heart thrummed in his chest.

"You're quite welcome," Bridgewater said. He tipped his hat and sauntered away.

Michael was stunned. Even in his perhaps slightly overblown regard for his acting ability, he'd never imagined he'd be able to pass as an *entirely different person* to a man who had bared his heart to him only a few hours earlier. Then he realized his calculations had excluded one critical factor: Bridgewater was a member of a very privileged class and, as such, regarded the people below him in the social strata as nameless, faceless bits of everyday ephemera—life's wallpaper, so to speak—and spared them about as much attention as one might the light switch in the loo or the disposable chopsticks at one's favorite Chinese takeaway.

His attention was diverted by Undine, who emerged from a fabric shop, causing both him and Bridgewater to jerk to a stop. The red-haired man laughed out loud.

Slipping away would have been smart, but Michael was unable to convince his legs to remove him from what might be his last look at her. He knew she saw him even though she didn't look his way. He could feel her *not* looking at him, in fact, which made him both a little happy and a little sad. It was as if they shared a secret no one else knew and yet they would never get a chance to take pleasure in their shared knowledge.

Undine smiled when she saw Bridgewater, and he hurried to her side. An intense conversation followed, with Bridgewater clearly communicating his concern about her disappearance and an unruffled Undine waving away his worry. If Bridgewater had raised his voice, Michael would have intervened, damp ravine or not, but the conversation was conducted with civility. He found himself a little disappointed, to be honest.

With a pang, Michael watched Bridgewater take Undine's elbow and lead her toward his carriage. He helped her in, followed on her heels, and the carriage pulled away. To Michael, it was as if the sun had pulled down its shades and closed for the season. He watched until the carriage was nearly out of sight, absently stepping one way or another to stay out people's way. And he would have stayed longer but a hand clapped him on the shoulder.

"Come," the red-haired man said. "Let me buy you a wee dram. Ye look a bit dour."

Sixteen

BRIDGEWATER CLEARED HIS THROAT, AND THE LOOK ON his face was one of great reluctance. "I need to ask for your help on a matter."

An uneasy feeling went through Undine. The carriage ride had been pleasant enough. Bridgewater told her his men hadn't found the bishop or any evidence of foul play and added that while he was glad to have found Undine safe, he'd have preferred her to have abided by his wishes and stayed in the house.

Undine had refrained from comment except to say that she'd needed to order some things for her wedding wardrobe. She'd asked demurely if he'd minded that she charged the bits of fabric and ribbon to him, and she'd almost felt bad for how much joy the question had brought him. Then she rubbed the knot behind her ear that his long-ago blows had given her and remembered she didn't give a whit how betrayed he'd feel when he discovered she hated him.

"You know my prophecy skills are lessened considerably by strong affection," she said. "I canna see things clearly for those I love."

This was the truth. Undine's powers were not infinite, though she worked hard to ensure men believed they were. She'd been born with some powers of foresight and learned to give every impression of the rest by reading people's faces and listening to the things they didn't say.

The carriage hit an unexpected groove, and they shifted hard to the left. His hand, cool and meaty, kept her from sliding away.

"You 'canna' see," he said with a smile. "Listen to you. You're practically a Scot yourself now. I know your friends are quite dear to you, and I can reassure you the help you give me will not in any way affect them."

"I'd prefer not to reduce the intercourse between us to that of commerce, John. 'Tis not a prudent way to begin a marriage."

His tongue had lodged in the corner of his cheek at "intercourse," and she could see him struggle to bury his response smirk.

"I know that," he said after a moment, "and I wouldn't ask were it not important."

"Important to the English?"

His eyes turned clear blue—so blue she almost believed what she was about to hear would be the truth.

"No," he said. "To me."

Undine debated how hard to refuse. She'd told him powers weren't as strong with loved ones, and he'd assured her the favor would not hurt her friends or advantage the English—not that she believed him. Even the most powerful love spell could not erase a man's fundamental character flaws, after all. Continuing to protest could raise his suspicions, which might raise him from the spell like water splashed on one's face raises a man from slumber—and yet she had a bone-deep revulsion to even hearing the reason for his request.

She shook her head. "I think it'd be better if we—"

"It's not even for me, in all honesty. You've heard of Lord Morebright, I assume?"

Simon Morebright was an elderly English nobleman, deeply in debt. There were rumors he had once run a secret and separate intelligence operation for Queen Anne unknown to those in her cabinet—of course, there were founded and unfounded rumors about many people in Anne's small circle of friends—but Morebright was unique in that his relationship with Anne seemed to have ended badly. He'd closed his London house, moved north across the border to his estate in Scotland, and hadn't been heard from since. Undine couldn't begin to guess why Bridgewater might be seeking help for a man like him.

"I have," she said. "He's a close friend of Queen Anne, is he not?"

"Oh, aye, though he's too old for the merriment of court anymore. He lives in Scotland."

"Does he?"

"Aye, near Perth. Charming estate. He's dying and I wish to help him."

Bridgewater looked at her, mournful. He'd certainly given her little room to say no with grace. She would, though, if she needed to. She could be quite immune to cajoling—ask any of her friends or even Bridgewater himself, whose beating had come when she'd refused to give him the information he sought.

And yet…

It struck her that Morebright might be involved in the messages, though it seemed unlikely. But the question to consider was who would learn more if she agreed to listen to Bridgewater's request concerning Morebright—her or her fiancé?

She touched her heart. "He's dying?"

There were enormous risks to playing this game with Bridgewater. She hoped she held the stronger hand.

"Aye," he said. "I've described the case to the best surgeon in York. The situation involves a tumor on his wrist, and the surgeon says he can cure him, though it may involve removing his arm. I'm sending a man from my solicitor's office in my carriage to bring him down to York with his manservant."

"I don't see how I can help you," she said. "I'm not a surgeon. I might be able to tell if he's going to die if I saw him in person, but the man is quite old, and any death I saw could be the same old-bones death any one of us might expect at that age."

"No, my dear," Bridgewater said with a smile, "we'll leave that to the surgeon. He assures me that Simon— Lord Morebright—can enjoy several more years of good health with the surgery, albeit with only one arm."

"'Tis very good of you to feel such concern," she said. "I didn't realize you knew Morebright that well."

"Oh, the man was like an uncle to me. My father was often away with the army, and when he was there… Well, let us say we did not always see eye to eye. Simon was there when I needed help or advice. There are some things, after all, one cannot share with one's father." He gave her a weak smile.

"A friendship like that can be such a blessing."

"Then might you consider aiding a dear friend?"

The warning voice in her head had not disappeared, but its cry was growing fainter. "I'm still not certain how I could help."

"But you'll do it if you can?"

She licked her lips. "Aye," she said. "If I can."

"Thank you, Undine. I can't tell you how much this means to me. As I said, I'm sending my carriage for him, and they can take either the northwest road through Peebles or set out directly north and go through Edinburgh first. 'Tis a bit longer through Edinburgh, but only a day or so, and the most important thing is to ensure the carriage is not set upon by brigands or…worse." He held up a calming hand. "Now, do not take issue with me. The clans are at war with England—"

"There is no declared war."

"My dear, you might as well say there is no declared sun. And if you assure me both roads will be safe, no one will be more grateful than I."

This was something she *could* sense, and her foresight rushed unbidden into the reservoir of her head. Like a cross between a galloping herd of horses and the gurgle of a borderlands stream, the silent rumble, cool and fluid and unstoppable, shook her. She could guide it or give way, but she couldn't stop it, not once it started.

The colors in her head swirled blue and green like the northern sky at Hogmanay. She turned her thoughts to the roads, each a formless blur, like a reflection in a wind-blown lake, but distinct from the other, and

Bridgewater's carriage upon them. No red, no yellow, no orange.

"There's no danger," she said. "The roads will be trouble free."

"Thank you," he said, relieved. "And will you give me your word you'll tell me if that changes?"

He'd said it lightly enough, as if it was the most reasonable thing in the world for a fiancé to ask. And it would be—if she cared about him or Morebright in the slightest. Instead, he was asking her to make an unbreakable oath. Once given, the word of a naiad could not be broken even if the naiad wished to. Did he know this? His face gave away nothing.

"Aye, of course, John." What choice did she have?

"Thank you. I knew I could count on you."

The carriage drove onto the ferry that would take them across the Tweed to Bridgewater's house. The sun was sinking low in the west, spilling its fire over the Cheviot Hills. Fingers of black and red stretched into the sky like tendrils of smoke.

She shook her head and the foresight receded.

"Our wedding awaits," he said when they'd reached the opposite side. "I'm eager to find the priest."

"I am too." And she was, though it wouldn't be till tomorrow, and Bridgewater would find no joy in his search for an officiant to marry them tonight. But he could discover that in his own time.

He settled into the seat. "I'm happy we're of one mind on this."

"'Tis truly the way of love."

Seventeen

"A WEE DRAM" SEEMED LIKE JUST THE THING TO Michael, though he had some misgivings about the man whose hand lay on his shoulder, guiding him through the door. He *did* have red hair, which Undine had indicated one of the two people would possess, but he was also quite imposing, being several inches taller than Michael, and he sported a short sword as well as an expression that suggested trying to run would be fruitless.

"Are you a Scot?" the man asked.

"You dinna think I sound like one?" Michael said, feigning amusement.

"A Scot, aye. A Scot from 1706, nae."

The hairs on Michael's neck lifted. "That's an odd thing to say."

The corner of the man's mouth rose. "And I've hardly begun." He led Michael into the tavern and closed the door behind him.

Michael blinked, his eyes adjusting to the darkness. The place was small and dingy. Four tables filled it. All were empty except for the one at which sat four men in kilts disagreeing loudly about a horse. Another man, also in a kilt, sat on a settee in the corner, drinking from a mug. A small fire burned in the hearth at the side of the room, heating a cast-iron pot from which the potent scents of garlic and onion rose. Saliva poured into Michael's mouth, and he took a step closer to see what it held. He hadn't eaten since…well, since two poached eggs on toast at breakfast, which was starting to seem like more than three hundred years ago.

"What do you say to a wee dram *and* whatever's in that—" Michael stopped. The red-haired man had disappeared, evidently through a curtained doorway to the side.

Michael sighed. He had a few quid in the trousers he'd left at the whorehouse, not that they'd get him anything here except probably burned at the stake. He wondered if he could wash dishes for his supper—if, in fact, they washed dishes at all in this place. The wooden trenchers on the table in front of the arguing men did not appear to be shining examples of household fastidiousness.

The man across the room adjusted the settee with a meaningful squeak, caught Michael's eye, and gestured to the space beside him.

Michael realized then that the man's hair was brown. He looked at the swinging curtains through which the red-haired man had passed and back at the man with the brown hair. It was certainly *possible* they were the couple to whom Undine had referred, Michael thought. Homosexuality hadn't just sprung up in the twentieth century, like jazz or fondue. It had been around for as long as there had been people.

Just because he *personally* wasn't aware of gay culture in Scotland in the seventeen hundreds didn't mean it didn't exist. If one was going to use Michael's knowledge of a subject as a requirement for that subject's existence, one might as well be willing to say goodbye to lace tatting, *Battlestar Galactica* fan fic, and the entire field of neurobiology.

Michael made his way toward the table, hoping he was reading the man's signal correctly, especially as the man seemed to have lost interest in him, staring instead into the depths of his mug.

"Er, may I join you?"

"Could you have made your approach any less subtle? Maybe carried a flaming torch or something." The man—a Scot too—downed the last of his drink.

"I beg your pardon," Michael said, lowering his voice and dropping onto the settee beside him. "I, er, didn't think they were paying attention."

"They're not. But the woman in the scullery is."

Michael swung around. The scullery—at least what he could see of it—appeared to be deserted. "I'm not sure how I could have approached with more subtlety. I mean, I just sort of walked over, usual gait and all that."

The man grunted, his disappointment undiminished.

"Undine told me to—" Michael clapped a hand over his mouth. "Am I allowed to say her name?"

"Too late now. Where did you see her?"

"Just now. At the whorehouse. Er, not in the way you're imagining," he added quickly, seeing the man's expression. "I mean, I don't know what you were imagining or if you were imagining anything, but it was just as a friend—an acquaintance, really. She took me there—I mean, brought me there. She said you'd help me… You and your, er, friend."

"My friend?"

"I don't know what you call him. The man I came in with. Your friend."

"What sort of help do you need?" the man asked.

"Let's start with a name, shall we?"

His brows knit. "You need a name?"

"No, I meant *your* name. What is it? I'm Michael Kent." He held out his hand. He'd decided to keep his Scots accent as a precaution.

"We generally don't use names," the man said, giving him a quick shake. "But you can call me Gerard. If I were you, I wouldn't mention Undine again."

"Fine." Michael was finding it harder to maintain a sense of anxiety about a tiny tavern inhabited by four drunks and two gay guys in the middle of effing Coldstream. "She said you could hide me."

"We can. Ship or wagon?"

"No, no. Here. In Coldstream."

"There's nothing here."

"Well, that's going to make your job harder, isn't it?" Michael laughed, but the man didn't. "I think she meant in your place."

"What's happening in your place?" The red-haired man had reemerged with two mugs and a stone bottle. He handed a mug to Michael, grabbed a chair from the closest table, and moved it over.

"Sorry," Michael said, getting up. "Would you prefer to sit next to him?"

The red-haired man frowned. "Um…nope." He uncorked the bottle and poured something brown in

Michael's mug, refilled Gerard's, and poured some in his own. "*Sláinte*."

Michael sat back down and drank. Whiskey, and a good one—strong and peaty, with bright notes of grass and orange peel.

"An acquaintance the three of us have in common suggested I could put him up for the night," Gerard said, addressing the red-haired man.

"It's going to be a wee bit crowded, no?"

Michael turned to the red-haired man. "I hope you dinna mind."

The man blew a puff of air from his lips. "Not a bloody bit. You're the one who's going to be uncomfortable."

Michael, midsip, choked. "I am?"

"I wouldna want to be the one on that thing," the red-haired man said. "'Tis big enough, mind ye, unlike some, but try to turn or move on it, and it feels like you're impaled on a stockade fence."

"It's not that bad," Gerard said, adding to Michael, who was beginning to feel dizzy, "Trust me. You won't even notice. Duncan likes to complain."

"Duncan?" Michael said, finding his voice again.

"Aye, that's me." The red-haired man extended his hand.

Michael shook it heartily. "You're Lady Kerr's fiancé."

"I am."

"Then you're not…" Michael's forefinger flicked back and forth between the two men.

Duncan frowned. "Not what?"

"Er, sleeping at Gerard's place tonight?"

"God no," Duncan said. "I'd rather sleep on the floor than on that mattress. In any case, her ladyship and I are off to see Chieftain Hay as soon as she finishes the last of her correspondence." He added to Gerard in a meaningful tone, "Undine summoned him. He's one of us."

"Wait," Michael said. "'One of us'? What does that mean?"

"Seriously?" Gerard said, brightening. "How are the Mets doing?" His Scots accent had evaporated.

"You're *American*?" Michael said, aghast.

"That's more surprising than being from the future?" Gerard laughed and turned to Duncan. "What is it with you people?"

He was from the twenty-first century *too*? Was anyone here who they seemed to be? Michael struggled to get his bearings. "Are you American like him?" he asked Duncan.

"Scot," Duncan said soberly.

Gerard said, "And he's got the least-believable accent of all. What about you, Kent? I thought I heard a little Brit there."

Michael was too flustered to know what accent he was doing anymore. "How did you two get here?"

Duncan stretched his legs. "Let's say Undine is not the most careful of spell casters."

"I was lifted out of a bloody performance," Michael said.

"A battle reenactment for me," Duncan said.

Gerard shook his head. "For me, it was a damned fine glass of whiskey. Of course, to be fair," he said, holding up his mug, "you never really know where a damned fine glass of whiskey is going to take you."

"How long have you been here?" Michael asked.

They gave the impression of having been in 1706 for quite a while, and he was starting to worry his interlude would be turning into something more permanent.

Duncan looked at Gerard, and they both smiled. "Long enough to know we're staying," Duncan said.

"You can't leave?" Michael said, feeling his worry grow.

"Oh, aye," Duncan said. "There may be some jiggering to it. But if you decide you want to go, Undine can generally get around to making it happen."

"Generally?"

"She hasn't lost one yet." Duncan refilled the mugs.

Michael relaxed a bit. He wouldn't mind saying good-bye to the National Rose, but that pub in Barcelona was another matter.

Gerard scratched his cheek. "So you're a musician? An actor? You look sort of familiar."

"Actually—"

"Abby said Undine called him to take Bridgewater's confession," Duncan said.

Gerard's eyes widened. "You're a *clergyman*?"

"You were right before," Michael said. "I'm an actor... Well, I used to be. I've been a director the last fifteen years."

"*Trevor Quince!*" Gerard said. "That's it. You're that old wizard guy, what's-his-name, in those movies!"

"Orlando Brashnettle. And thank you."

"Well, well, well, a famous actor in our midst."

"Not very famous. And not in your midst for long, I hope."

"Do you?" Duncan, who seemed to be the more contemplative of the two, regarded Michael with curiosity. "I wouldn't have guessed so, seeing you watch that carriage pull away."

"Why would Undine call an actor to take Bridgewater's confession?" Gerard looked at Duncan, confused.

"She thought she was calling a priest," Michael said. It seemed Undine hadn't told any of her friends about the wedding ceremony. *Odd*.

Duncan pulled his stool closer. "What did Bridgewater tell you?"

Michael swirled the mug absently. Bridgewater's feelings for Undine were a source of displeasure for him. "Not much. He loves her."

"Prick," Gerard said. "As far as I'm concerned, he deserves exactly what he gets."

Michael didn't disagree, but his attention had moved to the men who'd been arguing about the horse. They'd exchanged looks a moment earlier and fallen unnaturally quiet.

"If you ask me"—Gerard went on, and Michael lifted his finger to alert him and leaned his head toward the table. Duncan's hand drifted instantly to his sword, and Gerard, who had stopped talking, cleared his throat and went on in perfect Scots—"Queen Anne can kiss my hairy arse."

As Tybalt, Michael had stabbed Mercutio. As Cyrano, he'd fought a duel with Valvert. As Macduff, he'd killed Macbeth. As a director, he'd even stepped on Henry Higgins's foot hard enough to make him limp for a week after he'd heard him call Eliza Doolittle a bitch. But the last time he'd actually confronted someone with the purpose of doing him true bodily harm was in first form, when Robbie MacNair had taken the seat next to Tamsin Grey in art class, when Robbie *had known for a fact* Michael was the one in love with her, as he'd just confessed as much to Robbie over his ham sandwich at lunch. Michael had thrown a killer punch, but Robbie had had the last laugh, shoving the table so hard that it overturned, and Michael had had to go through the rest of the day with a chipped tooth, blue paint in his hair, and a shirt that looked embarrassingly like one of Jackson Pollock's canvases.

The closest of the men at the table had a pistol at his hip, but none of the others had weapons that Michael could see. Duncan had a sword, Gerard had a knife in his belt, and Michael had a lady's handkerchief. They were at a numerical and ballistic disadvantage, but they had one small, soon-to-expire advantage: the three of them knew something was about to happen before their adversaries knew they knew.

Michael jumped to his feet. "*You're* a fucking hairy arsehole," he said to Gerard in his best imitation of a belligerent, drunk Englishman. "Queen Anne wouldn't wipe her arse with the likes of you or any of your filthy countrymen."

Gerard snorted. "Aye, but only because she's too fat to wipe."

Michael grabbed Gerard by the shirt and dragged him to his feet. "Apologize, you ball-faced turd."

Michael pulled a beautiful stage punch that brushed Gerard's cheek but made a meaty noise against his shoulder. Fortunately for all of them, Gerard's shock at this passed easily for a post-punch daze. To Michael's great relief, Gerard turned out to be a fast learner. He threw a roundhouse that grazed Michael's chin just as Michael snapped his head back. Michael's *oof* was worthy of an Olivier.

He spun in a dizzying circle, milking every millisecond for its dramatic richness, while the four men stared, slack jawed, waiting for him to land.

Duncan, who had leapt to his feet as the first punch was thrown, made his way surreptitiously around the men.

But, like the way a spinning top sometimes does just before it falls, Michael found new balance, slowed, and came to rest in a fighting stance. He grabbed Gerard, whispered "Tuck and roll," and shoved him toward the men. Gerard landed on his side on the table, sending mugs flying in every direction. The table crashed to the ground, knocking three of the men to the floor with it. The fourth, the one with the gun, stood up, disgusted to have been doused with ale. He shook the foam off his arms, and as he wiped his face on his sleeve, Duncan slipped the pistol out of its holster and tossed it lightly to Michael, who promptly hid it in the waistband of his breeks.

The men were crawling to their knees, though Gerard was upright first and slipped through the curtained door.

"Get out of here, ye drunken English gowk!" Duncan said, grabbing Michael by the shirt and towing him into the street. Michael spun for a bit until the door closed, leaving the two of them alone.

"Nice move on the pistol," Michael said under his breath, offering it to him.

"Keep it," Duncan said.

"Who are they?"

"Men who would stop Undine and her rebels. Men who would do her harm. Are ye in?"

"Yes, of course."

"I thought ye might be."

Gerard appeared at the side of the building, giving the other two a thumbs-up.

For an instant, the three men looked at one another, then Gerard disappeared, and Duncan turned to walk in the opposite direction. "The priory," he said quietly to Michael. "But not until after dark."

Eighteen

"Sir?"

Bridgewater blinked, roused from his daydream. The rain had stopped, and outside the window, mists rose in billowing sheets from the warm ground. "Aye, what is it, Gillis? Do we have some word of the bishop or his associate, Father...er..."

"Kent, sir," the corporal said. "No. Nothing regarding either of them."

"Very strange, don't you think, for two church men to disappear on the same day? Most times I would call that a blessing, but today..."

"It's possible they were called back to the bishopric or even to York by the archbishop."

Bridgewater sighed. "Perhaps you're right. I'm sure we'll hear something tomorrow. Has my fiancée settled into her rooms?"

"Actually, sir, that's why I'm here."

Bridgewater heard the odd note in Gillis's voice. "Where is she?" he said.

The man licked his lips. "The lady wished to...avail herself of the river."

"What could you possibly mean?"

Gillis coughed uncomfortably. "She's swimming, sir."

"*Swimming?* In the river? With a brigand or worse possibly running through the woods? 'Twill be pitch-black out there in another quarter hour. Is someone with her?"

"No. The lady would not allow it."

"'Would not *allow* it,'" Bridgewater repeated. "Are you a child? Do you report to my fiancée?"

"No, sir."

"And I've made it clear she's to be guarded at all times."

"Aye, but—"

"But what, Gillis? What could possibly explain your failure to follow orders?"

"She's…naked, sir."

"Naked?"

"Aye, sir. Completely. I told her she was to stay in the house until the danger was past. She laughed. Then I told her that if she chose to disobey your request—I was careful to call it a request, as you said—that I would have to accompany her."

"And?"

Gillis reddened. "And she began to undress."

"She *what?*"

"'Twas only her stockings, but she made no show of any regard for my presence. Not the slightest. 'Twas as if I were a shade from the darkest removes of Hades."

"Oh, for God's sake, you sound like one of Colonel Thorpe's idiot daughters. What happened?"

"I ran, sir."

"And she went to the river?"

"Aye."

"Clothed or naked?"

"I couldn't tell you, sir. But you can see her clothes in a pile near the bank."

Bridgewater turned his gaze to the river. He could see a bend in the water, lit pink by the falling sun. The bank was too high to allow him see her, but her clothes were there, just as Gillis had reported. She was a strange woman, no doubt, but he found her strangeness intriguing. Always had. The idea of possessing her—of commanding her—in bed and out, sent a tingle of pleasure through him. She'd disdained him once, and it was those women—the ones who held themselves above him, despite being lowborn or worse—whose subjugation he most enjoyed, whom he pummeled a bit more roughly than necessary, whom he got with unwanted child and whose heads he held in submission over his lap as he caressed their gleaming hair.

It hurt him to have feelings like that about Undine, with whom he'd surprised himself by falling in love, but the truth was her wifely subjugation *would* please him. He would indulge the worst of his desires outside his marriage—it was the least he could do for a woman he loved—but as his wife, Undine would have to bend to his will. The idea drove him to such a degree of wild longing, he dared not linger on the thought in front of Gillis.

"Leave her," Bridgewater said. "I'll collect her."

"But that wasn't what brought me here."

A sharper reluctance had appeared on the man's face and Bridgewater's concern grew. "Go on."

"I was down the hall from her bedchamber at my post when this began. She left her room, wearing a cloak, and headed toward the back stairs. After a few steps, she stopped and went back in her room, and at that point I began to circle the floor. I think she'd forgotten a hair-brush, for that was what she was tucking into her basket when I stopped outside her doorway. She was surprised to see me naturally, and that is where our discussion took place, but I also saw a letter on her desk."

"And you read it?"

Gillis flushed deeply. "I didn't intend to, but when she started to remove her stockings, I didn't know where to look."

I would have known where to look, Bridgewater thought, imagining those ivory calves. "And?"

"Are you certain you want me to tell you?"

Was Gillis actually trying to appeal to Bridgewater's gentlemanly instincts after he himself read her personal correspondence? "Aye. That's exactly what I want you to do. And be quick about it."

Gillis looked as if he were about to read his own death warrant. "It said only two things: 'nine o'clock' and 'castle.'"

Now it was Bridgewater's turn to flush. Was his fiancée conducting a clandestine affair? That was the obvious conclusion and certainly the thought Gillis wore on his pockmarked face.

"Oh, that." Bridgewater cleared his throat. "She's meeting an acquaintance of mine in Edinburgh on Friday to read his fortune," he said, lying. "He hopes she can help him with his milling business. He's considering an expansion and wonders if the time is right."

"Ah." Gillis bowed. "I see."

Despite the man's words and carefully inscrutable face, it was apparent he *didn't* see, and Bridgewater's anger rose.

Gillis cast a nervous glance toward the river. "Do you want me to take a post near your fiancée?"

"Do I want you to take a post near my naked fiancée? No." Bridgewater returned to the report he'd been reading. "Are you familiar with the Orkneys?"

"The islands to the north of Scotland?"

"Aye. Captain Charles is looking for an aide-de-camp there. I thought you'd do well in that role."

"Oh... I... 'Tis a great distance from here, is it not?"

"To Inverness, where you'll hire a boat, aye. And even farther to the islands. The sea there is quite rough, I hear. You'd do well to lay in a supply of whiskey. 'Twill be good for the crossing as well as the time after you land." *Assuming the crossing doesn't kill you.* "You'll leave before dawn."

"B-but I thought we were heading to Lord Morebright's?"

"Keep your voice down," Bridgewater said, furious. "Have you forgotten this operation was intended to be covert?"

"No, sir, but—"

"*We* are going to Perth. *You* are going to the Orkneys. There's nothing more to be said about it. Pack your things."

Gillis stared, stupefied. *There. Serves you right, you bloody ignoramus.*

"Aye, sir. Th-thank you, sir."

"Don't thank me. Thank Captain Charles."

Bridgewater saluted and the man left. He'd have to write Charles in the morning about the assignment and hope his letter reached the Orkneys before Gillis did.

Bridgewater drummed his fingers on the desk, torn between disparate thoughts, each equally distracting: Undine swimming unclothed in his river and Undine cuckolding him with someone in Coldstream.

The blood in his veins had started to boil, and its hungry buzz filled his ears. Something needed to be done, and he was the man to do it.

Nineteen

With the night as dark as a sea around him and only glimpses of the lambent sky visible above, Michael approached the looming shape with caution.

Priory? Looks more like a pile of rubble to me.

And it was. The great building blocks of the priory lay crushed in heaps. Nothing remained of its former glory—if, in fact, its presence had ever been glorious. The one shape higher than his head—considerably higher, in fact—also turned out to be the only thing left that looked as if it had once enjoyed a stonemason's touch—a stout stone structure off which hung the remains of an iron gate, its hinges rusted and pocked. When the priory had stood, the towering spike at the top, flanked by metal pickets, had made it clear visitors had not necessarily been welcome.

A woman stepped from behind the gate and uncovered a lantern.

Pained by the light, he struggled to make out her face. When his eyes finally adjusted, he inhaled.

She was the dead spit of Duncan—hair like flames; high, feline cheeks; and piercing eyes. Had Undine turned Duncan into a woman?

"Duncan?" he said, dry mouthed.

The woman blinked. "I beg your pardon?" She was a Scot too.

"Are y-you Duncan?"

She held the lantern higher and searched his face, concerned. "Mr. Kent, have ye suffered a head wound? I'm a woman. Can ye not see?"

Gerard appeared, knife drawn. "Is there a problem?"

"He thinks I'm a man," she said.

Gerard returned the knife to his belt. "He'd be the first guy in Britain who did, if that's true."

"You look just like him," Michael said.

She laughed. "Now that's a wee bit different, isn't it? And your first guess wasna that I'm his sister?"

"Are you?" said Michael, almost more surprised.

"No. I'm his aunt."

"A family of very irregular breeding habits," Gerard said, taking a stunned Michael by the arm. "Now why would you think my wife was a man?"

Michael halted. "She's your *wife*?"

"Oh yes. For nearly a month now."

"You're married to Gerard," Michael said to the woman, trying to work out the connections, "and the aunt of Duncan, who's engaged to Lady Kerr."

"Who is my friend and Undine's," the woman said. "Aye."

"Are you from the future?"

"No," she said, shaking her head. "Nor is Abby—er, Lady Kerr."

Michael turned to Gerard. "But you and Duncan traveled here from the future like I did."

"Yes," Gerard said.

Michael did the math in his head. "Is this some sort of weird cross-century dating service?"

"Oh, aye," the woman said dryly. "We draw up a list of all the most sought after features—ye know, tall, handsome, penniless—and put clean linen on the bed just before we fling the fairy dust about."

Michael's jaw fell. "Are you pulling my leg?"

"We definitely need to work on your irony meter," Gerard said. "Everyone knows there's no such thing as fairy dust. The rest is true, though."

Michael wasn't sure what to believe. "I'm not penniless," he said, clinging to at least one thing he knew to be a verifiable fact.

Gerard chuckled. "You are here. Duncan and I rely on the generosity of our mates. Not a bad way to earn a living, though," he said, and ducked when the woman tried to elbow him. "Frankly, I feel I was born for this sort of assignment."

The redhead *tsked*. "He's talking nonsense as usual. My businesses rely on his—what do you call it, Gerard? Advertising acumen?—and Duncan's helping Abby get her clan's finances in order. I'm Serafina Innes, by the way."

She curtsied, and Michael gave her a low bow.

"Please sit," she said, lifting a parcel from a basket. "We brought you supper and another set of clothes. We thought something more tailored would be better."

"Yeah, my best frock coat," Gerard added rather unhappily.

In answer to Michael's quizzical look, Serafina said, "The men in the Red Stag will be looking for two clansmen and a laborer. 'Tis wise for you to look more gentlemanly."

"And the guy you punched in the street will be looking for a priest," Gerard said. "Any more altercations and the only outfit left to hide you in will be one of Sera's gowns."

Serafina unwrapped the parcel, and the smell of chicken reached Michael's nose. His stomach contracted. He'd hidden in the woods outside Coldstream for the last few hours and was famished. "Thank you."

She laid cheese, bread, and the chicken on a large rock and added a corked bottle. He sat down and bit into a leg. It nearly made him groan with pleasure.

"Gerard says you acquitted yourself rather well today."

"Acquitted himself?" Gerard said. "The man's a showman! It was like the Hulk versus Ultron. The only thing missing were the sound effect balloons. 'BOOM!' 'POW!' 'BLAM!' Though the sound of your fist hitting my shoulder added a note of realism to the proceedings," he added, rubbing the aforementioned body part.

"Sorry about that," Michael said, swallowing hungrily. "I figured it was better than breaking your jaw. What more can you tell me about the four men?"

"That," Gerard said, "is an interesting question. I did a little checking after we parted. It turns out they are in the employ of one Colonel Lord Bridgewater."

"He has _Scots_ in his employ?"

"Scots are nae so noble that you couldn't find a few

willing to line their pockets, even here in the borderlands," Serafina said with a note of disgust.

"What exactly is the deal with Bridgewater?"

Gerard laughed. "How long do you have? He's
from the richest family in northern England. His father,
General Bridgewater, was in charge of all the border-
land regiments. Bridgewater stepped into his father's
role when the man died not long ago. However, unlike
his father, who had some honor, Junior is a liar, rapist,
cheat, blackmailer, and two-faced bastard who uses the
army to further his own agenda."

"Which is?"

"Enslaving Scotland for England's benefit and filling
his accounts with all the gold he can squeeze or steal
from either side."

"Sounds like a charming fellow—a real plus one for
a dinner party. Can anyone tell me why Undine would
agree to speak to the man, let alone marry him?"

Serafina and Gerard exchanged a look. "Did you
ask *her*?" Serafina said, a hint of calculated caution in
her eye.

"Well, I…no, not exactly."

"It would be better if she answered that question,"
she said. "There are some things she may or may not
want you to know. In any case, when it comes to
explaining her choice of fiancé, a woman should have
the last word, I think."

"And the first," Gerard added with a grin.

*So they're happy to expound on Bridgewater but not
Undine?* The united and silent front stirred Michael's
already-simmering curiosity about the naiad and gave
him the unmistakable sense that anyone who crossed

her would find himself facing Gerard, Duncan, Abby, and Serafina in a dark alley.

Michael nodded. "As you say then." The priory, or what was left of it, stood on a slight rise north of the town. He could see the Tweed sparkling in the distance and, beyond that, a sprawling house with few lit windows. He pointed. "That's Bridgewater's house, isn't it?"

"He's let it till the fall," Serafina said. "It was Henry VIII's originally."

Michael had no interest in its history, only in the fascinating and fair-haired tenant who had taken up residence there. He looked from window to window, hoping for a hint—a tiny hiccup in his pulse—that might suggest she was within. But none of the windows suggested anything. He was no Undine, it seemed, when it came to divination.

"There is some news," Gerard said. "We have a source in Bridgewater's circle. He said there's been an increase in activity at the estate—carriages being prepared for a journey. And officers have been in and out all day with notes for Bridgewater. Something is being planned."

"A battle?" Michael asked. "That would explain the carriages too. He'd want Undine out of the way."

"Not that large scale. We'd have heard about that. But Serafina has sent a note to Abby, who as you know left for Clan Hay, just in case. Bridgewater also sent to the bishopric for a priest."

Michael stopped eating. "Indeed?"

"Yes. And according to our source, Bridgewater seemed quite urgent about it. We can't figure it out."

Michael stood, appetite gone. Lights twinkled in the windows of the estate. Was she married even now?

Serafina asked, "Mr. Kent, do you know why a priest would be needed so urgently?"

She had the same annoying insightfulness as her red-haired nephew. Michael shook his head. "No."

"Well, that's the least of our worries," Gerard said. "Bridgewater was also snooping in Undine's bedroom."

Michael wheeled around. "We have to do something. She's in trouble."

"Maybe," Gerard said. "Maybe not. Bridgewater would search his best friend's room if he thought he could get away with it, even without being under a spell. He's a very suspicious man. In any case, there's not much we can do."

Ram down the door of the house. Pull Undine from the danger. Set fire to what's left. "No, I suppose not," Michael said. In the distance, sparks of moonlight appeared on the Tweed, and at once he knew she was there, in the water. He could feel her almost like a charge in the air before a lightning storm.

Gerard stood. "Serafina and I have to go. There's more food in the basket and a sort of room there in the back of the ruins, in case it rains. I'm sorry we can't offer you better lodging, but we just can't risk bringing you back into town."

"You should give him a plaid too," Serafina said. "For a blanket."

"There's one on the horse. Hang on." He hurried off.

Michael was already making plans and didn't catch Serafina watching him until it was too late.

"It won't be as easy as you think," she said.

"I don't know what you mean."

"Mr. Kent, you may be a good actor, but you're not a very good liar."

"I can't seem to help myself."

He could feel rather than see her smile.

"Aye, well, I ken this adventure in the past may seem like a dream to you, in which anything can be ventured without real cost, but you will face real risk if you get involved."

"I don't give a damn about Bridgewater," he said.

"I was talking about Undine."

"What about Undine?" Gerard said, reappearing with a folded woolen wrap, which he tossed to Michael.

"Mr. Kent was just telling me how interested he is in learning more about the legendary powers of naiads."

Gerard snorted. "Real glutton for punishment, eh?"

"That's me."

Twenty

UNDINE SWAM FULL POWER AGAINST THE CURRENT, losing herself in the life-giving exertion. Here, in the dark depths, she could forget the world and clear her head. She rolled on her back, taking in the oppressively spangled sky. The water was cold and bracing, and the world smelled of dirt and lilac.

He was out there.

She could feel Michael Kent, even if she couldn't see him, and she was deeply annoyed by it.

Her life was smooth and unblemished, like the skin of a fish, which allowed her to move freely between the north and south, Scotland and England, war and peace, water and earth. The people in her life were weights, holding her down, river weed that tangled in her fins, clouded her vision, and choked her gills.

She could endure some of it. Abby's sisterly love warmed her cold blood. Abby was sunlight in the darkness, and Abby's group of friends—Duncan, Serafina, Gerard—had made the light shine even brighter.

But Kent was other.

Male. Stinking, demanding, maneuvering, immovable male.

When she allowed her mind to turn to him, it was as if he blocked out everything else. Why did women permit this—desire it, even? How could one think clearly with such…egregious virility banging around in their heads, snapping at their thoughts?

She heard the sounds of splashing around the bend of the river, at the ford. Men again, determined to master the water. First the crossing by foot, then the ferry. There would be a bridge there in time. She could feel the unformed scar already growing in the earth beyond the bank.

Grrr.

She turned again, paddling with her arms now too. Hard and fast—as fast as she could move. The earbobs felt like ballast. She righted herself, furious, and pulled them off. She would have thrown them into the darkness had they not been Abby's.

"Undine?"

She jerked and dove under the water. *Kent*, she thought angrily, *somewhere along the bank*. She was embarrassed, which made her even angrier. She'd never felt shame for her nakedness till now.

"Undine?"

"What?"

"It's me. Father Kent."

Father Kent. Ha. "You're hardly a father, are you?"

"Well, er…no."

The night was so dark and the tall banks so reflective of sound, she couldn't quite locate him. But his deep voice carried, disembodied, to the farthest edges of the water.

"In my defense, I did intend to tell you," he said.

"I'm so grateful. What are you really?"

She couldn't see him in the dark, but the sound of his movement came at the highest point of the bank.

"Don't come any farther," she snapped.

The movement stopped.

"I work in the theater," he said.

His Bankside "congregation"! Her cheeks warmed. "Oh, you certainly had your fun with me, didn't you?"

"It was not the sort of fun I intended—er, what I mean to say is, I had no desire to have fun at your expense. I was dressed as a priest and you needed one. I only intended to make myself useful to you."

Hm.

"I'm sorry," he added, rueful.

She sighed. "Thank you," she said, shaking off her pique. "Now you must leave. Bridgewater's idiot corporal has been following me, and he can't find you here. Nor can Bridgewater. And one of the two will be here at any moment to claim me. I'm surprised we haven't been interrupted already."

For a long moment Kent didn't respond.

"Did you marry him?" he asked.

"Of course not," she said, touched by the plaintiveness of the question. "We had no priest. Do you think the Earl of Bridgewater jumps over a broom when he's taking his countess? You must leave before he finds his ascetic churchman has reappeared."

"There's something I need to tell you," Kent said. "About Bridgewater."

"Don't say it now. There are ears everywhere. I'm getting out."

She emerged into the cool air, and he gasped.

"Your clothes…" he said, panicked. "Do you want me to…?"

"*No*," she said, stomping up the bank. No one would force her into shame.

Blood buzzing in her ears, she reached for her chemise, but before she could grab it, dry wool encircled her from behind, and Kent drew her into his warm arms.

"You must be freezing," he said, rubbing her shoulders.

"Where did you get the plaid?" she said. It was too dark even for her to see if she recognized it.

"Your friend, Gerard." The rubbing motion was sending sent tiny coals of fire through her.

"You met Gerard?"

She was used to drying by sitting until her bones ached with the chill. The advantage of drying by body warmth seemed dizzyingly obvious to her now. Why had she never thought to try it before?

"Yes. And Serafina. Nice people. They're the ones who told me Bridgewater searched your room."

She turned to face him. "How would they know that?"

"They have a source in Bridgewater's circle. Someone who keeps an eye on things."

Who was it? Damn them.

"You mustn't be angry," he said. "They can't stop their caring."

"They should have asked me."

He laughed. "I can't imagine why they didn't."

"Who is it?"

"They didn't say. And Bridgewater has sent for another priest."

She turned. "*What?*"

Michael turned her back around and used a corner of the wool to rub the moisture from her hair. His hands were large and gentle, and the thrum of the motion was calming.

"Let's hope the bishopric has lost enough men for the day and refuses to toss another to the wind," he said.

"If Bridgewater mentioned Father Kent by name in his note, they'll figure out something's amiss."

"I know." He released her hair and tucked the plaid around her neck. "What's that?"

"What?"

"There. In your hand." He gently opened her fingers.

She'd forgotten she was holding the earrings. She was grateful the night hid the warmth that filled her cheeks.

"Pretty," he said, though she could feel his eyes on her not the earbobs. "I can see why you wouldn't want to lose them." He took one from her and held it up. "How does it work? I've never seen an earring with a spring." Without waiting for an answer, he tugged her lobe lightly and slipped one into place. "I'll be damned." He touched the stone with his finger, setting the iolite swinging and sending a vibration that ran all the way to her toes. "Now, get dressed and you can tell me what I need to do to help."

He slipped away behind her, whistling as he went, until he'd put himself on the far side of a fat pine.

"Stop whistling," she called. "You're inviting trouble."

He laughed, a low, rumbling sound that made

her smile. She was reluctant to remove the plaid. She'd also forgotten the pleasure a pair of arms could bring.

It didn't surprise her that Bridgewater had been in her room. Despite his promises, she knew he'd never intended to allow her to live without his oversight. The question was whether his intrusion into her privacy was driven by a general lack of trust or whether it represented some shift in his perception, one that might be the result of the receding effects of the spell.

She loosened the plaid and ran it over her breasts and shoulders, removing the last remnants of water. Spy business was not for the faint of heart.

The rustling Kent was making in the distance reminded her spy business was also not for innocent outsiders. It wasn't that he lacked the spirit—he'd shown himself to be surprisingly brave and true—but she wouldn't allow him to risk his life for her.

"What can I do for you?" he called. "Tell me while you dress."

"What you need to do," she said, twisting the other earbob in place, "is leave."

Even in the dark, she could feel his disappointment.

"Why?"

"We don't know what Bridgewater's capable of. You don't know what I'm trying to accomplish. And—" She caught herself and stopped.

"And what?"

"I told you. I'd spend every moment afraid for your safety." Her neck prickled with embarrassment. "Now will you please just leave?"

The silence between them grew in length, and her ability to overcome it lessened. She listened for anything—a breath, a sigh, the sounds of his retreat— that would help her interpret his reaction, but all was lost in a long gust that whistled through the trees.

Begone then, she thought, irritated. *You're losing your focus. What are you letting this man do to you?*

"Nothing." She flung the plaid to the ground and reached for her chemise.

The pine boughs shook, and Bridgewater stepped into view.

"John!" She jerked the linen into place. Her heart was beating so hard she dared not say anything. What had he heard? Had he seen Kent?

"I beg your pardon," Bridgewater said. "I didn't mean to interrupt you."

"What are you doing here?"

"I'd ask you the same, but I know you well enough to know your affinity for water. Were you talking to someone?"

"Aye," she said, stooping for her gown. "My mother."

He made a show of looking around. "Your mother? I would very much like the pleasure of meeting her."

"I wish I could offer it to you. She died many years ago. But I feel her presence whenever I'm near water. I'm very grateful you took a home on the river, John. Thank you."

"I had only your happiness in mind. And you… speak to her?"

He wandered the edge of the bank slowly, hands clasped behind his back, peering carefully left and right. Undine hoped Kent had heard her exclamation and was putting as much distance as he could between him and this clearing.

"Do you never speak to your mother or father?" she said. "At their graves? Or perhaps in the places in which you feel closest to them?"

Bridgewater shook his head. "I confess I do not. My father and I weren't close. I doubt my voice would be much salve to him, or his to me. Did your mother make you angry?"

"Make me angry?"

"You spoke to her quite sharply," he said, finishing his inspection.

"Oh, that." She was relieved to see he did not intend to extend his search beyond the clearing in which they stood. "'Twas only her asking me what I'd done recently to help those around me and me responding as a sulky child. One tends to fall into childish ways sometimes. My mother was a good woman and has always guided me well."

Bridgewater made a polite grunt, reflecting agreement or disbelief, she couldn't tell. His gaze fell on the plaid puddled on the ground, and she inhaled. He snagged it and held it out to her. "I didn't know you partook in the ways of the clans."

"'Twas a gift," she said tartly. "From Abby."

"I have no objection to you having friends whose opposition to England is well-known, but even you must see that an English noblewoman—the wife of an English officer—cannot be seen wearing a plaid."

She snatched it from his hand. "I have not worn it. Nor would I."

"Thank you. Now I must entreat you to return with

me to the house. Not only is it unsafe for a woman to be out alone at night, but there are things you must attend to."

"What things?"

"I've received a note. We must take a journey. You'll have to give the maids instructions on what you want to be packed."

"A journey? Where?"

"To the north, near Traquair. I've received word Wooler is flooded, which means the man from my solicitor's office won't arrive in time to accompany Morebright to York. I intend to do it myself."

She didn't have the slightest interest in sitting in a carriage alone with Bridgewater for that long. "I must remain behind. I have things I need to do."

"Tomorrow, do you mean?" He met her gaze, curious.

"Tomorrow, and every day," she said, frowning.

"I cannot leave you here to face the unpredictable dangers of the borderlands alone."

"One imagines the guards on your estate might provide some help in that—or the army if it comes to that." She smiled sweetly. "I know the families of the borderlands would be relieved to see the regiments watching me instead of going about their usual unpleasant business."

"I will not marry you and then immediately appear to abandon you," he said, impatience growing. "'Twould be unseemly."

"Then I fear we will have no problem. Lacking a priest, 'tis unlikely in the extreme we shall be able to marry before you leave."

He caught her by the wrist and she gasped. She focused her thoughts like a pinpoint of white light on Kent. *If you heard this, do not turn around. You'll sacrifice us both.*

"Undine, I'm getting the impression you're not quite as certain of your feelings as you have led me to believe."

The pressure of his grip was like a red-hot band of steel.

"Then you should be a fortune-teller yourself. I'm on the verge of ending our engagement this instant. Whatever my feelings for you are, I could never love a man who forced me into anything," she said, furious. "Now release my wrist."

Bridgewater did, and she slapped him. As hard as she was able.

The shock delayed the inferno for a moment or two, but it exploded, full flamed, in the inky black of his pupils. He would either strangle her then and there or curb his impulses, but she didn't know which.

He fought to master his voice. "You…you…"

She braced herself for the blow.

"Y-you are perfectly correct," he said, making a choking noise and beginning to weep. "I'm so sorry. You must see I can't leave you behind. You must see. You must."

"John." It was the effect of the spell, not regret, though she was surprised how unhinged he'd become. She patted his back. "'Tis not worth your worry."

"If Simon were to see me newly married without my wife… Don't you see? He'd know everything my father said about me was right. Please, you must come."

If she went, she would be without friends, without recourse, and without Kent. But if she said no, there was no telling what Bridgewater would do.

"Please," he begged.

"John."

"Please."

"All right. If it means that much to you."

He held her hand against his sopping cheek, then pressed it to his mouth in a kiss. "Thank you. Thank you. You are so good to me."

Morebright's home. She shook her head. If Bridgewater had something in his possession here that would prove the army was involved in an attack, she'd best find it tonight.

Twenty-one

"I'M GLAD YOU'RE HERE, SIR," SAID A YOUNG SERVANT
to Bridgewater when he and Undine stepped into
the towering entry hall. "There's a man here. In the
drawing room. The housekeeper is looking for you."

"'Tis the priest," Bridgewater said with far more
excitement than Undine was feeling. "I sent for
another." He squeezed her hand and ran a few steps
ahead to the drawing room doors.

"Wait."

He paused, hands on the knobs. "Aye?"

"I'm not feeling well," she said, which wasn't a lie,
though her unsettledness was more of the spirit than
body. "I think I shall go to bed."

"Come in just for a moment. He can marry us in
the morning, but you should greet him. I insist."

He opened the doors, leaving no room for argument. The man warming his hands before the fire was
not a priest. He wore a dark blue frock coat, and the
straightness of his spine spoke of an overage of pride.
He pulled at a cuff fastidiously. A green tricorne hid
his eyes, but Undine expected to find a meanness of

spirit there, and the closely trimmed beard in the latest manner of Parisians suggested their visitor was a man more intent on his appearance than his character.

The solicitor, without a doubt.

As if he'd heard her thoughts, Bridgewater said, "You must be from my solicitor's office. Thank you for coming."

The man removed his hat and dipped an abbreviated bow, clearly in no way moved by nobility. "I apologize for my late arrival. The bridge at Wooler was out and my associate's carriage couldn't make it across, but I happened to be working for another client close by, which he knew, and he sent word to me. I'm Charles Beaufort, by the way. At your service, sir."

"Welcome, Mr. Beaufort."

Undine started. The man's eyes were beady and sharp, but a hint of something else lived there as well.

"Do I have the honor of addressing your fiancée?"

"Aye, you do. Undine, may I introduce Mr. Beaufort. Mr. Beaufort, this is, well, Undine. She has no surname—at least not yet."

The man took her hand and kissed it. It was if the touch of his mouth lit the fuse of a Chinese firecracker. When he lifted his lips and met her eyes, her half-distracted perception of events turned inside out.

Mr. Beaufort was *Kent*!

She started so hard she nearly gave herself away. She couldn't have been more dumbfounded if he'd turned into a goshawk and flown out the window. But how had he done it? It was like one of those trompe l'oeil drawings that look like one thing one moment and another thing the next. Now, so clearly Kent, and before, so clearly—

"…must be tired, don't you agree, Undine?"

She shook her head to remove the cobwebs. What had Bridgewater been saying to her? "I am tired," she murmured uncertainly.

Kent chuckled, that same enchanting rumble that seemed to vibrate through every bone in her body. "It seems as if your fiancée is as tired as I must look," he said. "Perhaps we should all go to bed, aye?"

The charged gray of his eyes made her breath catch, and she realized her hand was still dangling midair from the kiss. She thrust it under her arm. He shouldn't be here, and the plans she'd laid so carefully were being rearranged like a deck of cards being shuffled.

"We should," she said.

This time it was Bridgewater who laughed. "My dear, if I didn't know better I'd say Mr. Beaufort has transfixed you. Beaufort, take care now. I would not like any solicitor of mine to steal my fiancée."

"I should never attempt such a thing."

And just like that, he was Beaufort again. She stared at him as if to nail his persona in place. But she couldn't. It was inexplicable—and maddening.

"Come, Undine," Bridgewater said, "let me escort you to the stairs."

"I-I…" She wanted to protest, but her tongue couldn't work fast enough.

Bridgewater took her arm and called over his shoulder, "Let us confer in the morning, Beaufort. One of my servants will show you to your room."

"I'm certain I shall find everything I need."

Twenty-two

SHE'D SIMMERED LONG ENOUGH IN HER CHAMBER, SHE thought, waiting for the house's occupants to adjourn to their rooms for the night. Now she stood at the corner of the main upstairs hall, waiting for the inexorably slow footman dousing the sconces to finish his rounds.

When the hall fell dark and the last footsteps receded, she ran silently to Kent's door, opened it, and slipped inside.

"You have *magic*," she said, shutting the door with an angry *click*.

He was sitting in candlelight, by a heavily draped window, a book in one hand and a glass in the other. His beard lay beside him on the table. "I'd advise you for both our sakes to keep your voice down," he said, standing.

"You have magic," she whispered. "You're a wizard or a conjurer or a magus."

"I told you I work in the theater." He tossed the book on the chair and went to a table, where a decanter and pistol sat. He certainly hadn't been carrying a pistol before.

"You changed today," she said. "Before my eyes."

He grinned. "Did you like that?" He filled a second glass with something the color of burnished gold.

"He couldn't tell it was you. Neither could I."

"I can see you didn't care for that." He placed the glass in her hand and drank from his own.

"Mr. Kent—"

"Michael, please."

"Michael…Mr. Kent…I am not a woman who's easily beguiled. 'Tis clear you've used a potion on me—and possibly Bridgewater as well. And we aren't even addressing the foolish risk you've taken in coming back here against my instructions, using a pretense that may ruin the plans I already have in place."

"I'm your best option at this point."

"*The potion*, Mr. Kent. I demand you explain yourself."

"Fine. Let me see, if I fooled you, then I am, by definition, a sorcerer. Is that right?"

"Aye."

"Is it possible that when confronted with a bit of skilled acting, you were simply taken in, just as Bridgewater was? He may be a bloody awful man, but you could hardly argue you're more observant than he is, could you?"

"Aye, sir, I could. And I insist you tell me what sort of dark art you've practiced on me."

He rubbed his cheek, amused, and his amusement infuriated her.

"Dark art, is it? What makes you so sure I've 'practiced' anything on you?"

"Because I couldn't tell it was you, and it explains why—" She caught herself.

"Why what?"

Her cheeks grew hot. "Why I'm behaving so ridiculously." She tore off the earrings and threw them on the bed. "You put a spell on me."

"A *spell*?"

"A love spell. I'm well versed in the ways of potions. I know exactly what you've done. Remove it instantly. I insist."

He downed the rest of his liquor and put down the glass. He stepped closer, so close in fact she could see a tiny bit of glue stuck to his cheek. Then he pointed to her glass. "I suggest you drink that."

"Why?" She brought the glass to her lips and noticed her hand was shaking. She downed a generous gulp.

He took the glass from her and put it on the table next to his. Then he put his hands on her waist.

It was as if her body were a crucible in which a chemical reaction had begun—proof, if any was needed, of his damnable magic.

He stared at his hands, as if deciding what to do next. She marveled at the delicate black fringe around his eyes and the planes of his cheek, dotted with stubble. He was a skilled magus, for his touch held a powerful inducement. She knew this was how love potions worked, though she'd never experienced it like this herself.

There was important information to be gathered if she used this as an opportunity to observe and—

Ooh!

His thumbs brushed her hipbones. The magic was hard to monitor objectively.

His eyes found hers. "Let's say for the moment I am

a wizard—I'm not—but let's say for the moment I am.
What would you do?"

"I-I would make myself immune to your methods.
You are, and I have."

He bent his head so that his mouth hung just above
hers. She could smell the whiskey, earthy and rich, and
the soapy scent of his skin. The electric charge was the
strongest she'd ever felt. She was surprised to find her
fingers in the short, soft waves of his hair.

"So it's not possible to be lured into doing something you don't innately want to do?"

"No," she said. "I'm glad."

Their lips met. The effect was dizzying. How did
mere humans fight it? This wouldn't be the first time
she'd entangled herself physically with a man—and
while she acknowledged the appeal of the ancient,
primitive rite that was so desired by their sex, the
effect had been too fleeting to have the same impact
on her. What would it be like, she wondered, to
combine the stultifying emotional drunkenness of the
spell with the physical response?

They parted and he touched her chin. Her face
lifted without thought, a marvelous effect. She must
ask him when they finished if it was flag root or anise.

His eyes, so soft and warm, crinkled at the corners.
"What *are* you thinking about?"

"Is the effect the same on you as it is on me?"

He smiled. "Yes, actually, it is."

"Odd. A spell that works on the recipient as well as
the giver. You're very talented."

"Okay, I'll allow myself to take credit but not in the
way you think."

She lifted her mouth again and kissed him deeply. She broke away, awed. "The spell grows in power."

"It's not a spell."

Not a spell? 'Tis as if a team of oarsmen were racing through my belly. All she could think about was his hands on her, loosening her gown, lifting her breasts, spreading her thighs.

"What happens next?" she whispered.

"What happens next is up to you."

"Use your magic. I'm not afraid."

He took her cheek in his sturdy, warm hand. "I have no magic to use on you, Undine, except for the magic any lovers have when they're attracted to one another. I wasn't lying when I said I'm not a wizard. I'm just a man who wants to know you better."

"Know me?"

His eyes twinkled. "You're going to make me say it, are you? I'd like to take you to bed."

She nearly laughed. What did people think they learned in that ridiculous, brief, awkward tangle? And yet the look on his face made it seem as if his understanding of her would grow tenfold. Suddenly she felt her experience had been lacking. She'd never learned anything in bed worth the trouble, but with Kent— solid, unchanging Kent—she thought she might.

"I think we should," she said.

He removed the pins in her hair and loosened the strands with his fingers. "Those eyes," he said in wonderment. "I swear I see the ocean in there. When I taste you, will you taste of salt?"

"Naiads are river creatures, sir."

"Ah. Then earth and iron."

She wanted to remind him he had just finished tasting her and that any question he had concerning her taste should have been answered, but it dawned on her with a rush of heat that may not be what he meant.

He led her to the bed and undressed. The absurdly bright loin cloth he slipped off made her smile. His body was lithe and his arms and thighs ropey. And he wanted her as much as she wanted him.

Lovemaking was a foolish pastime—ungainly, risky, especially for a woman and even more so for a spy—and filled with small embarrassments. But she found she wanted to be a fool.

He helped her with her ties and gown, and she removed her chemise.

His gaze brushed her body appreciatively. Unlike many men, his eyes hid nothing. In them lived a heady mixture of desire, anticipation, and joy. It was far more revealing than seeing him naked, and yet he did nothing to hide his feelings. And not a single ounce of need to own her existed in his gaze.

The magic coursed through her veins, tickling the roots of her hair and the inside of her knees. Some of these things she'd felt before, but this occasion had a gravity to it that was new to her. It glided around her heart, warming it like a velvet cloak on an October night.

She wrapped her arms around him, her palms coming to rest in the smooth divots of his buttocks.

"Shall we lie down?" he said, his voice coming muffled through her hair.

"Aye," she said. They crawled in side by side.

The linens smelled of wood fire, and the hairs of his

chest rubbed her cheek. Using touch alone, she tried to draw out any lies or falseness in him, to bring them to the surface so that she might assess them in the candlelight, but all she found was the same Michael Kent she'd known since he arrived. He might be a priest or solicitor or actor, but the man beneath the costume was exactly the man he'd always shown himself to be.

The heat of their kissing scorched her. Their mouths roamed. He lived up to the implied promise in his earlier question, and she writhed, his tongue against her bud. The potion was so strong and her desire to shield herself from its powers so weak.

He was practiced and deeply attentive. She needed only think a thing before he was doing it or allowing her to do it. They were like seals swimming together, flipping and turning in a perfect, spellbinding unison. She felt free of earthly bounds, as if the world beyond his arms had disappeared.

His mouth trailed down her neck, between her breasts, and down deep, deep, to where he'd begun their journey.

The magic, near to boiling, threatened to unleash the last of its powers. She gasped. But the release, satisfying and expansive, didn't slake her thirst as it usually did—not even close. She folded her hand around his cock, and he groaned.

Her heart was leaping like a stag now. The foolishness of men and women. Stupid, ridiculous, enthralling foolishness.

She surprised herself by taking the length in her mouth—black art at its most potent. She'd seen the pictures in books, heard the grunting cries, witnessed the couples in empty closes, but she'd never done it herself. If he'd reached for her head, she'd have stopped immediately, but he merely twisted and panted, palms over his eyes, while she savored the pleasure she bestowed.

"You're going to kill me," he said.

And it was a sort of death. A death and a rebirth. But she'd never felt it until now. Oh, the lightning strike, aye, with its attendant cries and arching back and grasping fingers. That part had been familiar enough. But not the sense that her heart had been momentarily stopped, or even that she'd wish it to be.

She was drunk under the spell now, and she touched and tasted whatever her exploring hands found.

He brought her mouth back to his and held her in a hungry kiss until her toes curled.

Then he climbed between her legs and slipped inside her. His hand found the place where their bodies joined, and he moved in a steady rhythm, his chest brushing hers. This joining eye to eye flustered her, and it was only his gentle *shhhh shhhh* that held her in the moment.

He asked if she was ready with the lightest press of his fingertips, and she assented with a squeeze. His release lifted her nearly from the bed with a force beyond magic. They fell into each other's arms.

"I have a number of questions."

He chuckled. "I feel like I should be surprised, but I'm not."

"You're quite practiced."

"That's not a question. I'm not sure it's even a compliment."

"Does the magic impact your performance?"

He smiled. "Yes. Very much so."

"Why? Is it the reverse action of the agent, possibly when you were handling it?"

He brushed his lips along the inside of her elbow, and she inhaled, surprised. "Yes," he said.

"The spell didn't dissolve after I experienced my release. Was it supposed to?"

He shook his head. "No."

"Did yours?"

"No. I want you even more now, if that's possible."

She stretched against him. "We could…"

"We will," he said, bringing her hand to his lips, "but for now I just want this."

"What?"

"Us. Here. Talking and touching."

"Oh." The idea offered its own mystical power, and she entwined her legs with his.

"*Ow.*" She rolled away, looking beneath her, and he chuckled.

"You were lying on a thistle," he said, "two of them, to be exact. No wonder it hurt." He cupped the earbobs in his palm.

"They're Abby's."

"The symbol of her clan?" he asked.

"Aye. And all of Scotland, as you know."

He clasped her lobe and slid one of the earrings into place. "They're quite eye-catching," he said, tapping the dangling stone with his finger.

The skin on her arms prickled into gooseflesh.

"Come now." He touched her chin, and she turned her head as if he'd tugged a string. The second earbob went on. She felt a bit like she'd just been clapped in chains, but the sensation was not entirely unpleasant, especially given the dancing light in his eyes.

"When will it wear off?" she asked.

"The earrings?"

"The spell."

He wrapped a skein of hair around his palm and held it to his nose. "Never, I hope."

"*Never?*" She sat up, gathering the cover around her. "That can't be."

"It's not the sort of thing either of us can answer."

"Mr. Kent, 'tis one thing to exercise a spell of short duration on me. 'Tis quite another to make it irrevocable. And, in any case, I've never heard of a spell that can't be reversed."

"Michael," he said plaintively. "Please. I promise if you wish it to end, it'll happen, even if I wish otherwise. Please lie down. There's something you need to know, and our time here must be short."

She leaned back. "What is it?"

"Something is happening with the army. Nothing large scale, but officers have been in and out with notes for him. Also, the carriages are being prepared for travel."

She flicked her gaze to the guttering candle beyond him. "Oh."

He sat up. "You knew."

"He told me. At the river. After you left. We're heading north to visit an old family friend of his who's ill—Lord Morebright. Though his intention was to send someone from his solicitor's office. You, I suppose, or the man whose place you took. You had best be gone by morning unless carting around lecherous old reprobates is something you'd enjoy."

"Would you have gone with him—Bridgewater, I mean?"

"Aye."

"You'd go alone in a carriage with a man whom you believe to be violent and untrustworthy?"

"Michael…" She took care to use his Christian name, as he'd asked. She wished fervently to lessen the pain in his eyes. "It was unlikely to be dangerous. He's under a spell."

Michael frowned. "What sort of a spell?"

"A love spell. Like this one."

"It's not like this one, I assure you. What does it mean? What are its effects?"

"He cares for me. He desires me. He's blinded enough by his feelings to allow me some freedom to move around unmonitored. Which I need in order to gather information," she added quickly, seeing the argument rise in his eyes.

"You drugged him to gather information?"

"*I* didn't drug him. He stole a potion from me meant for someone else. And he took it. He thought it was an aid to fornication, and he intended to seduce the daughter of a friend."

"Did he?"

"Partly." She would not soon forget the sight of Bridgewater, breeks around his ankles, being fellated by the poor girl. "But it wasn't the result of my spell, only his own disgusting lechery."

Kent was exceptionally quick, and she could see the questions forming as he worked out the scenario.

"Then why didn't he fall for the girl?"

"Love spells don't work that way," she said. "One has to be inclined to fall in love with the person already. The spell simply pushes the taker over the edge."

"So he *loves* you?"

"He was *inclined* to love me. Believe me, I was as surprised as you are. But he won't hurt me, don't you see? As long as the spell has made him fall truly in love with me, I needn't fear anything."

"Right. Only his desire to take you to his bed. Tell me, has he, to your knowledge, ever used force on a woman?"

The question surprised her, and she tripped on the answer.

"No," he said, standing.

"What do you mean?"

"You can't go."

The anger must have shown on her face because he added, "I don't mean I won't let you. I mean no one in their senses should be willing to go. Think of your friends. Think of me."

Think of him? As if *that* were likely to result in clear-headed decision making. Her independence was the reason she could be a spy. If she worried about worrying her friends or the men who chose to spend an hour in her bed, she'd be frozen in place, unable to make any decisions.

"It isn't a matter of caring about people. It's a matter of doing my job. I have an opportunity now, at Bridgewater's side, to help the people who long for peace."

His face softened. "Undine, surely you know how

the things that are happening in Scotland are going to turn out? You can see the future, can't you?"

The buzzing in her head returned. History as it would be written; the hard work and desire of the people trying to change it; the tension, palpable to her, of what was and what could be—she could feel it all. Yet she believed the future could be changed. She'd seen it on a personal level—a friend she'd helped return to the love of his life in the future, restoring their happiness, a man changing his luck via a trip to another century. If that could happen, why couldn't these small things stack up into something much larger, like rocks into a bridge or bricks into a home? Her theory—for she'd spent many long hours asking herself why she felt driven by a force beyond herself to work against the treaty of Union—was that such a change required a coordinated mass of determination working for it, the sort that could only come from brother aligning with brother, neighbor with neighbor, and even enemy with enemy. She didn't know the size of the mass needed. She only knew she couldn't stop trying to gather it.

"Of course I know what happens," she said. "And it's because I know that I fight. But, please, I beg you. Don't talk about what you know. It clouds my vision and makes it harder for me to see the change that must be made."

He looked at her sadly, and she knew he was thinking of the history he knew. He took her hand and passed it across his lips. "Some fights may not be worth the sacrifice. That's all I'll say."

"Do you mean because the Scots lose?"

His eyes widened.

"Aye," she said. "I know what happens, but not for the reason you think. Tell me, if you found yourself at dinner with John Wilkes Booth before the play that night, what would you do?"

His face softened. "You're saying that by carrying on as Bridgewater's fiancée, you have the chance to stop something akin to John Wilkes Booth?"

"Essentially, aye."

He tugged her back to the mattress and into his arms. "But what I'm saying is you may be Abraham Lincoln."

A knock sounded, and her heart lurched.

Kent reached for the pistol. "Hide," he whispered.

Twenty-three

BRIDGEWATER HEARD THE DOOR SHUT JUST BEFORE HE rounded the corner of the darkened hallway.

Why would Beaufort be up at this hour? When he made the corner, the door was closed. If Beaufort had been awake, he'd just returned to his room. Or maybe he'd heard a noise in the hall.

Then Bridgewater heard Undine's voice—or thought he had. Just a note. Scarcely enough to identify her, but he hesitated nonetheless. He looked up and down the hall. He'd given one of his colonels permission to lodge his twin daughters in the house for the month. Perhaps it was one of them—or an errant servant.

He took a deep breath.

You're being absurd.

The French carpet and thick wood door blocked sound and light. There was no way to tell if Beaufort was awake, asleep, entertaining a guest, or performing with an acrobatic troupe, for that matter. Bridgewater could knock, of course, but how would he explain the interruption?

So sorry, Beaufort, I forgot it was this late.

My servant said you might desire a glass of sherry before sleeping.

Oh, is this your bedchamber? Forgive me. I thought it was the map room. One never knows where one is in a new house, ha-ha!

He waited a long moment and heard nothing more. Normally, that would have been enough, but the memory of the look on Undine's face when she was talking to the solicitor tickled uncomfortably at his memory.

He shook it off and walked to the top of the stairs, then stopped again.

Good Lord, you can just walk to her room if you're that concerned.

But he'd promised her he wouldn't press for an entrée into her bed until she was ready, and that meant keeping a respectful distance between them—he on the English side of the house, she on the Scottish.

It ground on him to play the obedient sweetheart. He longed for the day (and night) when Undine would be the one having to submit to demands. He'd never wanted a woman the way he wanted her, but want her he did, and until he had her, he'd never be happy.

In direct violation of his sense of dignity, he walked to the Scottish wing and crept down Undine's hall. The door was closed. He was about to put his ear to it when one of the little urchins who worked in the house came whistling down the hall.

"*Shh,*" he said. Abashed, the boy bowed and shifted the basket of candles he was carrying from one arm to the other, his uncombed hair falling across his eyes. The moment he was safely past Bridgewater, he ran.

When Bridgewater was alone, he put his ear to the door and heard nothing. She was probably sleeping.

Probably.

He retraced his steps to the top of the stairs, but he couldn't bring himself to go down.

What if she was in Beaufort's room right now, while he stood, a helpless cuckold, at the top of the stairs?

He growled, uncomfortably aware of being a hostage to this strange affliction.

He wavered.

I do need to talk to the man, he reminded himself. A solicitor from a firm bought and paid for with Bridgewater money was the only man he could trust to deliver his note to Simon.

He took a step toward the door.

The boy reappeared, his circuit of the floor evidently complete, and went straight for Beaufort's door.

Bridgewater busied himself with the watch on his chain—a man too preoccupied to be attending too closely to anything but his thoughts.

The boy knocked loudly. "I have your candles, sir."

A Scot too. Bridgewater reminded himself to speak to his housekeeper. She needed to be more fastidious when it came to hiring from local families.

❧

Kent opened the door prepared for almost anything except the brown-haired, basket-toting lad who stood before him.

"Bridgewater's watching," the boy said under his

breath. "Don't say anything, let me in, and, whatever you do, don't close the door."

Michael returned the pistol he'd had behind his back to the waistband of his breeks, cast a bored look down the hall, and caught sight of Bridgewater staring at his watch at the top of the stairs. Michael smoothed down the edges of his beard and waved.

Bridgewater slipped the watch into his pocket and began to descend. Michael watched him until he reached the bottom of the stairs, then he followed the boy in, leaving the door ajar.

Twenty-four

"What's going on?" Michael had sheathed the pistol, but he had no scruples about removing it again. The open door was making him exceedingly nervous.

The young man began collecting candle stubs, and his eyes went briefly to the unmade bed. He was twelve or thirteen, though a glimpse of the man emerging was visible in his bobbing Adam's apple and gangly arms. He carried himself with more sangfroid than Michael's business manager.

"Where is she?" the boy said, continuing his housekeeping.

"Who?" Michael had no intention of admitting anything to anyone.

"Undine, it's Nab," he whispered. "Abby sent me."

Undine drew back the drapes just enough to peer at him. She was back in her gown, Michael noted with no small relief.

"Good evening," she said. "Please tell Abby when you see her I shall have something to say about this."

Nab smiled. "She said you'd say something like that."

She gave an "it's okay" look to Michael, though she didn't appear to be very happy about it.

"His lordship was in the hallway," Nab said, "watching."

"*Jesus*." Michael's stomach dropped to his knees.

"What did he see?" Undine said.

Nab shook his head. "Nothing, I think. He circled, and I thought he wanted to talk to him." He jabbed a thumb in Michael's direction. "But then he went to your room and listened at the door. And then he came back here. He was just about to knock when I ran in front of him and beat him to it."

"Thank you for that," Michael said.

"*Och*, 'twas nothing." He gave Michael a sidelong look and said to Undine, "He's one of us, aye?"

"Well, that's a bit of an exaggeration, but aye, you can trust him."

Michael wouldn't have been more flattered if Queen Anne herself had called to offer him a knighthood.

There were more sounds in the hall, and Undine dove again behind the drapes. It was a footman on his rounds. He hesitated when he saw Michael.

"I would've preferred the candles when I called for them," Michael said sternly to Nab, "not an hour after I went to sleep."

"I'm verra sorry, sir. I was helping the cook."

"You were not. You were outside. I can see the mud on your trousers."

The footman cleared his throat and continued, and Michael understood why Nab wanted the door to be open.

"Well done, sir," the boy said, awe on his face.

"I just hope I didn't just get you in trouble."

"Nae," the boy said, waving away his concern. "That's Harry. He's the reason I'm muddy. We were playing dice in the kitchen garden. He reports all he sees directly to his lordship, though, and his lordship will certainly ask him about you."

Michael moved a few steps from the door and lowered his voice. "What makes you think Bridgewater didn't see Undine come in here? Or Harry for that matter?"

"Er…" Splotches of red appeared on Nab's cheeks.

"You can tell us," Michael said. "Don't worry."

"I ain't worrit," Nab said. "It's just that…" He sighed and looked at his feet. "I'm not entirely certain how these things work with grown-ups, but I figured if his lordship was *sure* Undine had come in here, wouldn't he have just knocked down the door and slit your throat?"

Michael rubbed his neck. "Well, there's that."

"But I know he's suspicious," Nab said. "Of Undine, I mean. And possibly you now too. He was searching her room this afternoon—while she was away. Are you really from his solicitor's office?"

The drapes made a loud snort.

"You may take that as a no," Michael said. "I work in the theater."

"An *actor*!"

Michael shook his head. "No such luck. A director."

"I saw the one about King Macbeth." Nab held the basket in the air. "I liked seeing the head on the spike!"

"'Behold where stands the usurper's cursed head,'" Michael said, the lines as familiar to him as a song. "Yes, I believe that's a natural reaction to spending time with any group of actors. Is there anything else we should know about Bridgewater?"

"He spent the afternoon seeing one officer after another," Nab said, and Undine drew back the curtain again. "Something's being planned, though I don't know what. I know he's eager to speak to you. He mentioned it to his secretary twice today."

"Do you know why?" Undine said.

"No. I cleaned the baseboards near his office for as long as I could, but I was afraid someone was going to notice. But there was one thing I did see. I was only catching peeks when the door was open, but after he sent some corporal to the Orkneys—"

"Ye gods," Michael said.

"—he opened a drawer and looked at something for a long time. But 'twas odd because he looked at it in the drawer, without putting it on his desk. And he jumped like a scared cat when the servant came in with his coffee."

Undine looked at Michael. "I need to see what it is. We heard that someone is planning an attack in Scotland and that the messages travel through this area. None of my sources in the English army can confirm an attack is being planned. In fact, they say the officers have been told to maintain peace at all costs."

"But you don't believe it."

"In this case, I do. They want nothing to disrupt the vote on the treaty. But the rumors haven't stopped."

"You think Bridgewater is involved."

"No question. Every fiber of my being believes it. But I need proof. It could be the letter I'm look-ing for."

"The drawer's locked," Nab said. "He used a key. I heard the scratch of the metal."

Undine made a dismissive noise. "I don't need a key to get into a drawer."

"You might need something to get into the office, though. There's a guard posted outside."

"We've got to let the boy go. If he spends much more time here, Harry's going to get suspicious," Michael said.

Nab pulled a handful of candles from the basket and dropped them on the table. "The footman makes regular circuits. The next time he walks past the stairs, I'll offer him a leg of chicken I lifted from the kitchen. That'd be the time to go," he said to Undine, "if you're planning to leave."

Michael cleared his throat. "Thank you, Nab. A pleasure to meet you."

The lad grinned. With a wink, he said in a voice that carried to the hall, "I canna apologize enough for my tardiness, sir. I do hope the rest of your evening is pleasant."

Michael doubted the second half would be anywhere near as good as the first.

Twenty-five

"I'm going to his office," Undine said.

"Makes sense. We're unlikely to get a better opportunity than now, in the middle of the night," Michael said, tightening her laces.

She shook her head. "You can't go down there with me."

"Right," he said, "because it'd be much nicer to be given the news you'd been thrown in the dock—or worse, the river—along with my coffee tomorrow. 'Pardon me, old boy, but things have gotten a bit sticky with my fiancée. I had the strangest sense you were taken with her, which was bad enough, but then I found those lovely, soft hands digging through my drawers. Normally, I'm all for that sort of thing, but I'm afraid these particular drawers are strictly off-limits and we've had to have her drawn and quartered. Now be a good fellow and pass the bannocks, would you?' Oh, that'd be a great end to my first twenty-four hours here."

Undine rolled her eyes. "John would never eat bannocks."

"Really? That's your only comment?" He continued the tightening.

"And is that how people talk in your time?" She sniffed. "'Tis very off-putting."

"I'm coming. That's that."

"I don't need help. I have my methods."

"And I have my pistol. We'll make a great team. We've already made one," he said, putting his arms around her and kissing her neck, "or have you forgotten?"

"You can give me the pistol and I'll have the protection you think I need."

"Nope. Sorry. We're inextricably linked, he and I. You can't have one without the other. By the way, you smell wonderful. Is that lilies?"

"Lilies? *Never.* I despise them."

"Really? Why?"

She hesitated. "I don't know. I just do. The scent you smell is gardenia. And how like a man to see a pistol as male."

He pulled the device in question from his waistband and examined the barrel. "There is a certain elegant similarity."

"Elegant?" She rolled her eyes and twisted away. "'Tis like saying a hippo bears an elegant similarity to a swan."

"I'm not sure I entirely follow, but I'm flattered by your choice of size."

She made a Scottish noise and began rummaging in the bedside table. "In any case, I can find my own weapon."

"I'm sure Bridgewater's guards have an innate fear of being swatted to death with a hairbrush or a copy of Caesar's *Gallic Wars*. You're being stubborn. Also, don't you think I'm involved?"

"You?"

"I, the man from his solicitor's office. Isn't it possible the man from his solicitor's office knows something?"

She paled. "I never thought of that. All the more reason to get you out of here."

"But I could help."

"You don't know anything."

"But he doesn't know that."

"You think you're that good of an actor?"

"I do, yes."

She sighed. "Well, that's all the more reason for you to let me break into his office on my own. As you said, you're supposed to be from his solicitor's office. You can't be found rifling his papers."

"And you're supposed to be his fiancée. How is that any less of a concern?"

She shifted. "Because if I don't find the proof I need to stop him, then you'll still have a chance to get it out of him in your meeting and take it to Abby."

"Oh, *no*. No, no, no, no, no. We're not dividing our effort in order to double our chances of success. Pardon me for saying so, but the problems of the people of Scotland and England don't amount to a hill of beans in comparison to your safety. Not to me."

She looked up from her searching long enough for him to see the hint of pleasure on her face, which she immediately hid. "A hill of beans?" she asked lightly. "Is that something from one of your theatricals?"

"Sort of. Do you like it? I stole it."

"Does the actor end up with his head on a spike?"

Worse. He ends up saying good-bye to the woman he loves. "Not in this one."

"Well, I'm glad to hear not everything you've done has an unhappy ending. By the way, you told Nab you're a director. What's that?"

"I'm the person who tells actors what to do."

"Someone tells actors what to do? That's strange. Do they listen?"

"Not really. It's a wee bit unsatisfying, if I'm honest. But it's made me rather skilled at working with difficult people." He watched her size up a letter opener as a potential weapon.

"Does that come in handy?" she asked.

"More than you'd expect."

"Well, you should care about Scotland, but I'm not surprised you don't. I doubt an Englishman's ever been born who really cares about Scotland." She'd laced the word "Englishman" with unmistakable disdain.

"You might be right," he said, "if I were an Englishman."

She wheeled around. "Are you not?"

"No. I'm a Scot. Born and raised in Peebles."

Even in the candlelight, he could see the surprise on her face. But it wasn't delight, as he'd expected. She smiled, but there was something manufactured about it.

"You talk like an Englishman."

"Drama school, I'm afraid. This," he said in his Borders accent, "is my real voice."

"You're very talented," she said after a moment, but it didn't sound like a compliment. "I had no idea. You hid it well."

"I didn't *hide* it. You make it sound like I didn't tell you I was married."

"Are you married?"

He shook his head, afraid his voice would betray him.

"But you were." She said this with a certainty he knew he'd be a fool to deny.

"Yes," he said. "A long time ago. Not anymore."

"She hurt you."

"There was a fair bit of pain, yes."

Like spotlights, those eyes traced the path of sorrow he kept hidden. He felt as if his skin were being burned from his body, but he didn't move and he didn't say a word.

The reflection of the candlelight seemed to quiver in her eye, and for an instant he thought… Well, he didn't know what he thought.

"Strong and ever present," she said at last. "How do you keep people from seeing it?"

"It's not easy."

"Your magic is indeed powerful." She touched his arm, and the scorching resolved into a gentle warmth. "People like us can carry it, but I think it's better to put it down."

The sounds of the footman returned. They had to act.

"The time for compromise has arrived," he said.

She crossed her arms. Her hair had been pinned up quickly, and the stray strands reminded him of what they had shared.

"And what do you mean by that?" she said.

"I'll limit myself to staying within earshot of you, so

I can come like the cavalry if you call. And you limit yourself to staying out of danger."

She pursed her lips, evidently searching for a hole in the offer and finding none. She extended her hand grudgingly. "That will do."

"Another shake?" He clasped her hand.

"Lately, I seem to have forgotten all my rules."

Twenty-six

BRIDGEWATER'S OFFICE SAT AT THE END OF A LONG hall visible through the doors of the drawing room. Kent was to wait in the garden off the drawing room's french doors, pleading an upset stomach and the need for fresh air if someone asked. Undine was going to divert the guard outside the office door. She and Kent had descended the stairs unobserved. Nab had done his job well. As she stood outside the drawing room, she took a deep breath. She had to trust Kent was in his proper place even though she couldn't see him.

That had always been a problem for her. There were few people in whom she could fully place her trust. Whether that was the fault of an overly independent nature, a necessity of the life she'd chosen, or a reaction to a series of disappointments and blows, she didn't know. She could count on Abby in all things, even if their political views sometimes diverged. And she was quite fond of their new friend, Serafina. As far as men, with whom the majority of her time was spent and who were by nature harder to trust, she could count only Duncan, Gerard, and one or two acquaintances from her youth among those she would put her faith in. And now Kent.

But Kent was different. He possessed powerful magic, that much was certain, though she knew her attraction to him had begun before the spell. The magic alone made him a worthy companion, though it hardly made him trustworthy. She should be incensed he used a spell on her without her permission, but somehow she knew no harm would come to her under his care and that he had no ill intent. Even more puzzling, she had no interest in removing herself from the magic's influence.

You're under a spell. That's why you have no interest in removing the influence.

It was true. But he'd excited a part of her she'd thought unexcitable. Not her body, she considered with a smile, though he'd certainly done that well enough, but her desire to be with another person. And for that, she was both surprised and grateful.

Closing her eyes, she listened for a sense of the night. The soldier was gray and adrift in her head. Bored with his post. She turned toward the staircase. Bridgewater was somewhere beyond—a jagged boulder tumbling down an endless hill. Even in his dreams, he pushed forward, crushing, destroying. She could also feel Kent. He filled the space around her with a beautiful, undulating blue, like water—there to catch her and hold her, weightless.

She entered the drawing room, holding her candle high. She saw the guard down the hall but ignored him, walking straight to a tall display of objets d'art in his line of sight. She looked longingly at the objects sitting on the highest shelf—three large, onyx elephants decorated with silver and pearls, a father, a mother, and a child. Given their size—the father was easily over a foot tall—they were also likely the heaviest of the objects on the shelves as well.

She walked a few steps back and forth, staring at the creatures, then looked around, letting her gaze come to rest on a small table. She put her candle on the floor and dragged the table to the bottom of the display. Whether or not she agreed with their politics—and she'd met a few Englishmen for whom she did not develop an instant dislike—she'd never met an English soldier who would not do whatever he could to help a gentlewoman in distress. She looked up at the elephants again and climbed as unsteadily as possible onto the table.

The man pelted down the hall. She stretched her arm for the elephants—

"Undine! For the love of God!"

Bridgewater caught her by the waist and swung her, breathless, off the table.

"Let me call a servant. It is the elephants? My God, you could have fallen. Thank you, Private."

The guard, who'd stopped a few steps behind Bridgewater, bowed and returned to his station.

She was too surprised to think. Bridgewater hadn't been tumbling down a hillside. He'd been coming down the stairs. Kent's spell had dulled her thinking.

"I can't believe you're still awake," she said.

"Nor I you. We'll be leaving very early, you know," he said, adding tenderly, "though you can sleep in the carriage if you need to."

The private resumed his position outside Bridgewater's office. The opportunity was lost.

"Are we still going, then? I thought since the man from your solicitor's office arrived…"

"I hardly know him. I've been thinking about it. 'Tis best if we go. Morebright will be happier. Are you here alone?" he added lightly.

"Aye, except you and the private," she said with a laugh. "I noticed the elephants earlier, and you'd said I should make myself at home. I thought the smallest one would be most charming on the chest in my bedchamber."

"I'll certainly ask a footman to fetch it for you in the morning. Come," he said, taking her hand. "Perhaps a walk through the garden will help us slumber."

"Oh, no, I-I shouldn't like the damp. Let's sit for a bit here."

He led her to the settee and went to collect the candle. "Have you seen Beaufort?"

Her heart thumped. Had he seen her enter Kent's bedchamber? "Not since you introduced us. Why?"

"I thought I heard him."

"You did," a voice said.

Undine turned.

Kent stood in the doorway, pulling at his beard. "I was speaking to the lad who delivers candles. I wish to have my wicks trimmed more closely."

Bridgewater gave Undine an exaggerated eye roll, as if to say "What sort of man is so particular about candles?"

"I see you can't sleep either," Bridgewater said.

"I was nearly asleep when I was interrupted, and now I feel as if I might never close my eyes again."

Even though Kent was looking at Bridgewater,

Undine repaid the indirect compliment with a smile and saw the corner of his mouth rise.

"I pray my candles weren't to blame," Bridgewater said.

"On the contrary," Kent said, "the candles were more than satisfactory. 'Tis the wicks that were lacking. But I do not hold the length of a man's wicks against him. I'm certain the boy will profit from my suggestions. My lord, as long as we're both awake, might we use the opportunity to discuss the matters that have brought me here?"

Bridgewater looked at Undine. "Well, I..."

"Oh, please do," she said, standing. "I can entertain myself elsewhere."

"May I suggest the garden?" Kent said.

"Oh, I-I-I would prefer to avoid the damp, sir."

"Nonsense. The night is warm. I suggest you keep close to the side of the house, though. It serves as a fine windbreak and there are some lovely lilies in bloom there."

Lilies? She met Kent's eyes, and he gave her an owlish blink.

Bridgewater led her to the door. "This may take a while, my dear. I suggest you see yourself up to bed when you finish."

"Take all the time you need."

Twenty-seven

"SHE'S A VERY HANDSOME WOMAN," MICHAEL SAID before Bridgewater could choose the course of the conversation. Michael intended to tackle his own agenda first. "There's no denying it."

Bridgewater preened. He was the sort of man who thought a woman's beauty the most important thing about her. The more beautiful a woman, the more it said about the man who'd won her. Undine *was* beautiful, but any man who thought that her greatest asset was a fool.

"With all due respect, however," Michael said with regret, "I must recommend you reconsider marrying her."

Bridgewater's brows flew up. "*What?*"

"She hasn't sworn her allegiance to England."

"She hasn't sworn her allegiance to Scotland either— or France or Holland or Hispaniola, for that matter."

"Her family is unknown to us," Michael added gravely.

"She doesn't need a family. An ancient name and title is what *I* bring to the marriage."

"And she refuses to give up her work." Michael said a silent apology to his hardworking mother and grandmother.

"She told you that?"

"She didn't need to. We've spoken to her friends and acquaintances."

"You've done *what*?"

Michael was close to getting himself bounced from the house. "News travels fast, my lord," he put in quickly, "and the job of our firm is to keep you protected. As soon as we heard, we sent one of our representatives here to gather information."

Confronted with an egregious invasion of a loved one's privacy, two reactions were possible. But Michael had little doubt which one Bridgewater would manifest. A man who wore battle ribbons in his own home was a man for whom ego was more important than integrity.

Bridgewater glanced over his shoulder and back at Michael. "What did you find out?" he asked in a low voice.

"Oh, a number of things."

"Where's the report?"

"Nothing is written down, of course. But I can tell you what we've found."

"Should we adjourn to my office?"

Michael inclined his head toward the brimming decanter on the side table. "For my own part, I'd prefer to stay closer to the whiskey." He added in a lower voice, "And farther from your soldier."

Michael had once convinced a highly paid and minimally talented Hollywood actor that the part of Claudius was more important to Shakespeare's fundamental theme than that of Hamlet and, as an added bonus, had fewer lines to memorize. By doing so, he'd saved the actor from embarrassment, the National Rose from a PR nightmare, and Shakespeare from an unsettled sleep, and he was still able to splash the actor's name over every ad drawn up for the play. Convincing Bridgewater to delay his marriage to Undine or abandon it altogether would be more challenging, but it would represent a much bigger coup. Undine probably would have preferred he spend his time with Bridgewater trying to extract the information contained in that letter, but her safety was more important to him. In any case, she might already have the letter in her hand, and even if she didn't, there would probably be another opportunity in the morning. Bridgewater had clearly sent for a man from his solicitor's office for a reason, and Michael doubted Bridgewater would head to Morebright's until he'd had a chance to discuss it with him.

"I can fetch you a drink," Bridgewater said with an aggrieved sigh. "But do begin. I want to hear the worst before Undine returns."

❧

Undine knew full well why she hated lilies, but it wasn't the sort of thing you told a man you'd known for less than a day. Lilies were what she'd smelled the afternoon the soldier had run her and her mother from their little house, and they'd traveled for days after that, always at night, their possessions lost to them, to find the place her mother called "the Wash." Her mother hadn't cried—her mother never cried—but Undine had. The loss of one's known world is a heavy misfortune for a five-year-old. She'd learned the only way to protect herself from such a staggering blow was never again to have a home she cared about—or anything else a soldier could take from her. Hearing the long, painfully dull story of Undine's first great loss would have been enough to send Kent running from the bedchamber.

Perhaps unsurprisingly, Bridgewater's gardens were filled with lilies—orange, pink, and yellow—stretching their spindly necks toward the south. On top of everything else, they chose England too.

She pushed the flowers aside to enter the path that proceeded along the back of the house. She spotted the men in the drawing room, Kent with his elegant, broad shoulders and Bridgewater with his laces and fringe.

The pain Kent carried inside him… She'd felt it as an inky blue—the bottom of a well or a sky without stars—and heavy it had been. She couldn't untangle the images. Despite what people thought, she wasn't a visionary. And in any case, it would have been rude to try to enter that guarded place without an invitation.

She walked briskly down the path and soon saw why Kent had encouraged a garden visit. The window to Bridgewater's office was open. Its sill stood about six feet above the path—too high to reach without something to stand on. She weighed the risks. Bridgewater might return to his office. That was where his papers were hidden, after all. But Kent was keeping him busy. And the guard might hear her and alert Bridgewater.

On balance, she thought it was worth the risk.

She grabbed her skirts and tied them in a tight knot between her legs. There were enough obstacles between her and her object—no need to add more in the form of linen and silk. She caught the corner of the window and gently pushed. It opened wider with a reverberant *screech*.

She pressed herself against the house. Bridgewater came to the window of the drawing room. She could see the gold of his hair in the candlelight. He peered into the garden, and she held herself motionless.

~∽~

"Did you hear that?" Bridgewater gazed out the window, looking a bit stupid, Michael thought, with his jaw hanging open.

"'Twas an owl," Michael said. He hoped Undine had made it inside. He also hoped she found what she wanted quickly, for her own safety, and because he wasn't certain how long he could maintain his calm with a man whose first questions after hearing his future bride's privacy had been grievously violated by his own legal firm had been "How many men has she taken to her bed?" and "Is it possible she's told any of them my secrets?"

"I'm going to take a look around," Bridgewater said.

"'Tis unnecessary. You may frighten your fiancée more than the noise did."

"I can hardly leave her alone out there."

"I bow to your superior judgment." Michael clutched his drink, trying to keep all 650 of his

muscles from launching him into a hard run for
Bridgewater's office.

Bridgewater ran out, and Michael hurried down the
hall toward the private, who immediately straightened.

"Your commander," Michael said, "he needs you
at once."

"What is it?"

"He heard a sound. It sounded like a shriek.
Outside."

The man pelted away, and the moment he was out
of sight, Michael turned the knob.

Unlocked.

He opened the door and found Undine crouched
by the desk.

"I heard your voices," she said. "What happened?"

"Bridgewater heard a squeak."

"The window," she said, hastily opening a drawer.

The room was dark, the window closed.
"Bridgewater's looking for you," he said. "And now
the soldier is too. We have to get out of here."

"Keep your head down in case they walk by the
window."

He dropped to a knee, pulled the pistol from his
trousers, and half cocked the hammer. His theater
training had come in handy.

"This has to be it." She lifted a locked metal box
out and placed it on the desk.

"Take it."

"It's too big. Someone will see it." She jumped to
her feet and, sticking close to the wall to remain out of
view, made her way to the hearth. "He'd put it within
reach. I know he would."

"What?"

"The key."

In the garden, Bridgewater called, "Undine?"

"We have to go," Michael said.

She lifted the candlesticks on the mantle one by one and looked underneath them. "Dammit."

"Try the flowers. There."

She turned around. A handful of lilies and roses sat in squat vase on his desk. She lifted it. Then she grabbed something and held it high, victorious. It was the key! Hands shaking, she slipped the key into the lock and turned. In an instant, the lid was up.

"I can't read it," she said. "It's too dark."

"We'll come back," Michael said, losing his patience. "We have to go."

"You have to go. He'll be looking for you."

"He's looking for you *right now*."

Bridgewater started to speak, and his voice was right outside the window. "Why has the pot been moved?" he said. "Check the window."

Michael balanced the pistol's barrel on his wrist and took aim.

A hand came into view. "Closed, sir," the private said. "Perhaps she returned to her room?"

"Go there," Bridgewater said. "I'll check my office."

"Undine, leave it or take it. We have to go. *Now*."

"If I take it, he'll know," she said, trying to catch the moon's light on the pages. "It's something about the upcoming vote to unite England and Scotland."

Michael tried to take the pages from her, but she held them out of reach. He clapped the box shut, turned the key in the lock, and returned the box to the drawer. He grabbed her arm and pulled her to the door as she stuffed the paper in her pocket. "We'll run." He pointed away from the drawing room. "Can we get out this way?"

She shook her head. "Only through the drawing room. The other wing is locked."

They flew to the drawing room but stopped when they heard approaching footsteps.

Michael pushed her into a room filled with paintings off the hall. "I can't save both of us, but I can save you. Slap me."

"*What?*"

He pulled her into his arms and bent her backward in a brutal kiss.

Undine shoved Michael away and slapped him. He cradled his cheek. He didn't need to turn to know Bridgewater had appeared. He could tell by the rigidity of Undine's body.

"Mr. Beaufort!" she cried.

"I desire you most ardently," he whispered.

"*Beaufort,*" a red-faced Bridgewater demanded, "remove yourself from my home *immediately*."

"You have no idea the devil's temptress you have in this woman," Michael cried.

Bridgewater's eyes bulged from his head. "'Tis only your connection to a most respected firm that is keeping me from killing you. I suggest you try my good nature no further. Be assured your connection will be severed the instant my letter reaches your employers." He raised his hand and brought it across Michael's face.

An explosion went off in his ear, and he wove a step.

Bridgewater grabbed him by the cravat. "Did

you hear me?" he said, nose touching Michael's. He slapped Michael again, and when Michael didn't respond, the slaps turned to punches.

"Stop it!" Undine commanded. "Stop it this instant!" She dragged Bridgewater away.

Blood poured from Michael's nose. He bore it for her.

"Get out," Bridgewater said in a growl. "Get out now."

Michael crawled to his feet.

"That cunt-faced little fornicator didn't even fight back," Bridgewater said to Undine. "Are you all right?"

"Aye. Let him go. He's not worth the trouble." She gave Michael a look of absolute heartbreak.

Bridgewater straightened the ribbons on his coat and looked at Michael. "If you say a word of what you told me to anyone else, I will hunt you down, cut off your stones, and choke you with them. Did you understand?"

"Aye."

Bridgewater lifted his boot and shoved him into the hall. "Now, run."

Twenty-eight

UNDINE PACED THE DRAWING ROOM UNTIL SHE HEARD the front door close. She couldn't get the image of Kent's battered face out of her head. She knew he'd sacrificed himself to save her. He'd had a pistol and could have used it but didn't.

The knowledge of that sacrifice bound her to him and distressed her deeply.

There are sacrifices that must be made for peace, you know.

Aye, but he didn't volunteer *to serve, did he?*

"The *blackguard*," Bridgewater said, downing whiskey. "To accost a man's wife in his own home."

"I'm not your wife, John. Not yet. And your reaction was brutish."

He swung around. "You criticize my handling of the situation?"

"I will not marry a man who cannot control his temper. If you can profit from that information, I suggest you do so at once. If you cannot, I'll go."

He shook with rage or the effort to control, she didn't know which. But she knew the only way to dampen his fury was to expose it, like an infected wound. The work of a spy wasn't meant to be easy or pleasing, but witnessing the attack on a treasured compatriot and facing the potential of violence to one's own self were the most unpleasant duties. She was overwhelmed and struggled to remind herself of the horrors the soldiers and clansmen unleashed on the innocent in the borderlands.

"You must learn to keep a civil tongue in your head, Undine." Bridgewater's fists were balled.

She said nothing. She'd said what needed to be said. She wouldn't be goaded into more. What she wanted was to excuse herself to her room, dig that paper from her pocket, and assure herself that the wounds to Kent's face were worth the information they'd won.

She held Bridgewater's gaze.

"Dammit, Undine."

"Give me your decision."

He lifted his glass to hurl it into the hearth and stopped at the last instant. With great effort, he brought his arm back down. "I will attempt to do better."

If the display at the river was any indication, he would cry now. The effects of the spell were beginning to stray further and further from normal, which meant she would soon have to end things here. As early as the morning, he could discover the papers were gone. Kent had positioned himself masterfully as the man to be suspected, but eventually, Bridgewater's reason would return, and if she wasn't away and hidden at that point, she'd be in very grave danger.

"Thank you," she said.

He pulled her into a demanding kiss. The transformation surprised her so much that she was momentarily paralyzed. All she could think about were the papers in her pocket. She lifted his hands to her face, and buoyed by her reaction, he deepened his kiss.

"Let me take you to my bed," he whispered. "Let me show the pleasure I can bring you."

She thought about what other secrets he might have stored there—correspondence and diaries—and debated what to do.

"I ache for you, Undine. Can you feel it?"

The thought sickened her, but what might she gain? *Do your proper job.*

The vision of Kent's gentle face would not be displaced. It hung like a bright light in the dark room of her duty.

"I… I…"

"Please, Undine. I beg you."

"I cannot."

The papers would be enough—they had to be.

She unbraided herself from his clasp.

"You destroy me," he said, breathing heavily.

"We will destroy each other—when it's time." She ran from the room and up the stairs, desperate to see what her adventure with Michael had brought them.

Twenty-nine

MICHAEL WIPED THE BLOOD FROM HIS FACE. HIS NOSE wasn't broken, though it hurt like a son of a gun. The blood was coming from a split lip and a deep gouge near his eye. Bridgewater's signet ring had raked him. Thank God the beard hadn't come off.

He stood in the shadow of a tree at the edge of the grounds, having been escorted as far as the end of the carriageway by a footman.

The intrigue had won them the letter, whatever it happened to contain, but his attention was focused on the woman he'd left behind. Undine was both cunning and capable—if he'd learned nothing else in his few hours here, he'd learned that—but Bridgewater was a dangerous and unpredictable man. Michael wished he'd been able to pull them both to safety, but he also recognized that her work to embed herself in the relationship with Bridgewater gave her the right to decide which risks to accept and which to avoid.

His thoughts returned to the confection of happiness and pain their time in his bedroom had brought him. The warmth of her body under his. The gleam of her shoulder in the candlelight. The scent of her skin. And the hobbling pain of remembering the past.

It wasn't that he didn't think of Deirdre on a regular basis—hardly a day went by when her face didn't occupy some moment or other of his thoughts—or that he hadn't come to grips with her death in the fifteen years since the highway officers had knocked on his door. But in that instant, when Undine had asked if he was married, he'd felt like a crab being jerked from a happy scuttle across the sand into a pot of boiling water.

And the last thing he'd wanted to do was burden a women he'd just made love to with the tragic story of his dead wife's accident.

The candles in the drawing room were still lit. He wondered what sort of conversation Undine and Bridgewater were having or if they were speaking at all.

His stuffed his hands in his pocket and was instantly reminded of the other thing he'd stolen when he'd stolen that kiss.

The letter crinkled as he withdrew it. Undine would be furious when she discovered he'd taken them from her pocket, but while he'd been willing—with great reluctance—to leave her with Bridgewater, he'd absolutely refused to leave her holding the evidence of her treachery.

The night was too dark for him to make out anything except a large, loopy signature at the bottom. Though perhaps if he sneaked closer to the light—

He froze.

There, in the window, Undine and Bridgewater were bent in a lingering kiss.

His heart thudded to a stop. Undine lifted Bridgewater's hands to her cheeks and held them there tenderly.

Michael's arm fell, and the letter slipped from his hand.

Thirty

THE CARRIAGE BUMPED AND BANGED OVER THE
rock-strewn road toward the home of Chieftain
Hay. Michael stared at the paper in his hand blankly,
as though the words were in Urdu. All he could
see, even in the day's bright light, was Undine in
Bridgewater's arms.

"Has the substance of the letter changed?" Serafina
asked.

Michael started, realizing she'd been watching him,
and folded the paper self-consciously. "No. It's still
about affecting the vote on the treaty."

"You look a wee bit raggit," she said. "Even apart
from that cheek and lip. Are ye under the weather?"

Michael shook his head. "Nae."

Nae? How odd. He'd only been in the borderlands
a day, and already the crisp BBC pronunciations his
vocal tutor had drilled into him at RADA were starting to relax their hold on his speech. As a young man
immersing himself in his career, he'd come to use the
sonorous BBC accent on a daily basis, as that was the
way of trained actors and the theater, and he'd loved

"I know."

"And you're certain she's with him now, going north?"

"Aye," Michael said. "To see some family friend of his who's ill. A Lord Morebright. They left just before dawn. I watched her get into the carriage. I watched them leave."

Gerard frowned. "What time were you escorted out? Didn't you say it was before midnight?"

"I wanted to see if their plans changed. We'd need to be able to react."

"You waited all night?" Serafina asked and exchanged a look with Gerard.

"It wasn't any bother." Michael had been too numb to feel anything. He didn't know the layout of the rooms or which room was Bridgewater's, so every candle that had been lit upstairs had felt like the stab of the knife. And then the flames had been extinguished, and the pain grew worse.

He'd awoken at dawn to the sounds of the carriages being pulled in front the main entrance. Undine had descended like a queen on Bridgewater's arm, her hair in a thick braid that encircled the top of her head like a crown. Michael had watched as they'd climbed into the larger of the two carriages, a vehicle gleaming with polished wood and brass appointments. He'd watched as their trunks and servants were loaded into a smaller and simpler carriage. He'd watched as the vehicles pulled down the estate drive and took the ferry across the Tweed. And he'd watched as the convoy exited Coldstream proper and disappeared in the distance.

He'd wondered if she'd looked for him as the

it. By the time he was twenty-five, his Lowland bu
was gone—forever, he had thought. He'd becom
known for his mellifluous baritone, and it had helpe
define his career as an actor. Hell, that was one of the
reasons they'd cast him as Orlando Brashnettle. Even
in his dreams, he spoke in the resonant, upper-class
sounds of his training.

But here, with Duncan and Serafina and the rest
of Scots, it seemed as if his past self was awakening
after a long slumber. Even Gerard, American by birth,
seemed to delight in what turned out to be the tongue
of his grandmother. If Michael stayed in Scotland
much longer, he'd probably be downing Irn-Bru and
rooting for the Hearts again.

"Now, there's a bit of a smile," Gerard said.

"I don't like that Undine is still with him," Serafina
said.

"She's got a job to do," Michael said. "We know
from the letter a diversion is being planned, but we
don't know where or what it is."

"It's dangerous. That man is a—"

"It's her choice," Michael said flatly. "For God's
sake, can we let her do what she needs to do?"

The carriage fell silent. Michael felt like an ass. "I'm
sorry. I'm…tired, I guess. We're all worried."

"You're right, friend," Serafina said, patting his
arm. "Worrying doesn't help her or us. And she's a
verra capable woman."

"Scotland's filled with them," Gerard said, poking
Michael's boot with his.

"Besides," Serafina said, "she'd never let Bridgewater
near her. She despises the man."

carriage had driven by. He'd had no sense of her doing so. It was as if whatever invisible connection that had existed between the two of them had evaporated. And even though he had no wish for her to accompany Bridgewater on his visit, her appearance on his arm and the man's pleasant demeanor meant he probably hadn't yet discovered his letter was missing. For that alone, Michael was grateful.

It was only then, when the carriage had disappeared from sight, that he'd sat down to read the papers.

By a request most urgent, you are to create a diversion at a time you believe the upcoming vote to be most likely to be shaped by such an event. Use the resources you deem necessary, though the diversion must in no way suggest the effort was preplanned or more than the result of an unexpected need to act. We depend on seeing the results of this action no later than Midsummer Day. Your service in this matter will not be forgotten.

The note was unsigned.

Midsummer Day. June 24. Less than a week from now. Michael drew his gaze from the increasingly barren hills outside the carriage window to the paper. It might have been an army order, but it wasn't an official one. He wondered why Bridgewater had kept it. Even locked up, it represented a danger if found—not to mention a risk to the mission.

Though the message was intentionally obscure, the "effort" to which the writer referred could only be an attack of some sort. That was what Michael had thought, and Serafina and Gerard had agreed when they'd found him waiting for them in the crumbling priory.

An attack on the Scots would fan the flames that already burned between the two countries to a ferocious intensity at a time when the Scottish lords were expected to vote on the treaty that would merge the two countries. Gerard and Serafina had described the river of secret money flowing from London to the noblemen in Edinburgh, bribes to cast their votes in favor of the union that was supposed to be a marriage of equals. But everyone knew, even in 1706, the union was going to turn into a snare that Scotland wouldn't be able to free itself from. And it hadn't, even three centuries later.

So why attack? Wouldn't that make the Scottish lords *less* likely to vote yes?

At first glance, yes. But Michael knew enough about history to know attacks weren't always what they seemed. History, they said, was written by the victors. If the English soldiers won, Bridgewater's story would be the one that carried the day. When he talked about it afterward, he could frame the attack any way he chose—the Scots attacked first, or the Scots had English hostages and he had been forced to attack, or the Scots had been planning some atrocity, but he'd found out first and stopped them. Sure, the Scots who survived, assuming some did, could contradict his version, but who in London—or, hell, who in the Scottish parliament already getting his pockets lined with English gold—would believe them? The attack might even seem to some to be just the sort of thing that would make it clear the clans needed to be brought under control by the invincible English army, something that could be easily done once the two countries were united.

"Michael," Serafina said, rousing him from his distracted reverie. "Abby will help. She'll be able to shed light on what's going on. The clan chiefs hear everything that's happening in the borderlands. If there's something to be done, Abby will know what to do. And more important, she'll know what to do about Undine."

There was nothing to do *about* Undine. She had to make her own choices. But there was one thing he could do *for* her, and he wouldn't be able to live with himself until he had. He'd taken the letter before she'd had a chance to look at it—and that might mean the difference between life and death for her.

"How much longer?" he said.

Serafina pointed beyond the carriage window to a castle perched high on the next hill that would have been at home in any gothic nightmare. "The seat of Clan Hay," she said. "That's where Abby and the other clan chiefs are meeting."

"It looks positively sinister."

"Aye, well, that might be part of how it's earned its name. It's called *Nimheil Faobhar.*"

The dozen or so Gaelic words Michael had learned from his grandfather consisted mainly of mild obscenities and different ways to describe an idiot. None of them sounded like the words she'd just said. He shook his head.

"It translates roughly as 'poisoned knife-edge,'" she said. "Most people just call it 'Black Blade.'"

Gerard lifted his palms and gave him a theatrical grin. "Great place to start a war, am I right?"

Thirty-one

UNDINE TAPPED HER FINGERS SILENTLY TO PRESERVE her solitude. Bridgewater napped on the carriage seat across from her, his head drooping so far down his shirtfront he ought to have suffocated. And yet he breathed on.

She knew what Michael had done and why but found herself unable to decide exactly how she felt about it. When she'd reached into her pocket after Bridgewater's unsettling kiss, she'd felt betrayed. Who was Michael to decide what risks she took? And yet the motivation behind it was clear. She wasn't used to having someone worried for her safety, let alone having someone with the skills to actually protect her.

Michael was a curious man. He knew little about the time she'd brought him to. He had no title, no colleagues, and no money, at least not here. His career was telling actors what to do. Yet he had proven himself capable of powerful magic that included not only love spells, but also the ability to turn himself into whatever sort of person it took to manage a situation. His guises were extraordinary—she herself

hadn't recognized him. And each seemed mainly to
depend on bodily changes—posture, voice, movement, accent, and phrasing—rather than costume or
face paint.

Talents. He had many.

She felt her cheeks warm.

Aye, she'd enjoyed their joining. He'd been a
caring lover as well as skilled, and the heat she felt
while thinking about it reminded her how potent the
spell was that still remained. In truth, she wished it
didn't have to end.

All spells end. You of all people know that.

They were either fulfilled, which ended them
instantly, or they slowly lost their strength. Spells that
damned the unlucky to a life of ugliness or one trapped
inside the body of a crow or pig only occurred in stories. Real spells depended on the power of their makers,
but they never, ever lasted longer than a few months.

She, in comparison, was a fairly weak spell caster.
The magic she possessed came from a book that had
belonged to the woman who'd taken her in when
she'd returned to northern England. The processes
detailed in the book had given her the means to pro-
duce magic, but she lacked the inherent power most
skilled magi were born with. That was why her spells
were often imperfect.

"Undine, what *are* you thinking about?"

Bridgewater, still muzzy with sleep, eyed her.
"Only my pleasure in seeing parts of Scotland with
which I am not familiar."

He snorted. "Aye, cold and empty. 'Tis quite
enthralling."

"I'm drawn to that which is sometimes unappealing to others. How long might we be staying with Morebright?"

He regarded her with interest. "Is there a reason you ask?"

"Simple curiosity," she said. "I know he's ill."

"Aye, well, I'll know more when I see Simon's condition. Do you see anything more regarding the road?"

For an instant, she didn't know what he was talking about. Then she remembered the promise she'd given him. She closed her eyes self-consciously. The easy blue waves had grown more dispersed, but nothing calamitous came into view.

"No," she said after a moment. "The journey will be safe."

"There's also a church on his estate—if you don't mind being a Scottish bride."

She'd forgotten about the wedding, and the reminder made her stomach knot. "Of course not," she said lightly. "I should be happy to be married to you under any country's flag, though I do wonder why the need is so urgent given that the papers that needed to be signed—the ones that awful Mr. Beaufort was supposed to be bringing—are not in your possession and are unlikely to arrive again until at least a week after your letter reaches your solicitor in London."

The mention of Mr. Beaufort cast a moodiness onto Bridgewater's countenance. While he had appeared to find her blameless for last night's kiss—she was in fact blameless for *both* kisses, but of course, Bridgewater would assert there was no blame to be found in the kiss he perpetrated—a certain coolness had crept into his behavior. She was half tempted to talk him out of his ill temper but decided that letting it slip away on its own meant she might enjoy a few moments of peace.

"My feelings about a wedding haven't changed," he said. "Have yours?"

"My feelings haven't changed either. You'll recall I'd told you quite clearly I wished to wait until my head caught up with my heart."

He crossed his arms and looked at her. "You are a bewitching woman, Undine. I'm astounded you agreed to be my wife."

There was the slightest friction in the words, as if the smile on his face couldn't quite coexist with the sentiment he was expressing. The hairs on her neck stood on end, and she waited for a follow-up comment, but none came, and after a beat, the hairs relaxed. She nodded her thanks and turned her attention to the landscape beyond the window, hoping to return to happier thoughts.

Thirty-two

ABBY LOOKED AT MICHAEL, SPEECHLESS. "ARE YOU telling me that Bridgewater, one of the highest-ranking officers in England's northern armies, is biding his merry way through Scotland a mere ten miles from where we're standing?"

"It depends on whether he took the road through Edinburgh or the northwest road," Serafina said.

Gerard pulled his gaze away from the striking ceiling. "Are we seriously standing under like five hundred razor-sharp cutlasses?"

"Yes," Michael said, answering both Abby and Gerard. "Bridgewater is taking her with him to visit Simon Morebright, some old, ill family friend. The man needs medical attention in York."

"Good Lord," Duncan said, "Bridgewater must have stones as big as soccer balls."

"But it's worse," Michael said, offering the letter. "He has orders from someone to attack."

"It's like a freakin' torture chamber in here," Gerard said, now running a finger over the spiked ball of a flail that was hanging over the hearth.

Duncan took the letter and held it so he and Abby could read it at the same time. The voices and plate banging of a large dinner party were evident on the other side of the looming doors. Michael had never been led into a room that felt more like a dungeon—no windows, no chairs, and an arsenal's worth of weapons. The chieftain of Clan Hay had an interesting idea of hospitality.

"Bloody hell," Abby whispered when she looked up. "I'm in there doing everything I can to keep the clans at bay, and Bridgewater's about to wave a sword under their noses."

"What are they planning?" Michael asked. A vision of the clansmen attacking Bridgewater's carriage filled his head.

Abby looked at Michael, clearly distressed. "I canna tell you."

"What do you mean, you can't tell me?" he demanded. "Undine's your friend. We came to you for help."

Duncan straightened, an unsubtle warning.

"They have no grudge against Undine," Abby said. "And they didna know Bridgewater was coming through their lands."

Michael met Abby's eyes. "Till now," he said coolly.

The words sent a pall over the small gathering.

"Aye," she admitted with just as much coldness. "Till now."

"I want your promise that no action will be taken that might harm Undine."

"I'm not a servant girl to be a handmaiden to your orders, Mr. Kent. I'm the head of clan fighting for its right to live in peace on its own land. If you weren't an Englishman, perhaps you'd understand that."

"I'm a *Scot*," he said angrily. "Born and raised in Peebles. My father is Clan MacLeod and my mother Clan Murray. I have no more love for England than you do. But that doesn't mean I'd betray a friend. I brought you that letter so you could help Undine, not put her in danger."

The door opened and a rotund man with long, white hair and a close-cut beard entered. He wore the plaid of a Scot and the scars of a seasoned clansman.

"Abigail, my dear, will you introduce me to your friends?"

Michael wasn't sure the word still applied, and Abby's awkward hesitation made the group's fraying nerves apparent.

"This is Donal Hay," Abby said, "chief of Clan Hay, our host here. Donal, this is Serafina and Gerard Innes—she's a merchant in Edinburgh with a shipping concern—and Mr. Kent. He's an acquaintance of Undine's."

A circle of bows and curtsies followed.

"You told me they brought news," Hay said, eyes narrowing. His gaze fell on the paper in Abby's hand. It was all Michael could do to keep from ripping the bloody thing right out of her grasp.

"They did," she said. "Bridgewater has unsigned orders to create a diversion before the vote is taken. The orders dinna say what the method of diversion will be nor the time and place it will happen, except to say it must happen by Midsummer Day."

Michael's anger rose. "I can't believe you're doing this."

"There's more," she said, undaunted. "Bridgewater's in a carriage right now, headed to the estate of Simon Morebright."

Hay's eyes trailed over the ragtag group of visitors, coming to rest on the one so obviously infuriated by Abby's statement.

"What do they know about what we're doing in the other room?" The "they" he referred to was Michael, Gerard, and Serafina.

Abby's eyes flashed. "Nothing."

"I dinna doubt ye, lass," he said. "You've always been as good as your word. But I hope ye'll not take it as an insult if I keep your guests here, under a close eye, until we complete the meeting we're in the midst of. The chiefs dinna take too kindly to having their plans get out. 'Tis the best way to ensure your friends get back to their homes whole and unharmed."

Abby couldn't even meet Michael's eyes. "Thank you, Donal. I agree."

Hay stepped outside to call his guards.

"This is the best way," Abby said fiercely, before Michael could speak. "You'll have to trust me. You know I wouldn't do anything to hurt Undine. That's the only promise I can give you."

"How can you live with yourself?" Michael said.

He took a step toward Abby, and Duncan inserted himself between them, which only made Michael angrier. He shoved hard and surprised Duncan. Duncan stumbled into the wall. He found his footing and grabbed Michael by the shirtfront.

Gerard flung his arms around Duncan. "That'll be enough of that, big fella," he said, wrestling him away.

"We don't want to be thrown in an actual torture chamber, okay? At least here, we have the weapons on our side."

Duncan shook his shoulders free of Gerard and adjusted his plaid.

Abby said, "*Nothing* will happen to Undine." Then she picked up her skirts and went out, with Duncan on her heels.

Serafina looked at Gerard, and Gerard looked at Michael.

"Who's up for some three-handed bridge?" Gerard said.

Thirty-three

MICHAEL STOOD BEFORE THE WINDOW OF THE TINY bedchamber he'd been assigned in Hay Manor, his meager bag flung in the corner by a guard. What a bowl of dog's meat he'd made of things. He'd thought coming to Abby would *help* Undine, not make things worse. And now he'd gotten the three of them locked up in this set out of *Dracula*.

The window afforded him a sliver of a view into the dining hall across the bailey, where the gathering of the chieftains was taking place. As his room was on the upper floor, he could see only the backs of their chairs and their lower halves. There had to be at least twenty-five of them at the long table, not counting the servants, whose lower halves could also be seen, though in their case, theirs were running to and fro, undoubtedly trying to cater to the multitudinous needs of their two dozen imperious masters.

"This is the best way. You'll have to trust me."

Bah. Self-important women clan chiefs were no less annoying than self-important male army officers.

He wished he knew more Scottish history. Had

there been a battle immediately before the vote on the Treaty of Union, a vote that had overwhelmingly favored the union? The odds were high. There'd been so many bloody battles fought in Scotland, especially along the border, you could barely toss a claymore without hitting a historical marker. His aunt had dragged him to most of them—Ancrum Moor, Bannockburn, Bothwell Bridge, Drumclog, Philiphaugh. And they all looked the same: majestic swaths of green with no hint of the unimaginable horror that had taken place on them.

He looked at the landscape beyond the curtain wall of Black Blade: an emerald valley as far as the eye could see.

Great news, mate. You may be standing on the exact site of a future historical marker.

There was no point in trying to pull up obscure battles from the cobwebbed corners of his brain. Even if he could have remembered their names, he'd never be able to find them in his internal map of Scotland. Hell, he couldn't even find his own location there.

The only location that could help him at all was Undine's, and he knew that one. She was ten miles from this delightful resort, sitting in close proximity to John Bridgewater. Michael had to get to her. He wondered if the guard at the end of the hall took a dinner break.

The doors to the great hall across the courtyard opened, and the clan chiefs streamed into the muddy bailey. Their faces were grim, and the little communication that occurred seemed to be limited to bracing shoulder thumps and terse farewells. His gut roiled. These were the faces of men—and at least one woman—who'd decided to take a stand against the English. He searched the crowd for Abby. How hard would it be to spot a woman in a sky-blue gown in this crowd of beards, plaids, and hairy knees?

He saw Duncan. The red hair was like a spot of hellfire in the pit of mud. Duncan saw him too. He put his hand to his brow and gave him a cheeky salute.

Eff off, my friend.

Michael scanned the line of windows along his floor. There was a large balcony outside of the room next door to his. He'd passed the room as he was being led here. No one was in it. He'd been able to see inside. And they'd put Gerard and Serafina together in a room in the other wing.

A knock sounded at the door.

"Servant, sor," an Irish voice said. "I have your supper."

"Come in," he said without turning. The chiefs were calling for their horses and wagons. If he could make his way to the balcony via what looked like a fairly sturdy ledge, he could probably hitch a ride to the main road. He had good balance and had been capable of some pretty impressive acrobatic feats in his younger acting days.

"I keep hearing a wardrobe door bang," he said, making up the first thing that popped into his head. "Would you mind letting the thoughtless gentleman next door know I'll be going to bed soon."

"Aye, sor. 'Tis rather early for bed, no? Especially with your bed warmer so far away?"

He frowned and turned.

Abby stood before him in the drab, gray dress of a servant, her hair hidden in a bonnet. She had a plaid and a black, knitted cap in her hand.

"I'm taking you to Undine," she said, closing the door. "Take off your breeks."

Thirty-four

"You don't mind taking the pass through the mountains, do you?" Abby said. "They'll be looking for us on the road."

The hike was straining Michael's legs a bit, but the vast, open vista with peaks as far as he could see more than made up for it. It had been a long time since he'd spent time in the angled turf of southern Scotland, rather than on the flat streets of London or even flatter boards of the stage. It felt like a tonic for his soul. He could almost smell the snow in the air up here, even in the warmth of summer.

"I feel terrible risking your relationship with the other chieftains," he said.

"*Och*. If only *they* worried as much. I make my own decisions, Mr. Kent. And if we manage this carefully, they'll never know."

"You must let me apologize. I treated you very badly, accusing you of the worst sort of…" He felt the heat climb again across his cheeks.

She smiled. "You were blinded by your emotion, Mr. Kent—it is Mr. Kent, aye? Not Father?"

"Yes. I owe you an apology for that too."

"Or perhaps Undine owes us both an apology, aye? I think there's probably more to the story than her needing a priest to hear Bridgewater's confession, isn't there?"

Damn these straight-talking eighteenth-century women. It was quite unnerving. "There might have been a bit more to it. I'm not at liberty to say."

She snorted. "She either decided to marry the brute to gain further access to his secrets or she needed you to get her out of marrying him because she got her nose too far into Bridgewater's business and got it pinched in the gate. That's what I think."

He couldn't help but smile. "You might be right. I couldn't say."

"*Mmph.* She takes too many risks."

"That seems to be a common affliction here," he said, tucking his small bag of belongings under his arm. "I wonder if it's something in the air."

"And she just lifted you out of whatever life you happened to be living?"

"It wasn't much of a life," he said, though the words surprised him. "Well, certainly not at the moment she called me back. Have you seen Shakespeare's *Romeo and Juliet*? I was playing Friar Laurence."

"You're an *actor*?"

"Was. A long time ago. I'm a director, which means rich people who don't know anything about the theater tell me what to do, and I take out my irritation on actors."

"And there's a living in that? How verra curious the future is. I don't know anything about directing, Mr. Kent, but I will say you're a braw actor."

The compliment warmed him—even after all these years. "Thank you. But please call me Michael."

"All right. Michael." She ducked her head and lifted her skirts to clear a particularly large rock.

He noticed that though she wore the attire of a servant, her boots were the hand-tooled leather of a noblewoman.

"Were you aware, Michael, that when Undine called Duncan out of the future to help me, I ended up falling in love with him? And that when she called Gerard out of the future to help Serafina, Serafina ended up falling in love with Gerard?"

He hid a grin in a readjustment of his plaid. "Yes, I believe I did hear something about that."

"Rather interesting, isn't it?"

"I couldn't possibly comment."

They'd reached a not inconsequential stream, and Abby slipped off her boots to cross barefoot. Michael followed suit.

"You mentioned you're of Clan MacLeod *and* Clan Murray," she said, apparently changing the subject, but Michael wasn't so sure.

"Aye." He heard himself saying the "aye" this time, and it felt right.

She lifted her skirts over her arm and waded in. "'Tis an unusual combination. Clan MacLeod, well, they're thinkers. You canna just start a war with the MacLeods. They need time to let the idea stew over the fire a bit."

He offered his arm and she took it. Clan MacLeod was his father's side and her description fit him perfectly. "That's a good thing, right?"

"Not if you're looking down the barrel of an Englishman's gun. But Clan Murray, they're like snakes that have been teased, even without the teasing. They're ready to lash out without the slightest thought."

"There's a lot of snake imagery in the Lowlands. Not sure what that means exactly. I tend to think doing anything without conscious thought is a bad idea."

She laughed. "I can tell whose side you take after."

"You don't agree?"

They reached the opposite bank and climbed out.

"I think ye need a good measure of both," she said, rubbing her feet in the grass. "There are times when you need to act and times when ye need to consider. And ye need to be canny enough to know the difference."

"Wise words."

"Michael, Undine is like a snake, which is not to say she's a member of Clan Murray or any clan for that matter. She would not take kindly to the implication. She has a complicated history with the clans and that one in particular." Abby sighed. "Perhaps she'll tell you the story someday. But like them, she follows her heart and acts without thinking. You…well, you have more inertia."

"Is that because I groaned when you said we'd be mountain climbing? Honestly, I do a lot of biking in London."

"What I'm trying to say is the two of you would balance each other well. I know I'm rushing things, but ye canna know how much time ye have here. Undine's most recent spell casting has been a bit… Well, there's no point in alarming you. Ye do take after Clan MacLeod, though, so I know ye'll benefit from a bit of a push."

They'd redonned their boots and returned to their slow climb.

Michael thought of the kiss Undine had shared with Bridgewater. He had no right to take exception to it. They hadn't made any promises to one another. Hell, even if they had made promises to one another, he'd have no right to take exception to any action taken by someone putting themselves in harm's way to bring peace to Scotland. His grandmother had been in Coventry during the Battle of Britain. Both his grand-fathers had served in the war. He'd listened to their stories—the ones they were willing to tell. He knew what it meant to be willing to do anything—anything at all—to stop the destruction of one's homeland. He'd never judge.

But the pain from that kiss was there.

One should never deny emotion. That's what he told his actors. If you have it, don't push it away and don't try to pretend it's something else. Unfortunately, he was holding two emotions at once. One of them wanted him to break into Morebright's house, drag her as far away as he could from it, and then lock her in a room no one could reach, with him beside her. And the other wanted him to run.

Neither of them was particularly practical.

"Look at that," Abby said, eyeing him. "I can see your mother's side in there, fighting to get out."

He gave her a weak smile. "You wouldn't have wanted to be on the opposite side of my mother in an argument. She saved my pathetic arse several times when the headmaster wanted to kick me out of school. He was just lucky she wasn't meeting him in a dark alley."

It seemed the only choice he had was to continue on the way he was, without thinking too much about anything at all. He'd go to that house, find Undine, tell her what he knew, and let her make use of it the best way she could.

"Look," he said, stopping. "We've been pussyfooting around this ever since you broke me out of the Hays' place. I intend to do whatever I can to help Undine. That includes telling her I think the clans are going to attack."

"That would be a verra dangerous thing for Bridgewater to hear."

He looked at those cool, unwavering eyes. Was she playing him?

"You have promises to keep and so do I—to myself, at least. I know there are things you can't tell me. I understand that. But *you* need to understand I'm telling Undine every damned thing I've learned or can guess at. Nothing you can say will change that. How she plans to use the information is up to her. But if there's some message you'd like Bridgewater to 'accidentally hear' then tell me. I'll do whatever I can for you. I owe you a lot."

The first voices he'd heard in hours other than his and Abby's reached his ears. They echoed up the pass from far below. Six men on horses, a quarter of a mile ahead. Even from here he could see the plaids.

"Just keep walking," Abby said.

"Who are they? Do you recognize them?" Their

faces were too distant to make out, but he wondered if Abby could tell something about them by their horses or their clothes.

"It doesn't matter. If we behave as if nothing is the matter, they'll ignore us."

"Stop," he said. "Is there a chance that those men will recognize you when we pass?"

She sighed. "They're from Clan Leslie, so aye. But I doubt they'll recognize me in these clothes."

"Come now. Let's be sensible. You need to turn around and go back. You have to get back to Duncan and your friends anyway. I'll engage the clansmen. By the time I'm done talking to them, you'll be out of sight and out of mind."

"I dinna think that's a good idea. You don't know the way and—"

"I can find Morebright's estate. I'm not a total imbecile. Half probably, but not total."

"We shouldna be stopped," she said, tugging on his sleeve and keeping her eyes on the men. "We'll draw less attention by walking."

"We can be a couple stopping to have a row. We're on the verge of having one as it is, it seems."

She sighed. "I don't want to leave you here on your own. I owe it to Undine to see to your safe passage."

"She'd be even more upset if I got you drummed out of the chieftain corps. Go. Now let me do what I need to do. I'll make it there safely. I promise."

Abby nodded. "Keep following this path till ye reach the river and then it's about a mile more to the east," she said. "Er, east. That's with the sun on your right, aye?"

He coughed. "Got it."

She extended her hand. "Good luck, Michael Kent."

He took her hand and leaned forward to kiss her on the cheek. "Thank you for your advice, Abby Kerr. You're a good friend."

She took a few backward steps, still looking at him. "Now, dinna forget you're a Kerr in that plaid."

"Is that a good thing or a bad?"

"The Leslies will like it fine. But take care with Lord Morebright."

He adjusted the knot that seemed to be the keystone to holding everything in place. "Duncan would probably kill me if he caught me wearing this."

"He's the one who gave it to me. He said"—her voice dropped into its lowest register for a dead-on imitation of her fiancé—"'If I have any clothes left by the time we get home, I'll be verra surprised.'"

He'd have to thank Duncan when he saw him next. But there was something more pressing he owed the man. "Abby, wait. Please apologize to Duncan for me. I don't know what got into me back there," he said, pointing vaguely in the direction of Black Blade.

"I know what got into ye," she said with a gentle smile. "And I suspect it's going to get worse before it gets better."

Thirty-five

"ARE YOU TELLING ME THE TRUTH, LAD?" MOREBRIGHT said to Bridgewater, spearing another hunk of boiled eel from the proffered platter. Undine's mind reeled thinking of Bridgewater as a "lad." The growth on the old man's arm was as large and misshapen as a summer squash.

"Aye," Bridgewater said. "The bishop was as drunk as a French lord. Naked. And lying on the floor of a whorehouse in Coldstream, claiming to have no recollection of the previous night. Is it any wonder we question the worth of the salaries we pay our churchmen?"

Lord Morebright laughed a gasping laugh that rattled the ring of keys at his waist and went on so long that Undine wondered if his nurse might have to be called. He'd spent the last hour behind the closed doors of his reception room with Bridgewater while Undine had spent the time walking the grounds, trying unsuccessfully to hear something through the closed windows and thinking about Michael.

Her thoughts had returned to the same subject when Morebright interrupted her pleasant reverie.

"Tell me, my girl," he said, "do you really read men's fortunes, or is that just something you say so that you might get them to tell you their secrets?" He bared his grimy teeth in an unpleasant smile.

Undine considered a number of replies, none of them acceptable in polite company, certainly not when one of the members of said company was the man to whom one was supposedly affianced and who was clearly sharing a secret with his host. Instead, she said, "You know what they say. If you want to keep a secret, you must first keep it from yourself."

The smile left Morebright's face. "I'll have to defer to you on that. I know you're the expert on keeping secrets. Don't get too close to my toes," he added sharply to the servant ladling boiled onions onto his plate. "They're as fragile as tinder."

Undine declined the onions and turned her attention to her soup. The earlier she could adjourn to her bedchamber, the better.

His lordship reached past her for the salt cellar. "Speaking of secrets, does John know of your past?"

Undine stiffened. Many of her customers in the borderlands believed her to be a whore, the sort of whore whom you knew, without evidence, to have slept with others and whom you told others you had slept with yourself. Undine had learned to live with the innuendo and even use it to her advantage, but if Morebright dared touch upon it here, as they ate their supper, he would find out how close to tinder those toes were.

"Simon," Bridgewater cautioned, "I don't think—"

"Shut up, Johnny. I didn't mean her moral

comportment. I'm perfectly aware those stories are untrue. I mean the story of her birth."

The blood in Undine's ears began to sing.

Bridgewater attempted to conceal his concern in a look of affection and opened his mouth to say something, then stopped and shook his head.

His chivalry knows no bounds.

"Have you not told him, Undine—or should I say, Miss Murray?"

Bridgewater wheeled toward her.

Undine's grasp on her goblet tightened. She wished the claret were rotting fish guts and that she might fling them in both their faces. "My father was a clansmen in Clan Murray."

"You're a *Scot*?" Bridgewater put down his fork, appalled for an instant before remembering his duty. "It doesn't matter, of course. Your mother was an Englishwoman. I know that. What was his name? I'm acquainted with a number of the men in that clan."

Undine's face grew hot. "I don't know his name. Nor does my mother."

The hint of a grin spread over Lord Morebright's face. "Her mother was raped, John. 'Twas a terrible thing. She came to the chieftain and demanded justice. The trouble was she'd never seen the man's face. And, unfortunately, none of the clansmen stepped forward to claim the honor. Integrity does not run deep in Scotsmen."

"My mother was also abandoned by her Englishman husband," Undine said, cold fire in her voice, "and the two of us were driven from our home by marauding English soldiers who stole our whiskey and set the place afire when they were done. So if we're looking to measure worthiness, perhaps it is *men* who fall short, not Scotsmen or Englishmen."

An electric silence followed, which was broken by a loud "Ha!" by Morebright.

"So you see, John, you are bestowing your name on a woman who will not only prosper by it but will be beholden to you for it. I call that a fine match. My own wife was the daughter of a butcher. She was always attentive to my needs, though she lived in a rather ridiculous fear that I would divorce her. And we always got the fattest geese at Christmas."

"Undine will never have to worry about anything," Bridgewater said, gaze darting, in a spineless attempt to both appease and contradict his host.

She leaned forward to meet Morebright's eyes and said in a voice loud enough to cause a maid passing in the hallway to turn. "Are you in your full faculties today, sir? Would you care to hear your fortune?"

Transfixed by the scene unfolding, the footman refilling Bridgewater's goblet forgot what he was doing and only kept himself from pouring claret onto the table by catching himself with a jerk.

Ignoring the servant's silent bows of apology, Morebright snorted. "'Tis no more than a Fair Day trick."

Undine waited.

"Nonetheless," he added, "you're my guest. I shouldn't wish to miss your performance. I've heard it's quite fine."

"Are you certain?"

"*Undine*," Bridgewater said.

He's finally found his gallantry, she thought. Too bad he was using to it protect Morebright.

Morebright waved off any concern. "I want to hear what she says, John. This sort of thing has taken the place of the castle fool for dinner entertainment. Let us be amused."

She took the man's unafflicted hand and turned it over to view his palm.

"You must close your eyes," she said, and he did.

She traced a finger lightly along the base of his fingers and then at the fleshy part of his thumb. He shivered at the touch. After a thorough perusal, she brought his hand to the edge of the table and leaned as close as she could to shelter it from John's view. Swaying a bit, she closed her eyes. "Men admire you for your foresight and business acumen. You're a man who does not shy away from risk and who reaps the rewards of such courage. You will soon find yourself at a crossroads, and the choice you make will serve you well. Do you see the line here?" She drew her finger across the base of his thumb, eyes still closed.

"Aye," he said, barely above a whisper.

"This represents a journey—and, of course, you're about to travel to York. There, you will meet a stranger who will offer you a great opportunity. Consider your options and trust your instincts. Things are not always as they seem, but you will see the answer clearly, even when those around you don't. On the whole, this is very strong fortune and betides both wealth and happiness." She released him and leaned back in her chair.

The man stared at the hand as if it were still tingling with the aftereffects of her magic. After a long pause, he shook his head. "Drivel."

"Your skepticism doesn't surprise me," she said,

adjusting her chain of silver and coral. "'Tis the lens through which the most intelligent men view the world."

"John, this must be a delightful diversion for you. Does she predict plump, blond nobleman's daughters for all of your unmarried friends as well?"

Bridgewater, who was eyeing Undine closely, didn't immediately respond. "One can always count on Undine for the most masterful sleight of hand," he said at last.

"Thank you, John," she said, standing. "Now, I must beg you to excuse me. I have to take care of a few matters before I go to bed."

A young servant appeared in the doorway. "I beg your pardon, sir. You have a visitor."

Undine's heart fluttered, and her gaze went immediately to the window, though it was far too dark to see anything.

"A visitor at this hour?" Morebright said. "Who is it?"

"A Mr. Peter Swift. He says you do not know him. Shall I ask him to return tomorrow?"

Undine hurried out of the dining room doors, hoping to see if the visitor resembled a theater director she knew, but the towering entry hall was empty.

"He's been moved to the reception room, milady," said the same servant who'd nearly spilled the wine.

She made her way into the library without comment, hoping her silence passed for haughtiness rather than a confirmation that she had indeed been curious about the man. It was only then that she allowed herself the pleasure of fingering the keys she'd lifted from Morebright's side during her performance. One of them, she hoped, would open a room in which she would discover the truth of what he and Bridgewater were planning.

She paged through an illustrated history of exotic flora, lingering on the eye-catching majesty of the *Java anthurium* with its proud and somewhat vulgar spike, while she waited with more nervousness than she cared to admit to hear a snippet of Mr. Swift's voice.

But her wait went unrewarded. Morebright entered the reception room, closed the door, and not another word was heard.

She reshelved the volume and exited into the hall. A hand on her arm brought her to a full stop.

"What was that in there?" Bridgewater inclined his head toward the dining room.

"I'm not sure what you mean."

"You know what I mean. You don't read palms. And you certainly don't give men fortunes like that ridiculous load of bilge."

"That's what he wanted to hear."

"But it wasn't the truth, was it? You saw his future, didn't you?"

She didn't care for Bridgewater's tone or the grip on her arm. Where was the inconvenient servant now, when she actually needed him? "I did."

"What was it? Why didn't you share it with him?"

"He had no interest in the truth. He only wanted to be proven right. So I gave him what he wanted."

"You should have given him his true fortune," Bridgewater said flatly. "He allowed you to read it. 'Tis not yours to withhold."

Her vision was not hers to withhold? She shook

her arm free. "If you feel so strongly that he should know what his future holds, you may deliver the news yourself. Tell him to make his will. The operation will be harrowing, and while he'll live to tell of it, a vessel in his neck will burst not long after, and he'll die in a pool of his own blood. His wife, by the way, loved him till the end and forgave him for the child he had by his factor's daughter. His factor, however, was not so forgiving, and if he ever wonders why his lumber concern never made back its investment, he need look no further."

She could tell by the surprise in Bridgewater's eyes that he knew some of this to be fact.

"Is there anything else?" she asked.

"Aye," he said, not chagrined by the edge in her voice. "Are you perhaps an acquaintance of Peter Swift?"

Her heart beat faster. Had he unmasked the man—or worse, hurt him? "No. Why?"

"The way you looked up when he was announced made me think you might know him. And when you left the dining room to 'take care of a few matters,' you came here rather than going to your room. Unless your matters include perusing Simon's collection of books, I'm not sure what this location offers other than a chance to run into Simon's guest."

Bridgewater was more sharp-eyed than she'd given him credit for. She would need to be more careful.

"Oh, look," he said. "Shall we introduce ourselves?"

She swung around, half-eager, half-afraid, to find Morebright exiting the reception room. The man who followed was half a foot shorter than Michael and twenty years older. Even then, she searched his face for a hint of those warm eyes and smile but found nothing.

"Good evening, sir. I'm Lord Bridgewater. May I introduce my fiancée, Undine... Well, I suppose we might as well say Lady Bridgewater."

Undine cringed at his use of that surname for her. And she'd never heard Bridgewater take the lead in introductions before. As a nobleman, others were introduced to him.

Peter Swift bowed deeply and Undine curtsied.

"A very good evening to you, sir," she said, feeling sorry for the man who, unbeknownst to him, was the object of such intense dislike.

"And how is it you know Lord Morebright?" Bridgewater asked.

"I don't—well, not verra well. I'm the new curate at Saint Kinian's. Lord Morebright sent for an officiant. Are you the lucky groom?"

Thirty-six

UNDINE LOCKED THE DOOR OF HER BEDCHAMBER AND collapsed against it, stunned. She felt as if all the air had been removed from the room.

But this is no more than what you'd assumed would happen.

Aye, but having an assumption and being confronted with the cold, awful reality were very different things.

She touched her hair, her dress. It was as if the world had lost its hold on what could and couldn't happen, and she needed to be reminded of the truth of things. Satisfied the strands hadn't turned to snakes or the silk to flames, she took a few rubber-kneed steps.

"I wondered if you'd be joining me at some point."

She jumped.

Michael stood in the shadows, wearing the dark blue coat of Morebright's footmen. His hair had been slicked back, and the false beard had been rolled into a queue, extending a few inches down his back and tied with a red ribbon. It looked just like the queues worn by all of Morebright's footmen wore. *He* was the inconvenient servant! She gasped, astounded.

"How did you…?"

He shrugged. "It's so hard to find good help these days." He'd rendered his wounds nearly invisible with some sort of face paint.

She threw her arms around him. The weight of him, solid and reassuring, steadied her, and it wasn't until she'd found her voice again a long, long moment later that she realized the arms that held her held her with palpable restraint.

"What is it?" she asked.

"I've seen Abby. I have news of the clans." He released her gently, but the air felt cooler than it had a moment earlier. And she knew without asking the clans weren't the cause of the chill.

"What?"

"When I was tossed out, I went to Gerard and Serafina, who in turn took me to Abby."

"In Black Blade?" He'd gotten himself into a meeting of the chieftains? For an instant, she had a vision of him as William Wallace.

"Aye. Very Scottish gothic. I expected a herd of vampire oxen to come charging around the corner at any instant."

"I don't know 'vampire.'"

"Like poisonous snakes, only with wings."

"I see."

It seemed to her the conversation they were having was taking the place of the one they needed to have. Nonetheless, neither of them seemed to ready to abandon it.

"What did Abby say?"

Michael hung his head and sighed. "Perhaps I shouldn't have told her, but I can't change that now—"

"What did you tell her?"

"I told her Bridgewater was taking you to see Lord Morebright."

"Oh my skies." He opened his mouth to offer an apology and she waved it away. "Abby and I have a peculiar relationship, you see. We occupy different sides of the conflict here often enough to make a policy of silence on certain matters a requirement."

"I'm sorry. I see that now."

Undine imagined the scene. Two dozen clan chiefs, whose men in the borderlands were harassed on a daily basis, finding out the man who oversees the harassing is trying to travel through Scotland without notice. Abby, herself the victim of a highly embarrassing blackmailing at Bridgewater's hands earlier in the year, forced by honor to reveal what Michael had told her and then arguing for a measured response.

Then it dawned on her that allowing Michael to come here might be part of a trap. "How did you get away?"

Michael told her the story, and when she heard his escape was Abby's doing, her eyes grew moist. Abby would not have used Michael to deliver false information. Responsibility to her people might require her to work at cross-purposes to Undine, but Abby would fight every clan chief in Scotland before she'd allow Undine or a man Undine cared about to be used unknowingly to foil the rebels' dreams of peace.

"And she led you all the way to MacDougal's Fist?"

"I must say the Scots have a peculiar way with names, but yes, she led me to a rocky hill almost in sight of the river that led me here."

Undine basked in the unique comfort that comes from a sister's care, even when that sister is not truly yours. It was a feeling as powerful as magic—perhaps more powerful.

"She's very protective of me," Undine said.

"Indeed, she is. More than you know." His eyes were like glass in the moon's light, but it was the blue of regret, not pleasure.

"What is it? Tell me."

"There's more."

"The letter. What did it say?"

"Bridgewater has been tasked with creating a diversion of his choosing before the vote. He was told to have it done by Midsummer's Day."

"That's soon." A shiver went down her back. She knew the sorts of diversions the English army created. The vision in her head was a cataract of orange and red, like the core of a blistering volcano. "Who tasked him?"

"We don't know. The letter wasn't signed—nor was it addressed to Bridgewater by name—and Lord Hay took it from me. I don't know who has it now." He sighed. "I'm sorry. I really blew it."

Despite her worry, she had to smile. "'Blew it'? I'm not entirely sure, but I think I can guess the meaning."

But her quip did not smooth the concern on Michael's face.

"If we're parceling out blame, there are a number of tasks I've 'blown' too," she said. "I shouldn't have let Bridgewater talk me into coming here. I shouldn't have risked the success of the mission by exploring his office with him so near. And I certainly shouldn't have brought you to here, into this mess. This is my battle, not yours."

"If I believed that, I wouldn't be here. But there's a different battle I'm fighting now—far more selfish, I'm afraid. I know you have…things you wish to accomplish here. And nothing would bring me more relief than to take you as far away from here as I could, but I know I can't ask that. I know that your mission requires you to…endure…be willing to…" He shoved a hand through his hair, nearly destroying the neat queue. "Screw it. I want you to leave here. Now. With me."

"Michael—"

"It's not safe. It wasn't safe before we found out the clansmen might be mounting an attack and now it's not safe at all."

"The things I do can't be influenced by safety. If they were, none of them would ever get done."

"Undine…" He shook his head. "Nothing changes. The Scots parliament agrees to the treaty. The Act of Union is signed into law. Scotland becomes a part of what we call—"

"I know what it's called," she said sharply. "And while it's a 'Kingdom,' it's never really 'United,' is it?"

"I think you underestimate the ties that can grow when two groups face hard times and fight a common enemy."

"Germany, do you mean?"

He blinked. He hadn't realized the extent of her knowledge. Good. Better that he knew.

"Yes," he said. "And France in the nineteenth century. And America later in this century. And Russia and Spain and the Ottoman Empire. Scotland and England have their problems, but they are truly united after the Union."

"Through the fighting of wars?"

His shoulders fell. "Yes."

She groaned. "Why is it men can only find common purpose in fighting others? Michael, I don't care if Scotland and England join or not. I want to defeat the men who can't rest until they control more, the men who trample the homes and lives of people who only want peace and a chance to keep their children fed and safe—and Bridgewater is at the top of my list."

"I told you this once," Michael said softly, his gaze fixed in the distance. "Exacting revenge won't bring you the satisfaction you think, and endlessly praying for it will destroy you."

"I don't want revenge, Michael. I want peace."

She regretted the words the instant they'd left her mouth, not because they weren't the truth, but because that same sadness had appeared in his eyes when he'd spoken, and she'd missed her chance to find a way to ask him about it by responding in anger.

"Bridgewater is the conduit through which the bribe money is coming," she said. "We know that. If I can find proof of it, the trust the people of Scotland have placed in their parliament will be broken and the noblemen there will be forced to vote the will of the people or face their ire. Scots do not forgive easily—and they never forget."

A wan smile appeared on his face. "No they don't."

"I can't stop, Michael. I can't."

His hands moved as if he were arguing with himself and knew he wouldn't win. "But you know what happens," he said at last. "To Scotland."

"I haven't given up hope. I've borne witness to things that have changed—here and in the future. Nothing as big as this. Nothing," she admitted with a pang, "even a tenth as big, or a hundredth. But that doesn't mean it can't."

He took a long, deep breath. "And you're willing to stay here to…do what needs to be done…and face whatever comes?"

"I am."

His eyes, open and uncertain, met hers. She could feel his struggle, though she didn't know its origin, and even thinking about it made her afraid. Dammit, she could face a hundred Bridgewaters and a thousand clansman but not this perilous divide that seemed to have sprung up between her and Michael.

"If you're willing to fight," he said, "then I am too."

"Oh, Michael." She caught his lapels like they were ropes for saving a drowning woman. His arms came to an awkward rest on her back. She lifted her mouth to him.

"We can't," he said.

"Do you not wish to?"

"Oh, God, how can you ask?" he said, groaning. "I want you so much."

"Kiss me, then. The magic will take care of the rest."

"The magic's gone." He tried to push her away, but halfway through he pulled her into a scorching kiss instead. "I can't do this," he said, voice choked, when he released her. "I'll do whatever you wish me to do, but don't make me do this. I can't watch you take him to your bed and feel this way about you. I can't. I'll die."

"Take him to *my bed*?" she said, shocked. "My God, I'd put a knife in his belly first—or my own."

"You kissed him. I saw it. I don't deny you your right to use whatever means you choose to help the cause, but I can't feel what I'm feeling, Undine. My heart's like a mortar about to go off in my chest. If I don't get it away as far and as fast as I can, I'll be destroyed."

"*He* kissed *me*—and it was disgusting. I'd rather kiss one of your vampire oxen. I stopped him instantly. I'm so sorry you saw it. I–I…should have known you wouldn't leave. I felt you there, but I couldn't bring myself to believe it."

"Why not?"

"Because I have so little experience of a man's kindness. Because your wounds were—Oh, Michael, they were so awful. And because, I think, I'd hoped for you to stay so much."

He folded his arms around her, this time with no restraint, and held her close. "I want to teach you to expect kindness—to depend on it."

Her heart swelled into her throat, and she dared not speak. Here, in his arms, she felt safe.

"And I dinna want you to sleep with him," he said huskily, sounding very much like a Scotsman. "I don't care if Roman centurions march into the streets of Edinburgh and threaten to clap every Scot in chains."

"Roman centurions?" She gave him a look of mock concern. "You know we'd have to do something."

"Aye, and I'd start with offering Bridgewater to them for their lions."

The scent of his skin and promise of his protection made her dizzy. The kisses he was applying to her neck and ears were only adding to the effect.

With a firm clasp on her buttocks, he lifted her to her toes. "Let me show you what else you can depend on."

She had a general idea what it was, being held rather closely against it.

He backed her onto the bed and rucked up her skirts.

She wondered what Bridgewater would think if he found her fornicating with a footman, but the wondering was brief, as certain movements of Michael's made it impossible to think of anything else.

The emotions that had carried her this far were more than happy to let desire take over, and their bodies scrabbled roughly to mine the pleasure. She wanted every thought banished from the tiny palace of happiness they were making for themselves within the four bedposts.

"I want ye naked, lass," he whispered. "But first I want ye surprised."

Surprise was hardly the word for this quaking, clawing hunger, but the great force of it, she knew, was not in this heated tangle of limbs but in the vows he'd spoken before they'd begun.

The embers had been licked into flames, and then, with an urgency that starved her of breath and thought, time stopped.

But he was true to his word, and when she caught her breath, he undressed her and then himself, and this time they made a slow dance of it. He held her as she moved, watching her with an unembroidered affection that made her forget everything but the warmth in his eyes and the rumble of joy in his chest. The moon was high in the sky when she arched against him and realized she'd found something she hadn't even known she was missing.

"No more, lass," he said. "I'm too old for this."

"How old are you?" she asked eagerly, rolling onto her stomach to look at him.

"Old enough to know better than to try *that* a third time."

"I'd believe you," she said, "if it weren't for that." She ducked her head in the direction of what appeared to be incontrovertible evidence of his will to continue.

"Have you heard of a piñata?"

"'Piñata'? Like '*pigna*,' pinecone?" She frowned, looking at the *pigna* in question.

"And she speaks Spanish. No. More like an oversize toy—"

"Oh, *aye*," she said, understanding.

"Oh, *no*," he said, catching her hand. "Made of paper and glue. Filled with sweets. And one takes swings at it with a stick."

"Oh, no."

"Now you're getting it. Once the sweets are gone…" He held up his palms.

"We make more sweets?"

"Oh dear. I can see I've made a terrible mistake. Theoretically, yes, but when you're as old as I am, one has to make do with a few days of thin gruel first."

"I don't care for gruel," she said, flopping petulantly onto her back.

"Aye, well, one never knows," he said, catching her hand and lifting it. "And I'll promise you the possibility of changing until I've tricked you into letting me put a ring on your—"

He stopped, and with an awful shock, Undine remembered.

"What's that?" he asked.

She tried to pull her hand away, but her muscles seemed to have lost their ability to respond to the commands of her brain.

"His ring," she said, her voice no more than a whisper. "You…*married* him?"

"It doesn't matter. It means nothing."

He let go of her hand, and the bed went cold.

Thirty-seven

MARRIED TO BRIDGEWATER.

If she had to help the people of the borderlands, Michael thought, why couldn't she build them a hospital or something? Why did her work have to involve putting herself in the way of a man like Bridgewater?

He stood out of the rain, under the eaves of the stables, his heart feeling like a large bruise inside his chest. He gazed abstractedly at the white-capped river, running fast, and thought that was about what he felt like doing too.

Logically, he understood her explanation of how it had happened. She'd wriggled out of Bridgewater's grasp enough times that one more time would have pushed him to the edge of flat-out suspicion. But emotionally, Michael was finding it hard to accept.

She'd sworn it didn't mean anything to her. And of course it wouldn't. She *hated* the man. Michael had no doubt about that.

But she was *married*.

There was something concrete and unchangeable about marriage—well, certainly his, at least until it changed completely—and even more in this time. One couldn't get a divorce in 1706, not easily, and in this case, not without the intervention of the House of Lords, which meant it wouldn't happen unless Bridgewater wished it to happen. It was almost as if Undine had been encased in a deep-sea diving suit. Michael could still see her and talk to her and even hold her, but there was a layer there now that hadn't been there before.

He kicked his small bag of belongings, still wedged where he'd left it, between an overturned trough and the stable wall.

Why did she call you here?

She needed somebody—anybody.

No. She needed someone with a special set of skills. More important, she needed a man she could trust.

Great. So I'm a man she can trust. Maybe what she really needed was a brother. Or a dog. Here, Toby! Good boy!

Oh, I see. So you're willing to help her, but only if she sleeps with you?

You know what? Fuck off.

Why did you come to Morebright's home?

To tell her what she needed to know.

Lord Hay had no messengers? Come, Michael. Why did you come to Morebright's home?

To help her.

So how has your job changed?

He groaned. But it had changed. It had. It didn't matter how long he argued with himself.

Was a marriage still a marriage if one of the parties went into it with no intention of it being real?

The answer was yes *and* no, and no matter how he tried, he couldn't find a way to sort that out.

He opened his hand and looked at what she'd given him.

A small twist of orange paper that, with a tear and a shake, she'd said, would take him back to the National Rose.

Thirty-eight

UNDINE LIFTED HER HEAD FROM THE BEDROOM'S SMALL desk and wiped her eyes. She was glad it was night. She didn't want to see what her face looked like. Even without the moon, which seemed to have left her at the same time Michael did and been replaced by a suffocating gray rain, she could sense her herbs and potions standing in orderly rows, the tall tin for the catchweed, the delicate porcelain for the clove, and, of course, the now half-depleted twinflower in its uncorked glass. She reached for the familiar sheets of paper, only to realize she'd wet them with her tears. She could feel the dampness where the dye had run onto the cotton mat below and could smell the poke and bitter bloodroot.

What a fool she'd been.

To have opened her heart as she had—she might as well have smashed it to bits with a rock. She knew full well the imprudent lengths men and women went to when their hearts became entangled. Had she not seen men give up wealth, and women freedom? Had she not seen family dynasties destroyed? What made her think she was immune to such stupidity?

Spies have no business caring for anyone.

She looked at the ring on her finger: thick gold, inlaid with an emerald the shape of a cat's eye, and the motto of the Bridgewaters—*Paritur pax bello*, "peace is obtained through war." She shook her head, disgusted—as much at herself as at Bridgewater.

When the ring had been put upon her finger, it represented no real burden to her. An inconvenience, aye, but no marriage can occur when one does not consent in one's heart, no matter what words were leaving one's lips. But now she might as well be dragging the chains of Prometheus beside her.

She'd forgotten not everyone built a protective wall around themselves with layer upon layer of the nacre of duty, drive, and independence so as not to be vulnerable. Michael believed a marriage vow was as binding and important as an oath of honor. He lived in a world in which words mattered and one acted with honesty and feeling. She found herself wondering what sort of woman had earned such a vow from Michael and what had broken it in the end.

With an irony too cruel to be reflected upon, her marriage to Bridgewater had meant Michael could return home. The task her spell had brought him to perform—keeping her from marrying Bridgewater—had been rendered moot. As there was nothing he needed to keep her from doing anymore, there was nothing to keep him in this time.

She'd prepared the mixture in a silence so heavy her fingers had shaken. She had no doubt the mixture would work. The tears of a naiad were said to triple the power of any spell, and she'd dutifully collected them, her back turned, so that he might have the assurance of a safe and easy passage. It was, she thought, the least she owed him.

Would he be at peace back at his theater? She wondered if magicians performed in theaters in the future and if he used his magic on actors. She closed her eyes and opened her mind to try to see him after he'd returned to his old life, though each instant spent in such an exercise was like a knife in her heart. She saw a churning orange and yellow. Change, she thought. Not pain. Not relief. And certainly not love.

But he'd survive.

And so would she.

At once, she was aware of him, and so strong was her sense of it, she nearly looked at the door. But that wasn't the source of her feeling. It came from beyond the window, and when she turned there, the sparkle of Morebright's keys in the candlelight reminded her that her time at present was not her own.

Thirty-nine

THE ENTRY HALL WAS DARK AND EMPTY AS SHE STARTED down the stairs. The first room she intended to search was Morebright's reception room. It was the room in which she and Bridgewater had married, which gave her a passable explanation for wanting to be there should anyone discover her, though she did wonder if women truly felt such a connection to the location of their vows that they would wish to revisit it just to reexperience the happiness of the time. She'd heard a clanswoman of Abby's say it once after a luncheon Abby threw in the ruins of the chapel on her land, and Undine had been so surprised, she'd thought the woman drunk, but Abby had insisted no liquor had been served.

Undine would certainly never be so sentimental about her quick ceremony to the loutish Bridgewater, who'd spent the entire time smiling at her like an addle-brained fool.

She stopped, horrified.

Oh God, do I look at Michael the same way?

She turned back and forth until she spotted the

silvered glass of a sconce at the bottom of the steps and ran to it. She peered at her reflection and thought of that first kiss.

Great skies, I look just as addle-brained.

There's a reason to be glad he's gone, she thought firmly, though, she considered with a sigh, she hadn't quite convinced herself.

She padded quickly across the marble floor. The footmen were making their nightly rounds. The reception room was just past the dining hall. She hadn't been in the house long enough to figure out where Morebright did his paperwork, but the reception room was where he'd met with Bridgewater.

She pulled the ring of keys from her pocket, careful to hold them still. She gauged the size of the keyholes on the double doors and then poked gingerly through the selection of keys in her hand. Most were too large. The three smaller ones were about equal size. She reached for the smallest one, but the movement overbalanced the ring and the thing fell to the ground with a horrendous clatter that seemed to echo down every hallway.

She bent instantly for them.

"Lady Bridgewater?"

She nearly jumped out of her skin. She straightened and stepped forward so that her skirts covered the keys. It was an older, dark-eyed footman.

"May I offer my congratulations on your marriage?" he said, catching the handles and swinging both doors inward so that she might enter.

They weren't even locked.

"You may," she said, producing one of her famed addle-brained smiles. "Thank you."

He bowed and waited for her to enter. "It must feel like a great change."

Aye. Like I've been thrown in jail and am being readied to be burned at the stake.

She put her foot on the keys and slid them into the room, coughing repeatedly to cover the noise. The footman, light-footed for his age, had his hair pulled into a ribbon. She leaned forward to look into the man's eyes. It wasn't Michael, but she checked again, just to be sure.

"Is everything all right, milady?" the man said, uncomfortable under the close gaze.

"Oh, aye. I thought you looked familiar. I dinna see well without my spectacles, which I am loath to wear."

"Let me remedy that." He gathered a candle from a table, lit it from an entryway sconce, and placed it in a nearby pricket. "Will that be enough, or shall I light more?"

"'Twill be sufficient. I only wished... Well, 'tis a bit embarrassing. I only wished to sit here for a moment and remember the ceremony."

"A momentous time." He smiled. "My Mary's gone now, but we often visited the chapel on the estate where we said our vows. I always said that quarter hour alone made the whole year worthwhile."

The reception room had a settee and two stuffed chairs as well as numerous tables, shelves, and books. There was no desk, nor any obvious place to hide something. On the wall, a large mural had been painted of the Battle of Bothwell Bridge, in which the English army had routed the Scots not far from here. And if she remembered correctly... Aye, there he was. Captain Simon Morebright leading his company into battle. The muralist had made it easy to recognize him. Not only was he carrying his family's flag, but he was also by far the largest, handsomest, and most heroic-looking of the men portrayed on the canvas, sitting astride a horse, saddlebags at his side, in a bright pool of sunlight, no doubt indicating God's favor. She rolled her eyes. The only thing missing was a contingent of angels led by Gabriel and his trumpet circling Morebright's head and a sign that read "Here's the hero."

If this is what Morebright put in his reception room, she forbore to think what he'd had installed in his bedchamber.

"Do you like it?" the servant asked.

"It's something I shall not soon forget."

"His lordship had it commissioned a few years ago."

"He did? I would have guessed it to be a gift from his regiment, to thank him for his extraordinary bravery in the defense of our country."

The servant lowered his head, providing the humility he imagined his master would have displayed. "No, milady. It actually hides a door to the dining hall."

"Indeed?" She stared at the figures, looking for the outline of a door. It wasn't until she picked up the candle and drew even closer that the outline became visible in the trunks of three closely set oaks, which, of course, grew nowhere near Bothwell Bridge.

"I am amazed."

He opened the door, and there was the dining hall and its long line of arched windows. She felt Michael's presence again but knew it was only the night, the moon, and her regret coming together to defeat her.

"There are times," the servant said with a smile, "when his lordship finds it more convenient to adjourn to the dining room than to meet those who have come to call unexpectedly."

Which suggested, Undine thought, that he spent time in the reception room alone.

"I'd enjoy the same thing myself every now and again," she said. "Perhaps I can induce a muralist to come to Bridgewater's family seat."

"Coldstream now, is it not? Or will you be returning to the estate in Cumbria?"

She would be doing neither, partly because no earthly power could induce her to retreat even farther from the borderlands with John Bridgewater, but partly because she knew events were counting down quickly to a time when she would have to leave to save herself. She and Michael had stolen the letter from Bridgewater's box, and the moment Bridgewater opened it, his not yet fully formed suspicions about her would take on a very concrete shape. If she found anything here to take, then Morebright would also be on the verge of suspecting her. In addition, she knew the spell Bridgewater was under was fading. She'd already seen signs of its wildly shifting effects. And last, but far from least, the ring on her left hand meant she was now Bridgewater's chattel to do with as he pleased, and a man like Bridgewater was not going to let a situation like that go unleveraged for long.

She shook off the horror of such a thought. "Oh, I don't know what John wishes to do next concerning a home," she said. "I expect he'll surprise me."

The servant nodded, and as their conversation was

at its natural end, he began to back out, catching each door to close them.

"Wait," she said. "What's your name?"

"Tom, milady."

"Tom, I wouldn't want anyone to know I'm being so silly. Not even John."

He bent his head and the whisper of an approving smile appeared at the corner of his mouth. "As you wish."

The instant Tom closed the doors, she scooped the keys off the floor and began to look around. The table between the chairs had a small drawer but no lock. She looked anyway and found a folded broadsheet, a pair of scissors, a handheld lens and a number of other odds and ends, but nothing of interest, not even the broadsheet, which was four years old and concerned the necessity of approving the cost of a new toll bridge in Glasgow.

She paced the perimeter of the room and peered at the items on the shelves—porcelain doves, a box of quills, a set of cups for coffee, a small painting of Morebright's sons and late wife. Nothing looked like something the rebels would find useful.

The door in the mural was intriguing, though. Of course, there was every reason to believe a nobleman would have callers he didn't want to see, and a secret passageway provided a very handy escape. But an escape to the dining hall? Surely a man as manipulative and scheming as Morebright could have thought of something more original—stairs to his lover's bed-chamber or an escape route to the outside, perhaps.

She opened the door again—one had to push it, as

there was no knob to pull—and examined it. It was thicker than most doors, since it needed to be as thick as the wall, and she ran her hands along the sides and top, but she didn't feel any gaps that would suggest a hidden panel. She did the same to the frame around the door. It wasn't quite wide enough to offer a secret passage—unless you were a very thin child, perhaps—and it didn't appear to offer any secret hiding places either.

She closed the door again, marveling at the precision between the wall and the door's front. She most certainly wouldn't have noticed it without Tom's help.

Heaving a sigh, she looked again at the key ring. There were eight keys—five large and three small. One was undoubtedly for a money box somewhere and another for where silver plate was stored. A third would be for the room in which wine and whiskey were stored. The largest was probably for the house itself. That left four keys unaccounted for. Where in this place would four more locked rooms or boxes be that Morebright himself would take a personal interest in?

She gathered the pricket again to examine the keys nearer the window. There was nothing out of the ordinary about them. Some were more intricately fashioned than others, no doubt done to match either a highly stylized box or lock plate. All were brass. None had any markings to indicate what they were for or who made them.

She was just about to blow the candle out when she thought she noticed an odd ridge in the mural. Not near the door. Closer to the other side. She put her hand on the wall and ran it along the mural as she walked, intrigued. The surface was varied—a result of both the application of paint and the texture of the walls—but there were no seams. Until she reached a ridge.

Bringing the pricket closer, she found a ridge and another to match it running down the edges of Morebright's saddle bag in the painting. With heart beating fast, she followed the closest ridge up the wall till its endpoint and found another line running between the two ridges. Digging her fingernail in that, she managed to get a small door to open a bit, but it slipped back. She put down the pricket and tried again using both hands. Success. A small door, almost a shelf, angled open. Inside was a silver box about the height and width of a servant's tray with an ornate lock and handle. A shiver of excitement went through her.

She grabbed the case and sized up the lock. The first of the smaller keys didn't fit, but the second did. She opened the lid and found a sheath of papers. A number were letters Morebright had received from others, but at least three were from Bridgewater.

Undine quickly scanned the first one. It appeared to be an answer to an entreaty from Morebright to do more in the borderlands than his command would allow.

> *Simon, stepping beyond the orders I've been given is possible but would have to be undertaken with extreme caution… As you know, I am entrusted to make decisions when certain unexpected situations arise… The "situation" will have to be carefully chosen.*

This was all she'd need to get the vote defeated! If the Scots learned of the maneuverings of one of the highest-ranking officers in England's northern armies, it would be deeply embarrassing to the Scottish lords who'd already formed a coalition with England on the treaty. All it would take was to change the minds of a couple dozen lords and the treaty vote would fail. But more important, if she made the contents of this letter known, Bridgewater would undoubtedly be removed from his command. She knew General Silverbridge, the officer in Northumberland to whom Bridgewater reported, or at least, she knew his reputation. He was a fair and honest man. If she found something that implicated Bridgewater, Silverbridge would act.

She didn't have time to thoroughly read the correspondence here. She needed to get out of the house, and then get the story to one of the broadsheet publishers in Edinburgh, who could get it distributed. The letters themselves would have to be hidden. They were more valuable and dangerous than gold. As long as they were on her person, she'd be in extreme danger. The question now was, did she take the time to pack her powders and elixirs, or did she walk straight into the night?

She had no time to consider the choices. She heard footsteps and thrust the papers deep into her bodice, put the box on the shelf, and closed the small door hidden in the mural.

When the room's door opened, Undine turned from window.

Bridgewater started.

"There you are," she said, and ran to his side to kiss him.

Forty

MICHAEL STARED FRANTICALLY INTO THE DARKENED theater, trying to get his bearings. He was onstage, in a scene, squirming under the gaze of a thousand rapt patrons.

Was he in costume?

What was the play?

Did he know his lines?

An actress beside him said something, but her mouth moved in a bizarre imitation of a fish, as if she were talking in slow motion, and the roar in Michael's ears kept him from hearing what she said. He was drunk or something like it. The play seemed to be about Spain, but the set wasn't right. The actress, a blond, clutched a silver box that seemed to open and close on its own. He tried to remember if Friar Laurence used a box in Romeo and Juliet, but he could barely recall the central themes of the play. Romeo and Juliet were lovers. He felt certain of that. But something happened. Something came between them. Was the friar the villain or the hero? He found himself hoping they'd be happy. They seemed to want it so much. Did they end up together? A great wave of unhappiness came over him as he pondered the other eventuality. Was he supposed to change the end? Could he do it if he wanted to?

Someone nudged his ankle.

The audience waited for his reaction. He tried to move, but his legs weighed a thousand pounds.

The person nudged harder.

"Mr. Kent?"

Michael opened his eyes to see a deeply concerned Nab standing over him under the eaves of the Morebright stables.

"You need to wake up," the boy whispered. "I think Undine is in trouble."

Forty-one

"When did she go in?" Michael said, peering at the window from behind an exuberantly trimmed topiary pig.

"About an hour ago, I think," Nab said.

"An hour?" How long had he been asleep? He remembered holding the twist of paper, defeated, and staring at the house, looking for a sign of Undine beyond the darkened windows. He'd reviewed their conversation in the bedroom over and over, feeling both traitorous and stupid. After trying so hard to get in that house to be with her, why had he given it all up over something as foolish as a ring from a man she hated that had meant no more to her than, well, a ring from a man she hated?

"A quarter of an hour or more," said Nab. "And Bridgewater went in a few minutes after she did."

"What makes you think she's in trouble?" Apart from the obvious, of course, which Michael decided he needed to stop thinking so much about.

"Tom—he's one of the servants—found her first. I thought, *och*, she's fine. The man's as old as Cairnpapple and kindly like. But the instant he left the room and closed those doors, up he went to Bridgewater."

"Bridgewater, you're sure? Not Morebright?"

Nab's cheeks puffed as he thought. "I dinna know. Bridgewater came down, fast as a hare, and in he went. So I went to look for you."

"Thank you for the footman's clothes, by the way. They proved to be very useful."

The lad shrugged and eyed Michael with envy. "I wish I was your size. The only parts I get to play are stable hands and kitchen boys."

"Your day will come."

Morebright or Bridgewater. It didn't really matter. Bridgewater was possessive and suspicious. Morebright was an unpleasant jerk with a history of shady dealings. Either of them could cause Undine a great deal of trouble. Michael looked again at the windows. The candles were lit, which suggested the two of them were still in there. No one was screaming. No shots had been fired. A few minutes before, they'd heard two strikes of the resonant bell of what Nab informed him was a fancy French clock in the shape of a man chasing a stag that leapt in the air when the chime sounds, a clock that sat on the mantle in the great hall, so Michael assumed if Bridgewater was murdering Undine or—being optimistic—she was murdering him, they'd hear it here by the porcine shrubbery.

"Our best bet may be to go on the offense."

Nab's brow furrowed, and Michael had to remind himself he was talking to a boy barely more than twelve or thirteen.

"That's, er, making a strike before they can strike

you. It's a way to confuse things for the other side and give your side an advantage. Especially helpful if that's the only advantage you have."

"Like us."

"Er, right. Hey, not to go all schoolmaster on you, but why are you doing this anyway? Why aren't you at home with your mum and dad?"

"My mum wants me to tend sheep," Nab said, scratching his nose. "Tending grown-ups is more interesting."

Michael laughed. "Certainly more varied. Though I doubt you'd ever be able to herd the ones around here."

Nab's eyes brightened. "Have you met Gert? She's the herd dog—and a braw hand at sheep. Best I've ever seen. Erland and I were playing with her tonight. He's the cooper."

"Jeez, when do you sleep?"

"Mornings," Nab said flatly. "Grown-ups don't do anything interesting before eleven."

The boy cast a quick sidelong glance at the trough against which Michael had been sleeping. "Did she throw you out?"

Michael shifted. "Not exactly."

Nab frowned. "You left?"

Michael wasn't sure if the boy's loyalty was to Undine or the cause, but in either case, Nab seemed to regard the possibility with disapproval.

"You know she married him?" Michael said.

"Aye."

If Michael had been hoping for a sudden show of shared understanding, he'd been mistaken. Nab's look was as narrow as ever.

"By a real priest," Michael said.

"You pretended to be a solicitor. I'm pretending to be a stable boy."

"Right, but now she's really married. To Bridgewater."

The boy seemed more confused than ever. "Were you going to marry her?"

"I-I… Well, I mean, I might have. It was rather too early to think of such a thing."

Nab's disapproval turned to curious scrutiny. "How long does it take before you know? My mum said she fell in love with my da the moment she saw him carry a sick calf on his shoulder. She said it was like being hit in the head with a picket."

"Well, there is that sort of thing, of course—you know, in storybooks or plays—the hero spouting tortured speeches at the darkest moment, the heroine swooning. But in real life, it's quieter. A real woman never swoons. And a real man doesn't run around doing stupid things, putting himself in danger, racing through the countryside, climbing through windows—"

The look on Nab's face made him stop, and Michael realized he'd done everything he'd just described in the last few hours. "Oh. Right."

The realization stunned him. As a Brit—even one with Scottish roots—the idea of falling into a mad, passionate love was simply unimaginable—certainly since that day the officer knocked. Yet, here he was, standing in the dark of the borderlands countryside, in a servant's livery, in the eighteenth century, with a pistol jammed into his waistband, ready to do battle for a naiad whose singular goal in life was to change everything he knew about Scottish history.

Nab elbowed him. Undine and Bridgewater had

wandered into view. Undine's arms were crossed, and Bridgewater spoke rapidly, gesturing with obvious agitation. Michael's heart faltered. Had Bridgewater discovered something? Was this a quarrel about something else? Undine displayed no fear—not that he'd expect her to, even if facing down a primed cannon—and her posture suggested a disdain worthy of a queen. He almost felt sorry for Bridgewater. Almost. The man might win the argument, but he was definitely going to lose the war. The trouble was men like Bridgewater were notoriously poor sports when it came to losing wars. And Undine might be able to fend off his anger with disdain, but she'd never be able to fend off a blow. How far should he let this go? How far *could* he let it go? What would Undine want?

Michael could feel Nab watching him.

"So what do real men do at the darkest moment?" the boy asked.

He groaned. "Wait."

Forty-two

"I THINK YOU'VE HAD ENOUGH TO DRINK, JOHN."

In fact, Undine thought, he'd had *far* too much to drink, and it was only making his erratic behavior worse. They'd spent part of the time since he'd arrived discussing—in sometimes heated terms—his concern that she needed to begin to dress "like the wife of a nobleman." He hadn't—yet—applied a description to her current style of dressing, though the employment of such phrases as "unbefitting a woman of your now elevated status" and "likely to confuse a man who was unaware of your marriage" gave her a very clear hint regarding his perception of it. In addition, he'd announced his insistence that she accompany him and Morebright on the journey to York, which she had no intention of doing, but as she intended to leave the moment he either left the room or collapsed in a drunken stupor, it hardly seemed worth fighting about. And now he was describing the absolute necessity of ending her fortune-telling and spell casting except in those cases he deemed appropriate.

All of it was like a cloud of midges flying around her head—mildly irritating but of very little consequence.

What was of consequence, however, was her strong sense that Bridgewater had come in here for a different reason—a reason involving the hidden drawer in that mural.

When he'd burst into the room, his gaze had cut instantly from her to that wall. Since that moment, he'd done everything in his power to *keep* from looking at it, even when he sat in full view of it, which he'd had to do when she'd insisted on taking a seat on the arm of the chair facing away from it.

The question in Undine's mind, and one she couldn't get a clear grasp on, was whether he suspected her of rifling the drawer, whether he was afraid she would discover the drawer, or whether he simply wanted to get into the drawer without her watching him. In any of these cases, he'd be at that drawer the moment she left his side. And unfortunately, she hadn't had time to relock the box when she'd heard his footsteps, so if he knew what he was looking for, he'd know instantly it was gone.

He poured himself another glass of whiskey—his fourth—and waved the decanter at her. When she shook her head, he said derisively, "Why is it naiads don't drink? Is there something in whiskey that's poison to fairies?"

"John, you know very well I drink."

This one he tossed back and then, after he was sure she was watching, poured another.

"One might think you wished me drunk," he said.

"One might think you wished yourself drunk. I wish you only the chance for a good night's sleep."

"Take care," he said, taking a more modest gulp.

"There are many ways a new husband might inter-pret that."

She stood, disgusted, and walked to the window, realizing too late the papers had shifted in her bodice. "I can assure you I said it with only one meaning."

She'd thought the movement she'd made to read-just the load had been imperceptible, but when she turned the look on his face had changed.

"June twenty-fourth," he said, standing.

She started, keenly aware that was the date stated in the letter by which Bridgewater's "distraction" had to be completed. "What of it?"

"You may have until then," he said, moving closer. "After that, you move to my bed."

"For skies' sake, have you forgotten I possess the means to render you incapacitated in this area?"

His gaze cut to his drink.

"Do you think I need a potion?" she said, looking straight into his eyes.

"Do ye think I need a cock?"

She refused to reply, and he lifted his arm.

"Raise your hand to me, and we'll discover exactly how deep your desire for a working cock runs."

He flung his whiskey into the corner, sending shards of glass exploding in every direction, includ-ing the floor around her feet. Whoever lived with Bridgewater would have to put in for a large supply of drinking glasses.

She picked up her skirts, keeping her arm tight against her side. "I'm too tired for this, John," she said, sighing. "It's been a long and mostly pleasurable day. Let us end this on a happy note, aye? I'll call for a servant."

She prayed he'd nip at the bait. She prayed he wanted to dive into that hidden drawer more than he wanted to stand here and make her miserable, and she'd take her chances that he didn't know what to look for in there. Even if he did, she'd use a key and be out the front door before he'd completed his search. A moment after that, she'd be out of her clothes and into the river. He could look all he wanted, he'd never find her there. She'd swim all the way to Glasgow if she had to.

"John?"

Bridgewater appraised her closely. She could feel him considering the options.

"*I'll* call for the servant," he said. "Stay where you are. We don't want anything happening to you."

Forty-three

"Did you hear that?" Nab said. "It sounded like glass breaking."

It had. And now a thousand scenes raced through Michael's head, each uglier than the one before—Bridgewater shoving Undine into a china cabinet; Undine throwing a vase at his head; a table overturning as Bridgewater—

Oh God, he had to stop this.

He strained to hear more, but the night had fallen eerily silent. The breeze had died, and even the crickets had stopped. The river's churning was the only sound he could hear.

Undine, come to the window. Show me you're all right.

Nab waited for a sign from Michael.

"Go," Michael said at last. "Find out what's going on."

Nab began to run toward the house.

"Wait!"

The boy turned.

"Don't do anything unless you absolutely have to."

The boy nodded.

Forty-four

BRIDGEWATER LEFT, AND WHEN THE DOORS CLOSED, she heard a faint *click*. Had he *locked* them? Her anxiety rose. She hopped over the glass and ran to the doors. Head cocked, she listened for his departure. When she was sure he was gone, she tried the doors. To her great relief, they were open. She slipped into the entry hall and dug in her pocket for the ring of keys. She ran to the towering doors, hands shaking. The largest key fit the lock, but as she turned, the papers in her bodice fell down through her dress and dropped to the floor.

She scrabbled to collect them. When she stood, she nearly jumped out of her skin.

"What are you doing here?" she whispered furiously to Nab.

He put a finger to his lips and pointed nearly imperceptibly in the direction of her midsection, indicating an unseen danger behind her. With a thumping heart, she listened but heard nothing. She had to assume it was Bridgewater.

"Did he see the papers?" she mouthed.

"Undine?" Bridgewater said. "What are you doing?"

"I beg your pardon, milady," Nab said loudly. "I should watch where I'm going." He added under his breath, "Give them to me."

"No."

"Where did you get them?"

"The mural," she whispered. "Hidden compartment."

Bridgewater hurried toward them. "Why is the door open?"

She turned, keeping the papers and keys behind her. "I thought I heard a noise out here."

Nab snatched the papers and keys from her hands and slipped into the dark beyond the door.

"He must have been singing to himself," she said, battling to keep her voice light. "I thought I heard something and opened the front doors."

"The doors were locked."

"I'm afraid they weren't. I think I alarmed the poor boy when I called him in. He dropped everything he was carrying."

Bridgewater looked at the lock, then stared into the night. She could feel his uneasiness.

"We have a bigger concern," he said. "The footman says Morebright has lost his keys."

"Are they the only set?"

"That's not the point. The point is he thought they were on his vest. But they were gone when he retired for the night."

"Can we help him retrace his steps?"

"The footman's doing that. What I'd like you to do is wait in your room."

"For what?"

"I see no issue with this, Undine. It's nearly one.

Just take yourself to bed. Something may have been taken, and this way, you and I will be removed from the equation."

"You mean I'll be removed from the equation."

Two footmen arrived with brooms.

"Please escort my wife to her room and wait out-side," Bridgewater said to them. "I'd like her to remain safely out of the way while the house is searched."

The men put down the brooms and waited.

Bridgewater stood between her and door.

"Thank you," she said, curtsying. "I'll feel much safer with you there."

She made her way to the stairs, footmen on her heels, and prayed Nab was already far, far from the house.

Forty-five

BRIDGEWATER STEPPED INTO THE NIGHT AND PEERED down the estate's rolling lawns.

Wretched little rat. Was Undine in league with the boy? And for what? An uncomfortable sense of having been betrayed burned in his chest, though in truth, he couldn't imagine Undine being responsible for the loss of Simon's keys. He didn't know what Simon had hidden in his house, though the man should certainly be experienced enough to know to destroy sensitive communications. Bridgewater wished he could search Simon's hiding place himself—and he would have if Undine hadn't been there. Now he'd have to wait for the excitement to settle.

He shifted and rolled his shoulders, but the thought of Undine working against him was like a broken blade under his skin. Forget the suspicion, he might, but every time he turned, he was reminded of it with a stab of pain, and some unlucky time, he was going to turn too fast and find the blade had cut an artery.

He felt like he'd forgotten something important about her—something he knew once, before he'd been blinded by her beauty and fierce independence. But now she was his. Treacherous land, hard won. And land hard won lived by the rules of the victor—and the harder the win, the harder the rules. If she'd betrayed Bridgewater or England, if she'd taken something from Simon and Bridgewater found it on her, she would find herself a very unhappy bride.

"Lord Bridgewater?"

He jumped. The priest from Coldstream stood before him, habit and all.

"Good Christ, man," Bridgewater said, "what are you doing here? You mustn't approach a man in the dark like that! What if I'd had a sword in my hand?"

"Then I'd have only received what I deserved. I do beg your pardon for interrupting you, but I've traveled all day to reach you."

"Well, I'm afraid you've come too late. Lady Bridgewater and I were married this afternoon." He marveled at the man's idiocy—traveling forty miles without a thought as to whether he was needed or would even be welcome.

The man's face burst into a jubilant smile. "May I wish you joy of your marriage! She's a handsome woman, very handsome. I take it you found a priest? I must apologize for my abrupt departure yesterday. I received a very alarming letter from the bishop, but when I got to Coldstream, I found the bishop to be, well, not quite in his senses. I do believe he'd suffered a mild fit. He was—well, perhaps 'tis better not to dwell on it. He's recovered now, though, you'll be glad to hear, and he urged me to come here at once."

Bridgewater groaned to himself. He supposed the

man would expect a tithing for the church for his unnecessary efforts or, at the very least, a place to stay till morning.

"Father, er... What is your name again, please?"

"Kent, milord."

"Father Kent, I will see the servants find you a bed for the night. I suppose it's too late to expect you to go to the inn in town."

"I would be much obliged, sir. Perhaps I can say a few words of blessing in the morning."

"I doubt that will be necessary. Wait!" An idea struck Bridgewater. "Now that I think about it, my wife was to make her confession, but she was too much engaged in her hair and clothing—you know how women are. Could you find time to hear it?"

Kent nodded. "Perhaps I could hear yours as well?"

"The priest heard mine, of course," Bridgewater lied, "but Lady Bridgewater still bears the burden of her sins."

"An inauspicious way to start a marriage."

"Father, I must be honest. I'm afraid Lady Bridgewater has been involved with some unsavory activities, including some that may involve Lord Morebright, our host here."

"Pardon me, sir," a voice behind them said.

Bridgewater turned and found a footman standing in glow of the now-lit entry hall. He'd asked the man to give him news of the search. Bridgewater gestured him to a private area past a hedge.

"Was anything amiss?" Bridgewater said in a low voice.

"He's still looking," the footman said.

"Good. Where?"

"The silver room, the gold chest, his office."

"The reception room?" Bridgewater asked with false lightness.

"Oh, aye. I forgot to mention that. I don't know what his lordship was looking for in there. The only thing of value is the liquor, I suppose. But he was in there with the door closed for several minutes."

"'Tis probably where he thought he'd left his keys."

"Indeed," the footman said. "I'm sure you're right."

So the old fellow has some secrets, does he? But Bridgewater was more concerned about Undine. The odd exchange he'd witnessed between her and the boy made him certain something was going on between them.

"Thank you for your report. Please don't mention my interest to his lordship. There's no point in worrying him further."

If the man was wise, he'd know his silence would be rewarded before Bridgewater took his leave of the estate.

The footman bowed deeply. "Aye, sir."

Bridgewater returned to the priest, who had turned politely to observe the heavens.

"Is something going on?" Kent asked.

Bridgewater explained the situation, leaving out his own interest in Simon's secrets.

"My wife has been involved in some unfortunate dealings," Bridgewater said. "This will end, of course, now that I have the ability to keep an eye on her. But her transgressions were serious—lying, stealing, using her wiles on men to extract information, and I'm afraid this time, she might be involved in something that may get her in some very serious trouble. She was conspiring with a troublesome boy here."

The priest stared, wide-eyed. "My lord, the things you're suggesting are…are…"

"Shocking. I agree. For her sake, you must get her to confess."

"I will certainly speak to her."

"Do it," Bridgewater said. "Now. Immediately."

The man took a step and stopped. "You do realize that if I get her to confess, I can hardly report the nature of her confession to you."

Bridgewater stared at the man, whose eyes had taken on an unpleasant adamantine hardness.

"*I* may be the only thing standing between her and prison," Bridgewater said hotly. "It's imperative I know *exactly* what's she's done. You may redeem her heavenly soul, but only I can redeem her here on earth. Do you understand me?"

The man's jaw flexed. "I understand you perfectly."

"And you'll tell me what she says?"

"I'll tell you exactly what you wish to hear."

He'd had gotten the man's agreement, but it seemed to Bridgewater that he hadn't gotten what he'd hoped for.

Forty-six

FOLLOWING BRIDGEWATER, MICHAEL ASCENDED THE stairs, vibrating with a mixture of eagerness to see Undine and anxiety over his earlier behavior toward her. Then he saw the footmen standing guard on either side of the door and stopped. He wanted to grab Bridgewater by the neck and shake him, but he wanted to get Undine out of this house even more. He swallowed his fury, but if he opened that door and found Undine had been harmed in any way, Bridgewater would regret it.

Michael said, "The footmen must leave."

Bridgewater, who was unused to rural clerics issuing commands, stiffened. But Michael had faced the wrath of noble personages before. After Lady Velopar, he felt like he could stand in the fire of a dragon and remain unscathed.

Bridgewater waved the men away. "Remember," he said to Michael, "I can only help her if I know exactly what she's done."

"I understand your requirements. Please open the door."

Bridgewater produced a key from his pocket, and Michael realized she'd been locked in as well.

Bridgewater turned the key and grabbed the knob. Michael caught the door before it opened.

"Go," he said. "I'll find you when we finish."

Bridgewater stalked away.

Michael slipped inside.

Undine had been at the window. She turned when the door opened, and the look on her face when she saw him reminded Michael that he'd rather jump from the top of Westminster Abbey than ever hurt her again.

She made a small noise, not quite the noise that would have sent him running to her arms, but it gave him hope, and with hope, he could speak.

"I thought I'd never see you again," she said.

"I wonder if you might have preferred that. I didn't do much to make you hope for my return."

Without the glow of candles, her features were lit only by the night sky, bathing her in ethereal light. But even without candles Michael could see the room was Bridgewater's bedchamber. His boots stood beside the wardrobe; his hat sat on a high chest of drawers.

Nothing matters but her.

"What can I do to help you?" he said.

Before she could answer, a tiny spot of light appeared on the wall to Michael's left and disappeared. He wasn't even entirely certain he'd seen it. Then all at once he knew what it was, and he was furious.

"Your husband says you are in need of advice," he said, strolling casually between Undine and the vanished dot of light.

Keeping his back facing the wall, he held a finger to his lips and met Undine's eyes. "Bridgewater is watching," he mouthed. Then he poked his thumb slowly against the center of his chest to indicate the hole in the wall behind him.

"I am," she said, nodding. "I am very glad you're here."

He wished he could see her eyes. He wished he could see if the words she spoke were aligned with her emotion.

"You disappeared, Father," she said, and he felt the shame of his betrayal.

"I was a fool. I ran because I was afraid. I'm quite ashamed of it. I didn't tell your husband that. I told him I had to respond to the bishop's note from Coldstream—and he did send a note, but I had already left you by the time I received it."

"You were afraid?"

"Of being hurt," he said.

"I see." Her fingers fluttered at her sides. She hadn't made up her mind about his return. "I can imagine the news was unsettling."

"It was," he said sadly, "but that's no excuse."

She let out a long exhale. "One doesn't often hear of bishops being attacked, does one?"

"No, but I should have had more courage."

"Perhaps you should've. Perhaps I should've made it clearer how much Bridgewater and I were depending on you."

"I came back to apologize and to help you in any way I can. I apologized to your husband, and now I must apologize to you."

"What did my husband say?"

Michael winced. It was one thing for him to refer to Bridgewater as her husband. It was like being strung out on a rack to hear her say it, though.

"Your h–husband said—" His voice cracked and he felt his cheeks warm. "How ill bred of me. I've completely forgotten to give you joy of your marriage. I wish you great happiness." He made a low, courtly bow.

"You are kind, Father." She didn't wish to receive good wishes on the occasion of her marriage any more than Michael wished to give them.

"Your husband said you're involved in some questionable activities."

"Did he?" she said tartly.

"I do not judge, your ladyship. But I know he wishes to help you. And I know he'll want to *hear* that you've confessed everything."

"Do you intend to tell him what I say?"

"That's a hard question, your ladyship. Both he and I wish to help you any way we can. He is well placed to do so. I wish you would give me leave to do what I think is best."

She made no response. He directed her to one of the room's chairs, where she took a seat. As his eyes adjusted to the dark, he could see the fire in hers. Poor Bridgewater. He was not going to like what he heard.

"What concerns have you?" he asked. "Only in unburdening yourself will you find peace."

Michael could see the look of amusement in her eyes as she considered the form her confession would take.

"The act of fornication is one to which I am fundamentally drawn."

Michael nearly choked. "We are grateful, then, you have taken a husband."

"I'm afraid there were many men before Bridgewater," she said with a rueful smile.

"Your ladyship, perhaps we should turn our minds to matters of—"

"Is fornication still a sin if I like it when I do it?"

He dabbed at his forehead, which had begun to grow moist. "I'm afraid so, aye."

"'Tis worse, I suppose, if one has committed the sin with two men at once?"

"I do not believe the sin doubles. A sin retains its essential nature no matter the, er, size of the cast of players."

"Then three is no worse than two?"

"No." He mouthed, "Stop it."

Her brows waggled minutely.

"But none of those men meant anything to you," he said, attempting to rescue the confession. "There was nothing of the deep and abiding love between a husband and wife in it."

"No. Not at all."

"So his lordship—"

"Well, except one."

Michael hesitated. "Oh?"

"One man made me feel a way I've never felt before—I beg your pardon, Father. Are you married or otherwise familiar with the joys of fornication?"

"Er, yes," he said, choosing not to clarify the question he answered.

"Then you know that many men can bring a woman pleasure. I don't mean at once, of course, though that *is* possible as well. I mean in the general course of things. But very few can marry the pleasure to a sense that one is safe, that one's thoughts and dreams can be spoken aloud without embarrassment or misunderstanding, that one will not be tossed aside at dawn's light for the next challenge, that one is simply...treasured."

Michael's chest filled with something both ancient and familiar. "You felt that?"

"Aye," she said softly. "Have you ever felt such a thing?"

"Yes. Once. And again, I think."

"With your wife?"

Undine smiled at him, her features lit with emotion, and he had the distinct impression he had just been proposed to.

"Aye," he said when he could find his voice.

"How wonderful."

Michael was having trouble remembering which character he was in or what he was supposed to be accomplishing.

"Were there other sins we should talk about?" she said helpfully, amused at his bafflement. "I should think my political work might provide fertile ground."

"Right. Yes. Let us concentrate on that for a bit." If he had any hope of satisfying Bridgewater's prying inquisitiveness, he needed to get her to confess to everything Bridgewater knew she'd done and plausibly deny the rest. Now if he could just keep her steered clear of fornication. Well, at least until they were alone...

"I have worked tirelessly for peace in the borderlands."

"I do believe your husband knows that. It was certainly well-known in the circles I traveled. Did you ever work against the interests of England?"

"I believe England is as interested in peace as I am."

Well done!

"Have you ever worked against the interests of your husband?"

"Aye," she said. "But not since he became my fiancé."

"Not now?"

"No, of course not."

A knock sounded at the door. Undine lifted her finger a fraction of an inch—a signal to wait.

"Father Kent?" Bridgewater called, impatient.

Undine accompanied Michael to the door.

"I stole papers," she said under her breath. "Nab has them."

"Not anymore—" Michael began but stopped when the door opened.

Bridgewater looked at them, eyes narrowed. "I just wanted to let you know," he said, "Morebright has searched everywhere, from the laundry to the great hall, including the reception room."

Michael could feel Undine stiffen, as if she were preparing for a blow.

"And?" she said.

"Nothing was found."

"Nothing was found?" Michael said. "Or nothing was found missing?"

"Both, I suppose," Bridgewater said. "The keys weren't found, and nothing is missing."

"*Nothing?*" Undine said.

"Did you expect something to be missing?"

"No. I'm just relieved for Simon."

"Aye, I can see that." He turned to Michael. "May I see you outside, Father?"

Michael bowed to Undine and stepped into the hall. "How is the confession?"

You know very well how it is, you prick. "Fine, fine. We're crossing some challenging ground."

Bridgewater raised a brow. "What?"

Michael could hardly lie since the man had been listening almost since the start. "Past fornications."

"How many?"

Did this man have a shred of chivalry in him? "She didn't say."

"Ask. I want names. Some may be spies."

Mud-wallowing pig. I wonder how you'd feel if I kneed your balls into your stomach?

"Has she said anything about treasonous activities?"

"Aye," Michael said. "She believes England to be as eager for peace in the borderlands as she."

Bridgewater snorted.

If this was a test, Michael had passed. He'd reported exactly what Undine had said, and he could see the growing confidence in the nobleman's eyes. Bridgewater would be quite surprised when his new wife disappeared with her lowly curate. Michael needed to figure out how to extract the confession well enough for Bridgewater to abandon his Peeping Tomism so that he and Undine could make their escape.

"Make sure you ask her about the boy," Bridgewater said. "I want to know what's going on there. I don't like it."

"I'll ask her about everything. Where can I find you when we finish?"

Bridgewater straightened the line of his frock coat. "Don't worry. I'll find you." He dismissed Michael with a nod and turned to leave.

"Have you considered the impact of your distrust?"

Bridgewater paused, as if he couldn't quite believe the words that had been directed toward him. Michael cursed himself for saying anything.

"I beg your pardon?" Bridgewater said.

"The impact of your distrust. You may learn what you want to know, but her ladyship will never forget what you've put her through."

"I don't want her to forget. 'Tis part of her rehabilitation."

"Remember that when—" Michael stopped himself before he said *she's gone.*

Bridgewater frowned. "Remember that when what?"

"When you're called upon to justify your actions."

"Before *God*?" Bridgewater said, as if he expected the Almighty to fall far below him in the order of precedence in heaven.

"Who else?"

"Aye," Bridgewater said, "who else?"

Bridgewater left with a snort, and Michael returned to Undine. The instant the door was closed, she said, "I took the papers."

"I know," he said quickly, knowing they had only a second or two. "I saw Nab. Before I came into the house. He had them, but he returned them—after he took them from you."

"What about the keys?" she said, desperate.

Michael put a finger to his lips, tilted his head to the hole in the wall, and said in a clear voice, "I'd like to talk to you about what's happened here."

"What's happened?"

"This business about a theft."

She crossed her arms. "The theft that didn't occur?"

"Lord Morebright's keys are missing, which, of course, means a theft may happen at some point in the future."

She laughed. "Are we investigating potential crimes now?"

"Surely you can understand Lord Morebright's concern."

"He's a doddering fool."

"He's not fool enough to endure the loss of keys without worry."

"And you think I may have something to do with their disappearance?" she said.

"Your husband rightly worries. And you owe him, and God, the truth. What's your relationship with the boy?"

Her eyes flashed. "What boy?"

Michael didn't get a chance to answer. A howl arose in the courtyard. Undine ran to the window with Michael behind her.

"Let go of me, you stupid arse!"

Nab.

A footman had him by the ear.

"Leave him alone," Undine said loudly.

If Bridgewater had any doubt about Undine's relationship to Nab, he wouldn't anymore.

"This is Lady Bridgewater," she called hotly. "I demand to know what you're doing to that boy."

"He's a thief, ma'am," the footman said.

Undine gasped. "The keys," she said under her breath. Michael put a hand on her back to steady her.

The footman dragged the boy roughly toward the stables. Nab was losing the battle to maintain his bravery. His cries had turned to those of a terrified child.

"We have to stop this," she whispered, then called to the footman, "What are you going to do to him?"

Morebright stepped from the shadows of the courtyard, holding a crop. "Lady Bridgewater," he said, "I beg you to make yourself easy. My men found the keys hidden on his person."

"Nothing was taken," she said, furious.

"*My keys* were taken. I shall teach him to regret the wickedness of his ways."

She caught hold of Michael's habit. "What are they going to do to him?"

"They're going to whip him."

"What if they kill him?" She was quaking now, and he put his hand on her arm.

"They're not going to kill him. They're not." As if to underline his certainty, the first crack of the crop echoed in the night, followed instantly by Nab's wail.

"They wouldn't beat him if they were going to kill him." He prayed what he'd told her was true.

"Oh *God*."

A movement in the courtyard caught his eye, and he turned her to see. Bridgewater strode toward the stables as the footmen and other servants, curious, began to populate the edges of the open space.

"Listen to me," Michael said, as the second and third crack sounded and Nab's cries increased. "We have to make his sacrifice count. He tried to help you. Make it count for something."

Her quivering stopped, and she looked at him clear-eyed. "You search the room here. I'm getting those papers again. We'll take them to Caddonfoot, where General Silverbridge is. He's Bridgewater's commanding officer. I trust him."

"Caddonfoot?"

"It's the second town to the south—along the river. I'll meet you there at dawn."

"No," he said. "We'll meet at the river." He swept her into his arms. "I left you once, fool that I was. I'll never let anything part us again."

Nab's tortured cry cut through the night like a chain saw.

"Go," he said.

Forty-seven

MICHAEL DIDN'T GIVE TWO SHAKES FOR WHAT Bridgewater had hidden in his room. He knew what the papers in the reception room contained, as Nab had shared a summary with him after taking them from Undine. He also knew Nab had snuck them back into their rightful place according to Michael's instructions so that Morebright would find them safe and sound when his search reached the reception room. If Undine could get her hands on them again, she'd have everything she needed to put an end to Bridgewater's career and possibly the hopes of England for the union. As such, Michael hoped she'd forgive him for setting somewhat different priorities in the few moments he had.

The number of maids, nightshirt-clad laborers, and footmen buzzing at the edges of the courtyard had grown by the minute, corporal punishment having apparently taken the place of feeding Christians to lions in the area of spectator sports in the eighteenth century, but the group fell silent and parted like the Red Sea to make way for the unhappy cleric striding toward the open doors of the stables.

The *thwacks* of the crop and the high-pitched screams that followed were like scourges on Michael's conscience. The boy's safety should have been just as important as Undine's to him—more, as Nab was a child.

A footman held Nab's wrists while Morebright, in his billowy, white nightshirt, swung the crop. Bridgewater glowered at the boy from the sidelines. Nab was curled into a ball, and his face was covered with blood. For only the second time in his life, Michael wanted to kill someone.

"Lady Bridgewater has confessed," he said loudly.

Morebright stopped midswing. "Who are you?"

"Father Kent of the bishopric of Newcastle. In the last quarter hour, her ladyship has made me privy to several pieces of very sensitive information."

Nab, gasping for breath, opened his eyes.

Morebright looked at Bridgewater, who stiffened.

"Does she know you're here?" Bridgewater asked.

"I believe at this point everyone in a two-mile radius is aware we're here."

The two men looked at Michael expectantly. Michael gave Nab a regretful look.

"For heaven's sake," Morebright said, "do you intend to tell us?"

"I do not. It's critical I confess one of her key conspirators—right now, alone. The fate of England may rest in the balance." He pointed to Nab.

"What sort of a woman did you marry, John?" Morebright said, and Bridgewater, the scoundrel, stood silent.

"I have every reason to believe the things she did

and planned were to help England." If her husband wouldn't defend her, then Michael would.

"What were the plans?" Bridgewater said.

"As I said, I need to speak to the boy alone. 'Tis a matter between him and God. I am but the go-between." If, after twenty-eight years of churchgoing, two full years of cursing his maker's name, and another dozen or more learning to forgive him, not to mention half a scene portraying Friar Laurence, Michael couldn't borrow the gravitas of the Almighty to save a young boy, then the world was a place in which he no longer wished to live.

"As you wish," Morebright said at last and gestured to the footman to release Nab.

Nab, grateful for the reprieve and likely sensing it might not last, ran to Michael, who put a proud hand on his shoulder.

The men began to disperse, to leave Michael and Nab to their makeshift confessional.

"No," Michael said, and the noblemen stopped. "You stay here—all of you," he added to the gathered servants. "The boy and I will go someplace private."

He took Nab's elbow and led him into the courtyard.

"Where's my wife?" Bridgewater asked ruefully.

Oh, now that I've assured you she's not a traitor, you'll deign to see her?

"She's performing her acts of contrition," Michael said. "Alone. She'll see you in the morning when she makes her confessions to you."

"Indeed?" he said, voice filled with tenderness.

"She has much she wishes to say."

Bridgewater's chest puffed, and Michael almost felt

bad. With any luck on Undine's part, Bridgewater would never see her again.

As the onlookers watched, he led Nab, limping, around the side of the house.

"Bunch of bloody arseholes," the boy said.

"They are that. How badly are you hurt?"

"Not at all."

The statement was visibly false, but it probably at least meant he could keep walking on his own. Michael looked him over briefly for broken bones.

"Bloody hell," Nab said, hurt but in awe, "you have a supply of lies that never ends."

"Well, I'm going to tell you the truth now." Michael stooped to face him. "You were as brave as any man I've ever seen. And I'm dreadfully sorry you had to go through that." He caught the boy in a gentle hug and was delighted to feel him hug back.

"All right, then," Michael said, straightening. "Based on my experience with audiences, we have about sixty seconds before the glow of the magic wears off. Get your arse as far away from here as fast as you can. Undine will meet me at the river as soon as she gets those papers again. Join us there. We're heading to Caddonfoot, the second town to the south along the river. We're going to meet with General Silverbridge there."

Nab shook his head. "The papers aren't there," he said, grinning. "I stole them again. You told me to put them back. I did. And when Lord Morebright finished his check of the reception room, I ran back in and took 'em again!"

"Well done," Michael said, though he wondered

how long Undine would look for the papers before joining him. "Where are they?"

"I slipped them through a slit in the stables window when I heard the footman coming. I can get them in the morning, when they unlock the door."

Michael groaned. "That's not going to work. This is all going to fall apart very soon, and when it does, it's going to be ugly. Undine will be gone. Bridgewater will figure out I'm no priest. He'll convince Morebright to send his men out looking for us. We don't need the papers. We can fight this another way."

"*Och*, they'll never find me—not again. I know where I can hide until morning."

Michael shook his head. "I can't leave you. And Undine and I can't wait till morning. We have to do our traveling by night. This isn't a game, Nab. I can't leave a child behind."

For the first time ever, he saw Nab's eyes start to glisten. The boy was brave, but no one goes through a vicious beating without having their defenses shaken, especially not a child.

"I know what to do," the boy said angrily.

"I'm not questioning your competence."

"Aye, you are. I've been doing this for a long time. Since before you arrived. Don't I deserve a say in the matter?"

Michael couldn't argue with that. The boy had earned his right to decide.

"Promise me you'll meet us at Caddonfoot? I have no desire to avail myself of Lord Morebright's particular brand of hospitality again."

Nab nodded. "I promise."

"Wherever your hiding place is, can you sleep in it?"

"Aye."

"Then do that, please." Michael longed for sleep himself. He knew the adrenaline propelling him through the last hour would evaporate soon.

The time had come. Nab stuck out his hand.

"Be safe, aye?"

The boy smiled. "You too."

Michael watched him jog off into the darkness. Unless Morebright used hunting dogs, he very much doubted Nab would be found again.

He dug his pack out of the hedges where he'd moved it and walked the path around the house until he could look into the reception room window. The front door to the house was closed, and no footmen were in sight. The room looked empty, but even if she was in it right now, it would have looked empty without a candle lit.

Had she already gone to the river?

He peered down the gentle slope into the darkness but saw only the flicker of starlight on the rushing ribbon of black. The people they'd left in that courtyard were growing restless. He could hear the increase in their murmuring.

He had to have faith Undine and Nab would make it to the river, but the ability to easily summon faith had been stolen from him a long time ago. With a heavy heart, he tucked the strap of his bag over his shoulder and began down the hill.

Forty-eight

BRIDGEWATER OPENED THE DOOR TO HIS BEDCHAMBER and his heart skipped a beat. She wasn't performing penance—unless leaving without telling him was the penance she'd been assigned. He ran to her room and didn't find her there either. He lit a candle and looked at the rows of bottles and boxes on her vanity, trying to assure himself that she'd never leave without the bits of herbs and paper she carried with her everywhere. But there was something that prickled at his brain about the way the wardrobe stood with one door open and the bed lay unmade. She might have gone to the river to swim, but in the middle of the night?

He decided he'd walk the banks. Tom the servant was supposed to be gathering the priest and boy, and they met in the middle of the stairs.

Tom shook his head. "Neither of them can be found."

Bridgewater went up a step, thought better of it, and then continued his descent.

"His lordship would like to see you," Tom said.

"His lordship can wait. I'm taking a walk."

"He's waiting in the reception room. Shall I tell him you'll see him on your return?"

Bridgewater didn't answer. He just waited by the front door until Tom unlocked it and slipped into the warm night. As he walked past the topiary and down the garden path, he wrestled with the problems before him. If Undine was gone, her absence would be publicly embarrassing as well as privately distressing. Simon would ask questions Bridgewater didn't want to answer. A search party would have to be formed.

All of this in the midst of a secret maneuver to help the treaty negotiations along.

Damn you, Undine.

He reached the river and looked upriver and downriver. The murky black rushed over the bank. The notes of primrose and heather mixed with the stench of rotting fish. He decided to walk downriver first. Even a naiad must prefer to follow the current.

Half a dozen steps later, he nearly tripped on something. He stooped to pick it up. It was the brown burlap of Father Kent's habit.

Had he vanished too? Would every religious man disappear in a puff of smoke until there wasn't a single goddamned one of them between Newcastle and Inverness? *The world would be a damned sight better off for it*, he thought.

That's what he told his heart, but his mind told him that no curate just disappears, and that it was far too coincidental for this curate to disappear at the exact same moment Undine did. Undine had been talking to the boy. He was in on it too. The three of them—

Bridgewater put a hand on his heart. His heart

raced, his cheeks flushed, and he started to feel nauseated. *You've been betrayed.*

Then, a worse thought occurred—far worse. What
if they'd fallen in love? Was it possible the intimacy of
the confessional had transformed into passion? Were
they even now fornicating somewhere in the woods
or garden? He listened for their animal sounds but
heard nothing. He could barely breathe.

He heard a noise and turned. Simon stood at the
top of the rise, his wispy hair blowing in the breeze
like pennant flags on a naval ship. Bridgewater trudged
up to meet him.

"Where's your wife?" Simon said.

"Walking."

"With the priest?"

"Aye."

Simon made a skeptical noise. "We leave in the
morning?"

"Aye. I'm to meet with Silverbridge in Caddonfoot
after breakfast. Then I'll be back to accompany you
to York."

"Bloody goddamned wrist. I feel like taking a knife
and cutting the thing off myself. What about our plan?"

"Everything is in place."

"Everything except your wife."

Bridgewater ignored the comment. "The servants
will take their carriage back to Coldstream. They're
leaving before dawn."

"Do they know?"

"Aye. I've just given the instruction. Now, the men
I've hired—"

"Clansmen?" Simon asked.

"It doesn't matter if they're clansmen or not so long as they *look* like clansmen."

"And who will report it?"

"The driver—Tom. He knows what will happen, and he'll be the only one to survive, so he can tell the story."

"You told the clansmen to do it as close to Edinburgh as possible? We want the news to travel quickly."

"Aye." Bridgewater felt as if he were being catechized by his old history tutor, the man who made him miserable for four long years.

"Well done. This will turn the tide on the vote. I promise you."

Four servants dead. A waste. But he reminded himself many more people would die if the treaty wasn't signed. With a treaty in hand, England could suppress the clans quietly and efficiently. "Remember," Bridgewater said, "nothing is to be said to anyone—certainly not anyone in the army. This is *not* an army matter."

"If you weren't so bloody concerned with a promotion, you might have proposed the idea to the army yourself. They'd have probably made you a general on the spot."

Bridgewater gritted his teeth.

"What do you intend to do if your wife doesn't return?" Simon asked.

"I'll decide that when it happens."

"Are you not concerned?" said Simon, who appeared to be taking some pleasure in Bridgewater's discomfort. "I could send my men out to look for her." He waited expectantly for an answer.

The thought of having one of Simon's men finding Undine in the arms of that man and then reporting it to his master… Bridgewater shifted uncomfortably, weighing the unholy mortification against the chance to have Undine back under his control.

Simon lifted a lecherous brow. "Perhaps you're afraid of what you'll find?"

"Watch your tongue, man."

"You fool! Why are you so blind? The woman has no affection for you. She can barely look at you. I thought to myself, the man must want to plow her fields more than life itself—'tis the only reason I can imagine for putting up with her serpent's tongue and sideways glares. But my servant says you didn't even take her to your bed after you married her. Are you incapable of the act? Is she a blind to make you appear a functioning man? Or do you prefer the company of men?"

Bridgewater's head began to hum—so loud he had to put his hands over his ears. He felt dizzy, thought he might retch. The world seemed to be spinning, only the ground before him hadn't moved.

"Christ Almighty, John, conduct yourself like a *man*."

The spinning grew worse. The sky turned red. Simon's face looked like a gargoyle, and then he was as big as an oak. Bridgewater fell to his knees and began to howl.

Thwack.

He flew over backward, head ringing from the blow.

"Get up," Simon growled.

Bridgewater sucked in the clean, cool air. The night resolved itself into crisp shades of black and gray. He could feel his anger rise—anger at Simon, aye, but more at that witch. The white witch. He closed his eyes. Had he actually taken her for his wife? Had she tricked him? Had she seduced him into marrying her with her powders and poisons?

He sat up. The ceremony—swift and unfeeling—came back to him with pointed clarity. He could feel her chilly hand as he slipped on the ring. Oh God, what had he told her? What had she seen? He'd be ruined.

He climbed to his feet and let out a breath filled with cold fury. "Find her."

Forty-nine

"HERE," UNDINE SAID, TIRED TO THE BONE AND shivering in the night air. "Now."

Michael slowed his walking long enough to give her a sidelong smile. "I've heard of forward women before, but that pretty much tops it."

"*Ha.*" Her feet ached, her shoulders hurt, and she was nearly asleep on her feet. But the patch of red clover they were walking through would make a fine pillow for her head. "If I could move a muscle," she said, kicking a few stones aside, "it wouldn't be to, well…"

"Do this?" He took her in his arms and gave her a thorough kiss. At once, her shoulders relaxed.

"You tempt me, sir."

"What if I told you that you wouldn't have to move a muscle?"

"Could you tell me I wouldn't have to remain awake?"

He laughed and dropped his bag on the ground. "Unfortunately, there's a rule about that in the gentlemen's code. But if you insist…" He lifted her into his arms, laid her on the mound of clover, and then settled beside her with his back against a tree.

She sighed and closed her eyes. "This is more comfortable than the bed of the Prince of Anhalt-Bernburg."

Michael made a noise that, if she'd forgotten, would have instantly reminded her he was Scottish.

"I'm going to assume that's a saying of some sort," he said.

"Oh, aye." She smiled and stretched her legs in the coolness of the stems and leaves. "It's a saying."

He took her foot, and she stiffened. "What are you doing?"

Michael slipped off her mule. She cursed herself for changing for Morebright's dinner. Her boots would have been far more comfortable. "Did the prince not perform his duty as a masseur?" he said.

"Masseur—? Oh *my*. What are you doing?" He was rubbing the ball of her foot between his palms. She arched her back and closed her eyes. "That's...that's... soul splitting."

"Naiads have souls?"

"Of course they do. What sort of a being do you think I am?" She sniffed.

"Slippery."

"Pardon?"

"Slippery. Like the silk on corn or the mists on water. Hard to pin down. Hard to know. Yet as immovable as Ben Nevis."

"That's not overly flattering."

"It's not? I rather like it. It's like reaching out and never knowing if you're going to touch velvet or the fur of a tiger."

With one hand on the ball and another on the heel, he twisted and turned her foot, releasing more of the soreness.

"You have a taste for danger, Michael Kent." She groaned with pleasure.

"I have a taste for something else as well."

Despite the hour and her feet, the hollow space in her belly began to fill. "Do you?"

He removed the other mule and squeezed her tender instep. She pressed her other foot against his thigh and could feel his long muscles move under her toes. His presence was an elixir like none she'd known.

"I gave you the most powerful travel herbs I know," she said. "Why did you not use them?"

"You sound disappointed." There was a smile in his voice.

"It used every bit of twinflower I owned—and that's not easy to come by."

"It sounds like you wanted to send me as far away as you could."

"I did."

It was the truth, or had been then, and she couldn't disavow it. Any man who wished to stand beside her needed to speak the truth and be able to hear it as well.

He made a small *hmm* and tightened the circle in which he rubbed.

"Seducing my feet will not force me to retract my statement, you know," she said, though, in fact, she would have promised nearly anything if he promised to continue this unorthodox rubbing.

"I am aiming somewhat higher."

She snorted. "'Twas a home-finder spell with marigold *and* naiad tears, and I wouldn't have been the least surprised to find you took half the residents of Peeblesshire with you when spread the herbs."

He held her foot between his palms in a long, apologetic embrace. "Well, that would have been a bit hard to explain. I wonder, is it even safe to have the herbs in my trouser pocket?"

"I can't say what might happen," she said. "I can only imagine you'll end up being led into the performance of some very salacious penance."

"Like rubbing your feet?"

"For a start. When I consider the power of your magic, I am half-inclined—"

"Undine, please tell me you know I hold no magical power over you. I should be very sad to have my acting overshadow the feelings—the true and unalterable feelings—you might have for me."

He spoke soft and low, and the plea in his words unnerved her.

"The way you've made me feel…" She shook her head, afraid to believe. "I've never felt anything that so radiated magic."

"But that doesn't make me a magician—just a man who fell in love with a woman who he hopes has fallen in love with him."

She looked at her hands and feet as if the answer lay in some external force. "'Tis a very powerful force."

"The most powerful of all."

She sat up and reached for him. This kiss was different from the others they'd shared. This kiss—as light and open as a ray of sun—sealed a promise.

"I misjudged you," he said, "and dishonored your work. I hope I'll earn your forgiveness."

She smiled. "Oh, I believe you might."

With a pleased sigh, she turned on her side and tried pushed her worries about Nab from her head. "You think he'll be there in the morning?"

"Aye," Michael said. "I do."

The Tweed gurgled a short distance from where they sat. For some reason, the sound made her think of her mother and all the things she'd lost.

"Tell me about your wife," she said.

His hands stopped, but only for an instant. "Young," he said wistfully, "beautiful, smart—*so* smart."

"Was she a director too?"

"No." He chuckled. "Nor an actor. She taught at the local school."

"In Bankside?"

"No, but not far. We lived in Lewisham. We had no money."

His rubbing had slowed. She'd opened a dam somewhere in time with her question, and he was making his way slowly upstream.

She turned around, laying the back of her head upon his thigh, and he began to comb his fingers absently through her hair.

"She died."

"I could see the pain," she said. "I'm sorry."

"In a car crash. 'Car.' It's sort of like a carriage without the—"

"I know what cars are." She patted his knee, hoping to help him through the current.

"Right. Of course. Well, we hadn't been married

very long. Four years. She was coming home from the chemist. She needed bandages. She'd burned herself cooking a stew the day before and wanted to cover the blister. She wasn't a very good cook, but she was determined to 'make her mark,' as she said. I wouldn't have cared if we ate biscuits and tea every night. Honestly. Anyhow, the bandages were on the floor of the car—after, I mean. I remember thinking how weird it was that the crash had killed her but the bandages were still there." He shook his head and sighed. "A lot of odd stuff goes through one's mind at a time like that."

She took his hand and laced her fingers in his.

"I can see her," Undine said. "Hair the color of warm coffee. Eyes like Grasmere lake. Ready smile."

"As I said, she was everything back then."

"I don't mean back then. I mean I can see her now."

His breath caught.

"She's quite content, Michael. They don't have the regrets we have, you see. She's around you at all times. She wants you to know she didn't feel or know anything when it happened. No fear. No pain."

Michael's hold on her hand grew tighter, and she knew he was crying. Undine didn't *know* everything she'd just said. That wasn't how the information came to her, in neat, readable summaries. But the colors of his young wife in her head were a mix of cool and settled violets, and one said what one needed to, to bring people peace.

Undine squeezed his hand. "She also says you're too good an actor to have given it up."

This happened to be Undine's own opinion, but

she had no doubt it was his wife's as well. The violets swirled and lit.

I shall care for him, she said. *You may rest now.*

For a long time Michael said nothing. And the next thing she knew, she was asleep. And the after that, he was asleep too, breathing steadily, arm wrapped tightly around her waist.

Fifty

NAB JERKED AWAKE TO THE SCREECH OF THE STABLE doors being opened. It was still black as pitch out, and he was so tired, but he knew he couldn't have slept more than a bit. This part of the stables' low-pitched roof was hidden by the trees. He could lie comfortably and still observe the entrance.

He sat up, waiting for his eyes to adjust to the dark.

"...why we have to leave in the middle of the night, I don't know."

"It's not for us to wonder. Just get the horses ready."

The second voice was Tom's. The first must be another servant.

"I hear old Morebright sent out a search party," the first said. "Do ye think Bridgewater's new lady threw him over? They were just married this evening! I don't think my wife threatened leaving until we were married at least a year."

"That has to be a record for men in your family."

"What's that supposed to mean?"

"Stop talking and get the horses, aye?"

Nab had slipped the papers through a narrow slit in

the wall closest to him. He hoped the papers hadn't ended up near where the tack for the horses was stored.

Silently, he climbed down the nearest tree, swallowing the groans his bruised ribs and legs were causing, and waited. The men worked near the far wall, and as his eyes got used to the dark, he could see part of a stall inside that would cover his movements if he was quiet.

The building was dark and smelled of hay and shit. The horses had begun to nicker and move in their stalls, surprised to be aroused at this hour, and with their noise, he ducked easily behind the stall wall. The floor at his feet was piled high with sodden straw, and in a pinch, he could dive into it, though he dearly hoped that wouldn't be necessary. He felt gently along the wall for the slit and found it at last over some brooms leaning against the wall. The men were consumed with their efforts to adjust an uncooperative buckle.

He ran his hands gingerly over the ground, trying to avoid the wettest sections. *Ugh.* He wasn't too particular, but even he was going to want to wash off in the river after this. He found the papers, which made a crackle. The men stopped talking. Nab held his breath.

"Do ye think that'll hold?" the first man said.

"It'll be good enough to get us to Coldstream."

Nab slipped out the door and edged quickly around the building until he was out of sight of the house and the men in the stables. Then, he folded the papers and stuffed them in his pocket. He was flushed with the success of his mission. The words on the paper would damn Lord Bridgewater to a fate worse than death—though death would be a pleasing proposition for a man planning to stage a clan attack on English soldiers. Kent assured him the uncovering of the plan would put a nut in England's plans for the treaty as well. But most of all, Nab was happy because he knew he'd have earned his place among the grown-ups in the secret group of rebels. He thought of his mother and how proud she'd be, and his heart ached a little. He wasn't a child anymore and didn't need to be taken care of, but he hadn't been to Langholm in a month at least, and he missed her and his baby sister.

He rubbed his hands on his breeks and jogged toward the river. A quick washup followed by a walk long enough to put him out of the reach of Morebright and Bridgewater, and then he could sleep for a bit and still meet Undine and Kent in the morning.

He shoved through a tangle of low branches and a metallic *click* made him stop.

"Good evening, lad," Bridgewater said and slapped a hand on his collar. "I think it's time for you and me to have a talk."

Fifty-one

GENERAL SILVERBRIDGE'S MAKESHIFT CAMP OUTSIDE Caddonfoot was appropriately busy for the morning, and a polite soldier directed them to the church in a town three miles away, where Silverbridge was holding office for the day. Michael hoped Nab would be given the same direction.

The morning was pleasant, and before another hour passed, he and Undine came to the town and made their way to the church. Michael felt his ire rise when he saw the poor clergyman standing outside, having, it seemed, been evicted from his home by a bunch of war-waging English soldiers.

"Good morning, Father," Michael said, bowing deeply. He'd decided to put on Duncan's plaid that morning, feeling very much a Scot when he woke, and the hem brushed his shoes.

"G'day to you, son," the man said, though he couldn't have been more than a few years older than Michael himself. He had jet-black hair mixed with gray, a friendly smile, and eyes as piercing as a hawk's. "Welcome to our town. Are ye and your wife traveling through?"

Michael realized the curate must know every face in the village and therefore knew them to be outsiders.

"We are, though she's not my wife," he added, finding himself unable to lie to a churchman.

"Not yet," Undine said with a smile and a curtsy.

Michael introduced them and explained they were looking for the general.

"*Och*, well, ye dinna have to look far," the clergyman said. "He and his officers have been camped out in the church since sunup."

Michael's eyes were drawn to the quaint, moss-covered roof, humble steeple, and ancient, arched side door.

"I apologize for my countrymen," Undine said. "They show their ill breeding and worse when they take what isn't theirs. And a church, no less." She clucked her tongue.

Michael started so hard his companions turned.

"That's Kirk of the Forest, isn't it?" he said, pointing to the church, shocked to the bone.

"Aye, it is," the clergyman said proudly.

"Th-that's where William Wallace was declared guardian of Scotland."

"Indeed, it is, sir."

Michael didn't know why he was so shocked. He'd spent his childhood half an hour away and had come many times to the place Scots held an almost religious fervor for. Then he realized why he was surprised. The kirk he'd visited as a child had been in ruins. The one before him now was fully functional—the kind of charming village church you'd find in the center of every Scottish town, from Gretna to John o' Groats. He spun around to look at the kirkyard and was instantly transported to shoving match between him and Rob MacBain that ended in an excruciating detention for both of them. It was a wonder he'd made it through school.

"Do ye want to go in?" Undine said.

"Oh, aye!" And there it was again, he thought, the accent of his childhood. If he stayed here much longer—

He stopped. Much to his surprise, he found he had no desire at all to return to London of the twenty-first century. Sure, it had theater and Indian food—any food at this point, really, as he hadn't eaten since the night before—and cars and full-bodied Tempranillos and clean, white sheets and the house he'd lived in with Deirdre—

Aye, even the house he'd lived in with Deirdre. He'd give that up to be here, with Undine, feeling useful again, feeling needed again, feeling alive again. And somehow, he knew Deirdre would approve.

Apparently, running for his life, going hungry, and sleeping rough was not too bad a hardship for him. He looked at the long, sensuous curve of Undine's neck and remembered how soft the skin he'd caressed there had been. If that was sleeping rough, he'd choose it over a real bed any day—even the bed of the Prince of Anhalt-Bernburg—the blackguard.

The clergyman, whose name was Mr. Fleming, led them to the door. "I willna venture in, but if you say the officer has an appointment with you…"

"I'm most aggrieved on your behalf, sir," Undine said. "And I will certainly say something to General Silverbridge about taking up residence in your church."

"Dinna fash yourself, lass. In truth, it probably does their souls good," he said, then added under his breath, "and I think they can use as much help as they can get."

Fifty-two

UNDINE KNEW SILVERBRIDGE'S REPUTATION FOR fairness—as fair as an officer waging war in the borderlands could reasonably be—but he turned out to be a man of even more thoughtful consideration than she would've believed possible. Perhaps it was the fact that he'd married the granddaughter of a clan chief, an act that had won him no joy from the queen. Of course, it's very hard to tell a nobleman whom he can and cannot marry, especially when he had as much money as General His Grace, the Duke of Silverbridge.

"What assertion are you making then?" the duke asked after he'd heard their story. He was young for a general but sharp-eyed and kept his hair short over the collar of his officer's coat. He sat at a makeshift table piled high with correspondence. A carved whale on the church's small lectern rose out of its fashioned sea behind him, as if it were one of the supporters on his coat of arms.

Undine knew to proceed with caution. "I've told you the general nature of the threat. One of your officers"—she had taken care not to name Bridgewater yet—"has conspired with a wealthy Englishman prone to meddle in crown business to create a diversion before the vote, a diversion we believe will involve impersonating Scots and attacking your men."

The duke rubbed his mouth with the back of his fist. He undoubtedly heard outlandish stories every day about the things the army did or that Scots were going to do—few of them invested with any truth.

"With no evidence?" he said.

"*We've* seen the evidence," Michael said. "A letter in the officer's possession told him he must create the diversion prior to Midsummer's Day."

"But you no longer have the letter?"

"No." Michael shifted uncomfortably. "It was taken from me by a clan chief."

"Whom you refuse to name."

Undine leaned forward on her stool. "General, we're taking a risk coming to you."

"Indeed you are. You're accusing one of my officers of treason."

"With respect," Undine said, "*you* could be the person with whom this man is conspiring. This could be an attempt organized by the army to put the Scots in an unfavorable light."

The duke leaned back in his chair. "The Scots seem to be able to do that quite well on their own."

Undine clasped her hands to keep from banging them on the table. "What I'm trying to say is we believe we can trust you. That's why we've come. We believe you wouldn't want an unfair attack on either side at this sensitive time."

"Or at any time."

"Or at any time," she said, agreeing even if she didn't quite believe it.

The duke's gaze went to the guard at the church's entrance, who was speaking quietly to Mr. Fleming. The door had been propped open to allow the breeze into the sticky interior, and the sun illuminated the clergyman from behind as if he were a saint.

"Hallum," the duke called.

The guard turned instantly. "Aye, sir."

"Get my guests something to eat, will you?"

The man was smart enough to understand the implicit meaning of the order and exited, closing the door carefully behind him.

"Speak clearly and openly," Silverbridge said. "No more obscure references. You have two minutes to convince me I should believe you."

"And if we can't?" she said.

"You're wasting your precious minutes."

She looked at Michael, who said, "It's your call."

What choice did they have if they wanted to stop an attack? But complete honesty meant she was putting herself, her colleagues, and Michael at great risk.

"I would like an assurance from you—"

"Undine—may I call you Undine? I know of no other name to use."

She nodded.

"Your work's well-known to the English army," he said, "and near universally despised. And yet many of my men go to you to have their fortunes read. Some think that foolish. I certainly do. Even if you *can* tell them what will happen, what secrets and plans do they unintentionally reveal to you in the questions they ask?

I'm not so foolish as to believe you can't cause even more problems for the army than you already have. And so I'm willing to listen to what appears to be your deeply held concern. I pray you can convince me, for I should not like what I shall have to do next if you don't. Who is the officer?"

She took a deep breath. "Colonel John Bridgewater."

The duke's face didn't change.

She licked her drying lips. "We believe he's conspiring with Simon Morebright to prepare a violent attack that can be blamed on the Scots. I stole the letter from Colonel Bridgewater's desk. It had no address and no signature except the letter *S* and, therefore, could be from or to anyone. As I was indisposed, Mr. Kent took the letter to a clan chief, whom I refuse to name, to see if the violence could be stopped and, I believe, because he was concerned for my safety."

Silverbridge's eyes cut to Michael, and the general seemed to reconsider whatever assumptions he'd made so far about him. *You're not alone in that, sir.*

"Lady Kerr," the duke said, filling in the unspoken name of the clan chief involved. "We're well aware of whom you count among your friends. But go on."

Undine refused to let this unsettle her. "I've also seen a letter in Colonel Bridgewater's own hand in which he acknowledges he has the power to 'do things' outside his immediate purview in the army but that they—he and the person to whom he has written this letter—must proceed cautiously. This letter was in Lord Morebright's possession and hidden."

The general must have been a damned fine card-player. His face did not betray his feelings.

"Can you show me *that* letter?" he said.

She made a private groan. "No. Not yet. 'Twas taken from me for safety's sake. We expect to meet the person who has it this morning."

Silverbridge gazed at her with curiosity. "It sounds as if you make yourself quite a nuisance as a house-guest. In this tale of yours, are Lord Morebright or Colonel Bridgewater aware that you're in possession of their stolen letters?"

She shook her head. "No."

"Yet now we can assume every clan chief between here and Inverness is aware both of the plan and your part in uncovering it?"

She hung her head. "I would have to assume that, aye. And there's more." She made a small prayer of forgiveness to Abby. "It's possible the clans are planning their own, real attack. The chiefs were very angry about the abuses—potential abuses—wrought by Colonel Bridgewater and his regiments."

The general tapped his thumb. "You've put me in a very awkward position," he said. "And I regret to inform you, you're now the temporary guests of the English army—at least until Midsummer's Day."

Her heart fell.

Michael said, "Why are you holding us? She told you everything."

"Let's say there are aspects of her story I should like to investigate further. Who's the man who's bringing the letter?"

Undine crossed her arms. "I've said enough."

The general chuckled. "Rather too late for cau-tion, wouldn't you say? As you wish. I'll put my men out on patrol. We'll find the man and deal with him."

A knock sounded at the door.

"Enter," Silverbridge called.

Hallum stepped in cautiously, holding a tray of food. The duke waved him over and stood. "Put them in the back room after they eat," he said to Hallum, "and post guards." Turning to her and Michael, the duke added, "I appreciate your honesty. 'Twas eye-opening indeed—though perhaps not for the reason you were wishing. We'll move you to the room I occupy for now. You'll understand, I hope, if I remove my papers before you enter." He gave her a wan smile.

"I've told you the truth," she said curtly.

"I hope so," he said. "'Twill be the only thing that saves you."

His bow was foreshortened by the appearance in the doorway of another officer, who looked as if he carried upsetting news.

The duke hurried to the man's side. The officer looked at Undine as he murmured into his general's ear. The duke gave a brief order under his breath, and the man disappeared. The duke returned to Undine and Michael with a new sharpness in his eye.

"Perhaps your stay with us will not be as long as you think," he said. "Or your stay as guests. It seems I have a visitor. 'Tis the man of the hour, Colonel Bridgewater."

Fifty-three

NAB STARED SULLENLY OUT THE WINDOW. GEORGE AND Harry, two of Bridgewater's oldest and nastiest servants, sat on either side of him, and the carriage bumped roughly across the uneven path.

"I'm hungry," Nab demanded.

"There's no food for thieving little shites," George said. "You'll be lucky if we don't eat *you*."

Eliza, the cook, an older woman with round, pink cheeks, gave Nab a regretful look. "Once the master doles out his punishment, we'll give you something to send you on your way."

Her daughter, Grace, a year or so older than he was and with dark ringlets, suppressed a smile.

The master—Colonel Bridgewater—had questioned Nab roughly about his friendship with Undine, and Nab had thrown every piece of information about her that everyone in the borderlands already knew the arsehole's way, adding tears for effect—Undine was a fortune-teller, Undine saw men alone in her home, Undine was friends with a goddamned Scottish clan chief named Abby Kerr. Bridgewater had been furious, but he'd finally given up, and Nab had thought he'd be free to go, but the man had grabbed him at the last minute and shoved him into the servants' carriage, which had been readied for the early return to Coldstream. Bridgewater had told George and Harry that Nab was not to leave the carriage until they'd reached Coldstream, and then he was to be locked up until Bridgewater returned later in the day and decided what to do with him.

"We ain't giving the lad a meal, Eliza," George said sharply.

"When you run the kitchen, George, you may set the rules. Until then…" She folded her chubby hands around her basket.

Grace met Nab's eyes, amused, and returned to the book she'd been reading.

There was something about the way she looked at him with that superior smirk on her face. He found it extremely annoying but also something else—something that made him want to take that book from her hands and toss it out the window. It also made him want to pull the letter out of his pocket—the one that would make him a hero—hold it in front of that upturned pink nose, and ask what she'd done to bring about peace in the borderlands. Bridgewater thought he was so high and mighty, but never once in his rant about Undine did he think to look in Nab's pockets.

"What's 'Nab' short for?" Grace asked suddenly.

Nab's face exploded in heat. How could she have known to ask the worst question in the world?

"Nab," Harry said. "It's what ye do with criminals, aye? Ye nab 'em!" He grinned like a fool, and Nab wished he could knock Harry's few remaining teeth from his head.

Grace gave the man the same look she'd given Nab and dug into the parcel beside her.

"The lady asked you a question," George said. "Answer her."

Lady? Ha! She was a servant. At least Nab had a proper job and no one to call boss except himself.

Grace closed her book, taking care to keep her finger on the page she was reading—Lord knew she wouldn't want to miss a word, Miss Snooty Nose—and regarded him with mild curiosity.

"'Tis short for Norbert," he said through gritted teeth, ears ringing with shame.

"Oh." She opened her book and went back to the story.

Bloody goddamned girl.

"I need to stop," Grace said after a moment.

Harry and George looked at each other and rolled their eyes. Girls and their pissing. Nab hoped there might be some stinging nettle in the woods to brush her when she—

A very strange feeling came over him at the notion, and he found himself fighting to keep his eyes fixed on the view beyond the window rather than on her face.

George banged on the ceiling. "Tom! Stop! One of the ladies needs to take a walk."

The carriage rattled to a stop, and Grace unfolded herself.

George jumped out to hold the door, and Grace bent to check the laces on her boots before stepping down. She unfolded herself in a swirl of fabric, and Nab felt something round being pushed into his hand.

She jumped onto the road, ignoring George's hand, and Nab shoved the plum into his pocket, flushing hard.

"I'll go with you," George said to Grace.

"The hell you will."

Grace flounced off, while Nab stared, speechless, at that shapely back.

"How far are we?" Harry said, exiting the carriage himself.

"Nearly to Edinburgh," George said.

The plum was cool and smooth, a bit like Grace's hand, and he began to plot a way to savor his gift.

Fifty-four

UNDINE SAT AT THE SMALL DESK OF THE CHURCH office, the room that the duke had been using as a makeshift bedchamber. She touched the desktop, wondering if the evident goodness of Mr. Fleming had imbued the wood with its warm glow. In any case, it was better than considering the fiery and charred colors she saw in her vision regarding what was coming next.

"Are we rubbing this for good luck?" Michael asked gently.

She gave him a weak smile. He made his way to her side and laid a hand on her shoulder. "You know you can share what you're seeing. I've been watching your face, after all."

Were her feelings so clear? Around him, she was losing the masking skills she'd worked so long to nurture. She squeezed his hand.

He said, "My gran always told me, 'Shared joy is doubled; shared sorrow is halved.' I can bear my half."

She shook her head. "I see unhappiness," she said, hurrying to add, "but my powers are far from perfect."

He laughed. "You hardly need to tell me that. I was the person who got yanked out of the twenty-first century, after all."

She couldn't help but smile.

"You've never asked me to tell you what I see," she said. "About *your* future, I mean."

He pulled up a stool and sat close enough to tuck her hand between the two of his. "I rather thought of it as the thing other men did, the ones who weren't trying to impress you."

"Impress me?" she said, lifting a brow. "Is that what you call that hellfire scolding you gave me when you arrived?"

He shrugged. "You haven't forgotten, have you?"

"No. Nor am I likely to." She brought his hand to her cheek. "You're very hard to read, and I wonder if it's your training or…"

"Or what?"

The dizzying effects of this lust-filled attraction, she thought. It was as if a cloud had settled over him when she brought her mind to him. Oh, she saw color—vibrant, jeweled hues that swirled seductively, filling her senses and blurring her sight. None of it made sense, and almost all of it made her want to crawl into his lap and beg him to bed her.

He looked into her eyes, seeing more than she wished.

"I see," he said, the corner of his mouth rising. He leaned forward, putting his mouth to her ear. "I should very much like to repeat what we did this morning," he whispered, drawing his thumb across her palm.

"In a locked room?" she said. "With guards who could open the door at any moment?"

"Oh, aye."

She caught her breath—barely—and found her hands grasping his knees through the soft wool of his kilt.

"*Mmm*," he said, irritatingly smug.

She found his cock and balls and cupped them, which instantly wiped the smugness from his face.

The flesh tightened into warm steel in her hand.

"*Mmm*," she said.

"Take care, lass. I have it in my head to take you up against that wall, and too much more of that will make it far more hurried than you'd like."

She leaned back and opened a knee—an invitation.

He tumbled her skirts into her lap and found her bud. She curled her fingers around the arms of the chair and closed her eyes.

"I should very much like to see the top of that gown loosened," he said matter-of-factly.

She did as he said, but only enough to allow a hint of the rose-colored circles to appear.

"You're a temptress," he said, his cheeks ruddy now.

Her breathing quickened. "I am just as interested in a show as you are."

With a flick of her hand, she brushed the flap of his plaid over his knee. His thick cock swayed in the light.

"This is getting a wee bit dangerous, don't you think?"

"Ye have no one to blame but yourself. Can ye finish me with that?"

"Is that a challenge?"

"Oh, I know you can finish to your own satisfaction—I've never met a man who couldn't. But can you finish me to mine?"

He stood and pulled her up with him. He gazed at her, lust and love in his eyes. His fingers brushed hers, and her heart thumped.

"I won't leave you," he said. "Not as long as ye'll have me. And I'll die to protect you."

"I know," she said, surprised at her certainty. "I can feel it."

"What do you see? For me? For us?"

His presence, so close and so intense, filled her head, clearing the clouds. The suffusion was so violent, she winced. And then she wished she hadn't seen what she saw.

"Undine."

"I–I—"

"Tell me."

She wanted to push it out of her head, this distant, dark emptiness she saw—gray and cold. Like a frozen sea in the dead of winter—

She opened her eyes, and he was back—warm, fleshed, alive. But he knew. He'd seen her face and he knew.

"I don't see what will happen," she said sadly. "Men think I do, but I don't. I see a feeling—a sense of the future. The rest is just magician's tricks."

"Tell me," he said.

"I went to your future," she said sadly. "Alone or… worse. There's nothing of joy there."

His arm fell, and he took in a long breath. "I've been alone all my life," he said. "Dead would be a blessing. But for now, here, with you, I'm alive."

He kissed her, and in it, she felt acceptance and hope. Her mouth searched for forever, but all the world would give her was now.

"I want you," she said.

"And I you."

He pressed her against the wall, and she tugged up her skirts. He entered her slowly, reverentially, his head bowed to touch hers. They moved together, trying to capture the connection and hold it in their hearts.

When the gasp came, Undine clasped his stubbled cheek. He held her there—in the place between love and loss—as long as he could and then found his own release.

She tucked herself into his arms, cold now despite the warmth of the day.

"Michael."

He touched her lips, silencing the hunger for something that couldn't be.

"Mr. Fleming will not thank us for this," she said, voice shaking.

Michael chuckled, still holding her tight. "Perhaps we can point the finger at the duke?"

She felt a tear well and wiped it away. "I've never had this…easy intercourse with another."

He squeezed her waist and she could feel his smile. "I'd hardly say it was easy."

She laughed. "I want you to know how much this has meant to me—knowing you."

He cupped her chin and lifted it. "I see nothing of my future. I have no special skills in that area. But nothing you've told me has convinced me that I won't be with you forever and—"

Voices rose beyond the door, and they broke apart.

The door banged open, and the general looked at them, cold fury in his eyes. He looked at the scene before him. It would be obvious to anyone whose experiences were broad enough what had just transpired, and he shook his head.

"You might have told me Bridgewater is your husband," he said to Undine, and added to Michael, "And you might have told me you two were on the run."

He slammed the door and paced to the window.

"We have a few moments, no more. Your husband has demanded to have you returned to him, Lady Bridgewater, and I have no recourse but to do what he asks."

Michael opened his mouth to protest, and the duke silenced him. "He's asked for you as well. I told him he could press charges if he wished, but he had no right to take you from here."

"He has no right to her either," Michael said. "Even if she loved him, which she doesn't, nor he her, she has the right to leave him if she wants."

Undine shook her head, fully aware of Bridgewater's rights in the eyes of the law.

"Naive fool," the duke said to Michael. "You're lucky I believe her story."

She straightened. "You *do*?"

"Aye. We've been watching Bridgewater for a while, but we weren't sure what he was planning and we certainly had no proof. I've had my own men following him, talking to the men he talks to, asking questions. We've had to tread carefully because he's an officer and a nobleman."

Michael snorted. "Must protect our own."

"We hold ourselves to a higher standard," the general said. "I regret if a man who has omitted inconvenient truths and formed a relationship with the married wife of another man finds that distasteful."

"Take care, Your Grace," Undine said testily. "I've read the souls of noblemen and simple men alike. I've never known a man more good than Michael Kent. If you'd like me to make a public proclamation of the stains of your fellow officers and noblemen, I can, and will, if you continue on in this vein."

The general sighed. "You are exactly as my intelligence officers have described."

"I take that as a compliment."

"I'll tell you what we know. It's the least I can do, and if your wish is to be free of Colonel Bridgewater, I believe it will be fulfilled soon. Morebright used to be in the queen's intelligence service. He fell out of favor and moved up here, but he's kept a circle of very unpleasant friends in Edinburgh and London— men who still work in service to the queen but who sell their country's secrets to each other and others. Morebright and his friends have profited on the unrest. He's gotten Bridgewater to hire a group of criminals to pose as clansmen and attack a carriage carrying some of Bridgewater's servants. We believe the carriage is heading from Lord Morebright's home to Coldstream this morning. The disguised men will murder the occupants, leaving one man to describe the horror of the clan attack. But you're wrong about the motive. They're not hoping to convince the Scottish noblemen to vote for the union. They want to provoke Scotland and England into a war that will never end."

Her head spun. Attacking the English army was horror enough, but attacking his own innocent servants?

"You have to stop the attack," she said.

The duke stuffed his hands into his pockets and hung his head. "I can't."

"Why the hell not?" Michael asked.

"Because many more people will die if we don't find out the names of Morebright's sources," the duke said hotly. "And if we stop this small attack, Morebright will know he's been compromised. Ask Undine or her rebel friends what they'd rather do—save the lives of a handful of people or finally remove the men who generate war for profit."

He was right. She knew he was right. This was war. They had the chance to really turn the tide. Even a union between England and Scotland would be tolerable if peace, that rare jewel, came along with it.

"He's right," she said to Michael with regret. The thought of that carriage...

"I wish it didn't have to be this way," the duke said. "'Tis the most awful sort of decision a man in my position has to make. Believe me, I have little desire to sacrifice lives—"

"Servants' lives, you mean," Michael said. "It's only a 'small' attack, as you said. You and your army would tear the borderlands to pieces if it meant saving the lives of noblemen."

"*Michael.*"

"I won't be saving any noblemen," the duke said, sighing. "Certainly not these two. I'll be damning them both to hell—and a few more besides for good measure. But any regret I might have in helping to destroy the trust our country has placed in men of wealth and position is nothing—*nothing*—compared to the loss of those servants. But it must be done. And that's the burden I have to bear."

"We all do," Undine said, nauseated.

"Can't you hold Bridgewater?" Michael said.

"For what? We have suspicion but no proof. Not unless your man shows up with the letter." The duke crossed to the window and scanned the hills. "Removing Bridgewater from his office, and Morebright and his colleagues from their profiteering, is the most important thing I can do to bring peace to the people who live here. My family seat is in the borderlands, you know. My people suffer too. I need those names. Once I have them, we'll have enough to arrest Bridgewater *and* the others."

A knock sounded at the door.

"That's your husband," the duke said. "I don't know exactly what you meant to achieve by marrying him, though I think I can safely guess. I'm sorry I can't help you any further, but I have every confidence you have the resources to keep the ruse going until we've done what needs to be done."

"You can't hand her over," Michael said. "The man's a *murderer*."

The general looked at Undine, and with a nod, she accepted her assignment and released him from any guilt he might have.

"*Undine*."

The door opened, and the hairs on Undine's arms immediately stood on end. Nothing in Bridgewater's appearance suggested anything beyond the faintly discommoded, but there was a dark energy in him, invisible to others, that had been lacking for the past few weeks. The man she could see was a barely concealed beast, ready to tear into anything that got in his way with razor-sharp teeth. She looked at Michael and the general. Did either of them see what she saw? Michael, of course, looked ready to kill him, which warmed her heart, but neither he nor the duke seemed to sense the danger.

"I think I should like to lie down for a bit before we go," Undine said, crossing her arms to hide the shaking.

"You may lie down in the carriage, my dear," Bridgewater said. "Our time here is over."

He took her hand to pull her out, and Michael lunged for him, but the duke stepped between them.

"Hold him," the duke said to his guards, who took Michael by the arms. It pained her to see his sorrow, but she also knew keeping him away from Bridgewater would save him. She was doomed.

"You watch yourself, you bloody blackguard," Bridgewater sneered. "I'll see to it you pay the price for your villainy. You won't be smiling when I meet you next."

"That's enough, Colonel," the duke said. "Keep a civil tongue in your head. Your wife is back in your possession. 'Twill be up to you to keep her there. If you wish to press charges against the man, press them. I want your wife to report to me here tomorrow."

"Why?" Bridgewater demanded.

"I'd like to ask her some more questions about her work with the rebels. 'Tis nothing to be concerned about. I know she'll be willing to help us given her new status as an English noblewoman and wife of an officer."

It was the general's attempt to ensure Bridgewater stopped short of wounding or killing her. She doubted Bridgewater feared any retribution at this point.

Bridgewater could hardly refuse his commanding officer, at least not to his face. When he had Undine to himself he could do what he wanted. "Aye. Of course."

"Good. Morning would be fine."

Bridgewater bit back whatever he was going to say, saluted the duke, and pulled her out the door.

Fifty-five

MICHAEL ACHED TO PUNCH SOMEONE, AND THE DUKE would do. He shook himself free of the guards.

"Don't be a fool," the duke said, but he held up a hand to still his men.

"Why not?"

"You're a free man now. That could change."

"I'm not exactly free," Michael said. "How long do you intend to hold me?"

"Until I hear their carriage go."

Not long at all. With effort, Michael relaxed his fists.

"She'll be back tomorrow," the duke said. "And if you're concerned for her safety, you don't know her as well as you might. She's disabled more men in my regiments than I'd care to admit. Not carrying a pistol doesn't make her innocuous."

Michael took this in with as much dispassion as he could muster.

The duke frowned. "Are you concerned for her safety?"

"No. You're right. She knows how to take care of herself quite well."

"Good. And do I have your word you'll leave them alone? As I said, she'll return tomorrow."

"Yes."

The duke returned to the window. "They're leaving." He inclined his head toward the door, as if a mere bend of his noble head was all Michael needed to leave. "I don't know what part you're playing in all this," he said, "but the best thing you can do for her is to find the man with the letter."

Michael nodded. "Until then?"

"Aye. Until then. You know where to find me."

Michael gave him the courtliest bow he possessed.

Fifty-six

MICHAEL WAS IN A DARK MOOD, AND HIS FISTS ITCHED for a way to lighten it. He'd had just about enough of people telling him what to do and far more than enough of men whose power was keeping him from Undine. He'd lost a wife, given up every dream of happiness, sacrificed a sizeable portion of his working life to give England the theater she deserved with barely a thank-you, and now to be told by Undine herself—though he absolutely refused to believe it—to be told that he wouldn't end up with her? *No.* He wouldn't have it. Someone was going to pay. The only question in his mind was who—but he had a very strong candidate for the role.

He jogged toward a soldier, who stood by horses hitched to a post.

"I beg your pardon," Michael said, "do you see that carriage there, the one just disappearing over the rise?"

"Colonel Bridgewater's?" the soldier said.

"Aye. I'm afraid he left his orders on the table. The general is hoping you can stop him."

"Are you sure?" The soldier looked uncertainly toward the church.

"You can check, but I know His Grace will be unhappy if that carriage gets away. Perhaps I should go…?"

"No, no, I can do it. I just—"

"Excellent! Let me just let the general know that— what is your name, Private?"

"Littleton, sir."

"Let me just let him know Private Littleton has agreed to save the day."

The soldier lifted himself onto the closest horse, gave the beast a bit of heel, and flew off.

Michael waited a few beats, lifted himself onto another horse, and geed him into a trot.

The soldier, too intent on his mission to notice the man behind him, made it to the front of the carriage in record time, and waved the driver to a halt just as Michael arrived in the man's blind spot on the other side of the carriage.

"What's going on?" Bridgewater said, opening the carriage door closest to the soldier.

Michael jumped off the horse and opened the door near him.

"Get on the horse," he said to Undine, who was pale as a rabbit.

"What the *fuck* are you doing?" said Bridgewater, who'd spotted Michael.

"Get on the horse," Michael repeated. "*Now*."

Undine did as he commanded.

Michael met Bridgewater as he rounded the back of the carriage and punched him in the nose, sending a spray of blood over both of them. Bridgewater howled and his hands flew to his face.

Michael grabbed the pistol from Bridgewater's belt and tossed it to Undine before Bridgewater had time react.

She aimed it at Littleton who was reaching for his own weapon. "Don't," she said. "Get off the horse and throw your pistol as far as you can into that field."

Littleton gave her a stubborn shake of his head. Bridgewater looked in shock at the blood on his hands.

"Would you prefer to be the reason I shoot your colonel?" she said. "'Twill not do much for your career." She cocked the pistol.

"For Chrissake," Bridgewater said with a hiss, "do as she says."

The soldier complied.

"Who *are* you?" Bridgewater said to Michael. "You're not a priest. You're not a Scot. You're not—" He stopped midsentence and his eyes widened. "You're Beaufort!"

"Nope. Wrong on that too. I'm Michael Kent, and I'm the man who's taking your wife from you."

Bridgewater swung and caught Michael's chin. Michael reeled backward, and Bridgewater reached for his knife.

"Put the goddamned knife down," Michael said, finding his balance. "If you want to fight me, fight me like a man."

The soldier stared openmouthed, waiting to see what his superior officer would do in the midst of this surprising domestic drama.

"If you have balls, use them," Michael said, "not

your knife or your position or privilege. Find out what a real fight's like."

Bridgewater's eyes bulged, and he reached for the hilt.

Michael flew shoulder first into Bridgewater's groin. Both men landed on the ground. Bridgewater rolled away and vomited, clutching his stomach.

"Just as I thought," Michael said, stumbling to his feet. "No balls. She doesn't love you. Never has. And you'll never see her again."

"Oh, I'll see her again," Bridgewater wheezed. "If she wants to see that thieving urchin of hers, she'll have to come to me."

Michael's stomach dropped. "What thieving urchin?"

"Nab."

"Where is he?"

"On his way to Coldstream," Bridgewater said, "which is where you'll bring her if you know what's good for you."

Michael wheeled to Undine. "Nab's in the *carriage*."

He turned back, but it was too late. Bridgewater had found his knife and, with a gleeful groan, jammed it all the way through Michael's foot.

Michael bellowed, the horses reared, and the one belonging to the soldier took off like a shot.

It felt like an acetylene torch burning his flesh. He tried to move his foot, but it was pinned to the ground. He could hear voices, but all he could think about was stopping the monstrous pain. He grabbed the blade, screamed an obscenity, and pulled it out. He thought he'd faint. The blood poured into his shoe. His foot was soaked. He could feel the sloshing.

Bridgewater was climbing to his feet. He eyed Michael with murder in his eyes and Michael lifted the blade in the air.

An explosion went off in his head.

Undine had shot the pistol.

The knife was still in Michael's hands. Bridgewater looked at his chest.

Undine brought the barrel of the pistol down from where she'd been pointing it in the air.

"Too many people have died," she said. "No more."

In an instant, she'd brought the horse to Michael's side and extended her arm. He put his good foot in the stirrup and got in the saddle behind her. Bridgewater tackled their legs and it took a furious round of kicking to free themselves from him.

Undine slapped the horse and it took off like a Derby winner.

"Are you all right?" she asked.

"We've got to get Nab."

Fifty-seven

UNDINE HEARD MICHAEL'S SWALLOWED GASPS EACH time the horses' hooves hit the ground. He wouldn't die from bleeding to death—though she'd seen it happen even with a wound in the extremities—but he might from the infection that would follow, and she'd have only herself to blame. She'd brought him here, to this world, and he'd come to Morebright's home to protect her. Thank the skies he had. And thank the skies he'd stopped the carriage. Bridgewater had been in the sort of fury she'd only seen once before, and that time it had taken almost a month before she'd been able to walk again.

Michael's arms were around her waist. She laid her hand on top of his to get a sense of him. She didn't possess healing powers. There were women who did—and men too—but the closest one was in Jedburgh, miles from here. There were things she could read from his touch, though, because she was a naiad—and because she was a woman.

He started when their hands met, and she wondered for an instant if he'd been passed out.

"What are you doing?" he said, his voice strained but amused. "I'm not yours for the taking."

"*Ha*," she said, adding, "What makes you think I'm taking something?"

"You're hardly the first woman who's wanted me for my aura."

"I have no idea what an aura is, but I can assure you, I don't want it."

"Oh, you'd want mine."

There was illness there, she thought, and the sharpness of pain as well as warm, glowing affection and—she flushed—ravenous lust. Sorrow and the soaring blue of joy lived there too. It was a beautiful narrative of his person, though she wished she could ease the jagged pain. When she wiped away the surface layer of what she sensed and reached deeper, she saw the gnawing emptiness and sorrow. The sadness was a shiny void, as tall as a cliff and as sleek and cold as black marble, and she could see herself in it as well.

She released his hand.

"We can change what you see," he said.

She wanted to believe him and that what he said was true, but what she'd sensed was an immovable as anything she'd ever seen or felt. "Aye," she said, "we can."

"We'll fight."

Did he mean the army, Bridgewater, or the vision? Of the three, only one truly terrified her. "We'll do what we can every moment that we are able. 'Tis all anyone can do."

They'd reached the road that ran between Morebright's home and Coldstream.

"North to Morebright's," Michael asked, "or south to Edinburgh and Coldstream?"

She felt danger in both directions, but one was worse.

"Right," she said with a sigh. "There's going to be trouble."

"Let us be the ones making it."

Fifty-eight

DOES SHE KNOW THE EFFECT SHE HAS ON PEOPLE? MICHAEL thought. *No wonder powerful men are in awe of her.*

His arm still buzzed with the aftereffects of her touch. He felt as if he'd been stripped to his essence—just the base desires and failures of a man who'd lived an unexemplary life except for having fallen in love with two exemplary women.

His foot throbbed. Every step the horse took was like the whack of a small hammer on it. More concerning, he was starting to feel warm. He needed to attend to it. But he needed to attend to Nab and the people in the carriage first. The risk of certain death before the risk of potential death. That's how they triaged it in war. And now he was in one.

"What do you think the duke will do when he finds out we disobeyed his orders?" he said.

"He'll issue a warrant for our arrest. I can hardly blame him."

"Nor can I. There'll be no evidence to arrest Bridgewater or stop Morebright. I don't suppose your rebels are going to be very happy either."

She shifted in the saddle. "I've failed them. But I can't sacrifice Nab or any of them. Not for a principle."

"Let's save them. We can worry about the rest when we finish." *If we finish.*

A short time later, Undine brought the horse to a stop, and Michael focused his attention on the road before them. They'd passed a number of wagons and people walking in the last few hours, but no carriages. The last mile or so had been through a high, thistle-filled pass between two mountain ridges. He'd been too bleary to untangle what part of the Lowlands they were in, but now they stood at the highest point, looking down at the road curving out of sight into a densely wooded pass by a slender burn.

"Look," she whispered.

At the edge of the road stood a carriage.

"It's them." She guided the horse to a place out of sight. "That's one of Bridgewater's carriages."

Michael gazed at the carriage, so still, and a chill went through him. He could feel her worry. She had had the same thought he'd had. The horse flattened its ears and nickered unhappily.

A man in breeks and a cap burst from a tangle of briars near the carriage. He had a pistol in his hand.

She began to dismount and Michael caught her.

"*No,*" he said flatly. "Suicide."

The man opened the carriage door and began to speak, though they couldn't hear what he was saying.

"They're alive," she said.

"Someone is."

The carriage was a hundred yards ahead of them. They couldn't mount a sneak attack on horseback.

The only way was on foot, and the trees reached almost to where they stood.

"Through there," Michael said, pointing. "We'll be hidden. We'll have to leave the horse."

She slipped off and secured the ties.

Michael followed, landing on his good foot, but the first halting step on his other foot made him ill with pain.

"Let me look," she said, staring at his blood-soaked shoe.

The foot had swollen in the wet leather. "After," he said. "If I don't think about it too much—"

"If you don't think enough, you'll die."

"Well, there's a happy thought."

She met his eyes. "What can they do in your time?"

"Forget it."

"Michael, your wound is serious. I've seen men die from less. Will you die if you go home? You may die here."

"Not of the infection," he said sadly. "But I will of a broken heart."

She opened her mouth to argue but stopped, overcome. "Damn you," she said. "I don't want to cry. Not now." She swiped at her eyes angrily. "And I don't want you to leave. But ye can't ask me to watch you die. Ye can't."

He felt as if a knife was sawing him in two. "And you can't ask me to leave the only happiness I've known in years."

The carriage door slammed, and they turned. The man in the cap strode to the front and climbed on the driver's box. But instead of gathering the reins or picking up a whip, he stood up and looked down the road in one direction, then in the other.

"I recognize him," Undine said. "That's Tom, one of Morebright's servants. He's the one who told Morebright I was in the reception room."

"That's going to complicate things." Michael took a painful step forward. "I wonder what he's waiting for. Do you see that overhang?" Michael pointed to a rocky outcropping ten or fifteen feet above them, extending from the cleft of the hill beside them. "Let's see what we can see from up there."

They slipped quietly up the rocky slope—Michael, with his gasps and sharp inhales, considerably less quietly than Undine, who moved like a mountain goat, jumping from stone to stone.

At the top, they had a view that extended for miles, but the only people they saw were a few men fishing at the shore of the burn beyond the woods.

"What do we have in the way of weapons?" Michael asked.

"We have a spent pistol and no more balls or gunpowder. There's a sword on the saddle."

"We can't stop an ambush with that. Our best bet is to sneak down and free whoever's in there."

"And if the false clansmen arrive?"

The answer was obvious, and Undine sighed.

"Speed is our friend," Michael said. "Let's go before anyone else arrives."

He followed Undine as they made their way back down the side. When he got to the bottom, he heard a *click*.

Bridgewater grabbed Undine from behind and held

a pistol to her head. "Sorry to interrupt your plans with the carriage," he said. "Where's the letter?"

"Leave her alone," Michael said. "She doesn't know."

"Oh, she knows. Morebright's man found me at the church. He told me a very important letter went missing. Where is it?" he demanded, shaking her.

"I don't know what you're talking about," Undine said.

He swung her in front of him and boxed her jaw. "Does that help you remember?"

Michael leapt on Bridgewater's back, but Bridgewater jammed his boot on Michael's foot, sending searing bolts of pain through him. Michael crumpled, and the orange twist of paper flew out of his shirt pocket and beyond his reach.

He looked. Bridgewater hadn't seen it. But Undine had.

"Try that again," Bridgewater said, "and you'll have her brains all over you."

Bridgewater tied Undine to a tree with rope from the horse. He tightened the rope around her wrists until she gasped.

Michael's foot was bleeding profusely now, but all he could think about was Undine and Nab. Was Nab in that carriage? Did he have the papers? Would any of it matter? Michael pulled himself to sitting against a rock. The effort nearly made him pass out, but it brought him close enough to reach the orange paper.

Bridgewater was watching him, and his eyes narrowed.

Michael did everything he could to not let his gaze be drawn to the herbs.

A movement behind Bridgewater caught Michael's attention.

Nab looked at him over the edge of a boulder, eyes wide with alarm.

Two women stood behind him, peeking too—one old, one young. Nab pulled a folded piece of paper from his pocket and held it so Michael could see. Was it the show of a successful mission or the offer of a tool to use for a reprieve from his present circumstances? The question in Nab's eyes gave him the answer.

No. Michael made a barely perceptible shake of his head. The last thing he wanted was for three more people to be in danger.

Go, he mouthed.

Bridgewater grabbed a handful of Undine's hair and pulled her chin up. "Where is the goddamned letter?"

"I have it," Michael said.

"What?"

"The letter, you imbecile. You take your orders from a decrepit old lech now? I'm sure General Silverbridge will be happy to learn it. You pathetic fool."

Bridgewater's eyes glowed with fury. He released Undine and came to Michael. Michael braced himself, palms on the ground—one over the twist of paper. "Where is it?"

"You'll have to search me, I guess."

"I shall do that then," Bridgewater said, stepping on the hand under which the paper lay. "But perhaps you'd prefer just to tell me where it is."

The pain overwhelmed him, and Michael felt something in his hand snap. Bridgewater shoved his hand in Michael's shirt pocket. "Nothing there. Take off your plaid."

"I'll need my hand," Michael said.

"Use the other."

Michael unbelted the wool and it puddled to the sides of his shirttails. Bridgewater jerked the wool free and shook it. "Now your shoes."

Michael's heart fell.

"Take them off."

Michael extracted his throbbing hand from under Bridgewater's boot and pulled the shoe off his good foot with his good hand. The second had to be torn off his swollen foot. Michael swallowed a cry as the sodden leather came free.

Bridgewater checked the heels and then threw the shoes aside. "I don't see anything. Which leads me to believe the letter is somewhere much more interesting." He returned to Undine and cupped her breast.

"Ah, how I wished this could have happened in a more leisurely way. I would have enjoyed having those legs wrapped around me while I took my ease. But tied up will work nicely too." He tore the fabric of Undine's bodice open, exposing her breasts. "Nothing in there."

Michael grabbed the closest shoe and managed to peg Bridgewater in the head with it.

Bridgewater grabbed another length of rope from the horse, shoved Michael onto his stomach and tied his wrists.

Michael wished he were dead. He knew soon he would be. He thought Bridgewater would keep Undine alive, though he wondered if that would be worse for her than dying. He rolled to his side and began to work the rope. He'd played Houdini once in a play that had closed after three performances. He'd spent more time learning the lines than he had in front of an audience on that one, but he remembered quite clearly a trick that had involved escaping from bonds using the rope's slack.

Bridgewater searched Undine roughly—down her thighs, under her skirts, and thoroughly within her bodice. The pleasure Michael would have expected him to take in this seemed to be replaced by fear as each potential hiding place was found to be empty. Bridgewater searched the horse next.

"Where is it?" he demanded. "*Where?*"

He raised the pistol to Undine's head, but before he pointed the barrel, he came to a stop. "The *boy*," he said, realization exploding on his face. "*He's* got it."

Bridgewater looked at them both and must have seen the truth on their faces. He began to pelt down the road toward the carriage.

"He can't go down there," Undine said.

"Nab's safe. He's in the rocks over there. He has the letter. Nab!"

"Thank the skies! But we still can't let Bridgewater go there. The clansmen… Oh, Michael, you have to stop him."

Michael, who had far less interest in protecting Bridgewater from his hired clansmen than she did, felt a piece of the knot give.

"Where is he?" a voice demanded.

Michael turned. The duke stood beside the horse Undine had stolen. He saw the front of Undine's gown and averted his eyes, muttering an oath.

"Who?" Michael said. "Bridgewater?"

"I don't give a damn about Bridgewater," the general said angrily. "At this point, you're as much of a problem to the army as he is." He went to the back of the tree and began to untie Undine. "I want to find your colleague—the one with the letter. Or was that a lie too?"

"Don't say a word, Undine," Michael said. "The letter may be our only leverage."

"You'll need it," the duke said. "You're both under arrest. You've ruined a critical operation and destroyed what may be our only chance for peace. You're under arrest until I decide what to do with you, though I'm tempted to give you both to the rebels. You'd not like what they do to traitors."

"*Michael*," Undine said urgently, looking at the carriage.

Did she truly wish to save Bridgewater? Then Michael remembered the other servants, the people the carriage driver was talking to.

The loop slipped free. He clawed his way to his feet and ran, fueled by Undine's desire, as his body was too battered to carry on, on its own. Bridgewater had taken the road, but Michael followed the path through the trees, which he hoped would let him reach the carriage a few seconds earlier. Every other step was like a hot spike in his flesh. He heard the sounds of men's voices coming from the direction of the burn. And he heard the crack of wood on wood as Bridgewater flung open the door of the carriage. He wouldn't be first, but he may still be able to stop him.

Two men stepped out from behind a tree in front

of him, one with a pistol. Michael recognized one as Tom, the servant at Morebright's estate.

"What do you think you're doing, laddie?" Tom said.

"We have to get to the carriage," Michael said. "Bridgewater's in trouble."

Tom laughed a brutal laugh. "Bridgewater's at the army camp with the general."

"Kill him," the other man said.

In one part of his head, Michael heard labored thrashing through the trees behind him and Undine crying, "Stop, Tom!" In another, he heard voices of the clansmen near the carriage. "There it is," one said.

What he hadn't expected was the electric shock of the ball tearing through his side or the charred, fleshy scent of the smoke that wove its way around him like a death shroud. He fell to his knees, then onto his face.

He knew he was dying.

"Michael," Undine cried, her voice cutting through the slow-motion pain. "Go *home*. Please. Do it for me."

Her face, so beautiful, and the duke's behind it. He had a vague sense of something in his hand. He looked and almost smiled. The orange paper. Had she even told him how to use it? Then he remembered.

He lifted the paper, tore it open with his teeth, and shook it as the world went black.

The last thing he heard was a barrage of pistol shots and a terrified scream.

Fifty-nine

PALE SHADES OF PINK AND GOLD. THE COLORS OF HER skin. The softness of her touch. The luxurious cascade of her hair. His mind, unhinged from the exigencies of the real world, flitted among the slivers of joy, painful and pleasing. Tumbling aimlessly. Adrift. Alone.

"Mr. Kent?"

He jerked to attention in his seat in the front row.

"Are you ready?"

As ready as he'd ever be. His foot throbbed and itched in equal measure. Healing. *Ha.* Returning to its former state, perhaps, but not healing. Nothing would ever be healed.

The hole in his side was different. His chest was empty and aching. As if a part of him was missing. *That* he would feel forever. He stuffed his hand in his pocket and clutched the embroidered handkerchief. With a sigh, he adjusted his foot on the folding chair before him.

Eve, who'd been watching him closely—she'd been watching him closely since his return from the hospital a week ago—sat down beside him.

"Pretty weird having you disappear right in the middle of *Romeo and Juliet*," she said, voicing at last what had clearly been on her mind since his return.

"It was irresponsible, and I'm very sorry. I think what you'd call it is a breakdown. Between Deirdre and the responsibilities of the theater…" He damned himself for using Deirdre's death as an excuse, but he thought she wouldn't mind.

"Okay, that I can buy," Eve said, "though how you did it in front of hundreds of people, I'll never understand."

"It was a simple magic trick. I was out of my senses. I'm sorry. I know I left you holding the bag."

Eve gave him an interested look. "But that's not even the weirdest part. The weirdest part is you return after several days and collapse onstage, barely dressed, long after the theater has closed for the evening, and you've apparently been stabbed *and* shot."

Michael had refused to allow his surgeon to say anything about his condition to her, and Michael himself had been closemouthed. Eve was guessing. But then again, she was the one who'd found him and called the ambulance.

"I've been sort of embarrassed about it," he said, "but to be honest, I didn't even notice. Yes, I'd had my wallet stolen, which I also hadn't noticed. But the guy must have had a knife too. It felt like a stitch in my side. I guess it was worse than I thought."

"And he stabbed your foot?" Eve said, crossing her arms.

"I think he'd been considering stealing my loafers too. Balenciaga, you know. I can't explain it. People are strange."

"Uh-huh. You know what's even stranger? I gave the ambulance driver your wallet."

Shite.

The next actress walked into the middle of the stage. Michael knew before she began that she wasn't right. Helen of Troy needed to be both striking and imperious—the sort of woman men would fight a war for, the sort of woman a man would do anything for. That wasn't something that could be acted. One had to be born with it. Only one or two women he'd ever met had it…

The woman started her piece. "Not even close," Michael said flatly to Eve.

"Thank you," Eve called when the woman finished. "We'll be in touch." Then to Michael: "That's the forty-third actress you've dismissed one line in. At least five of them were great, and one was freaking perfect. What's going on?"

"They don't have the presence to play Helen," he said. "It takes gravitas and bearing and the sort of mythical beauty that—"

"Fine. You're back. You're recovering. And you've decided to stay in London and become the most miserable director to work with on earth. Got it. Well, we have one more actress to see today—and she happens to be great. I saw her in *Three Sisters* last year. But I'm sure you'll hate her, so I guess I'll call a different casting agent and ask for another round for tomorrow."

"She needs to be perfect."

"Sounds like an unwinnable quest."

Eve motioned for the next actress, and Michael bent to readjust his foot.

"Primrose Longacre?" Eve said loudly, reading from her list.

"Jesus Christ," Michael muttered. "I hate her already."

"No," the woman said. "My name is Undine."

Michael unbent.

Undine stood next to a confused redhead who clutched a script.

"*I'm* Primrose Longacre," the redhead said.

"And my assistant director here says you'll be perfect," Michael said, shocked into a happiness he could barely express. "Eve," he said, the script falling as he stood, "would you cover the contract details with Ms. Longacre while I…" He hobbled to the stage with all the speed he could manage, where Undine—in jeans!—met him in a violent and unbreakable embrace at the bottom of the stairs.

"I thought you were dead," she said, crying.

"I wished I were. Where were you? What happened?"

"Slow down," she said, smiling and burying herself deeper in his arms. "We have all the time we could want."

Sixty

THEY WERE DRESSED—BRIEFLY—LONG ENOUGH TO EAT the fine Catalonian sardines the landlady had left outside their door. Beyond their window, the Mediterranean waves rose and crashed under a cloudless blue sky.

Per als joves en l'amor, the landlady had said. *For young lovers.* Michael made a private smile. Not so young. But definitely in love.

"Tell me again." He watched with a shiver as Undine sucked the salty oil from her fingers.

"How many times do you want to hear it?"

"Until I can truly believe you're here with me."

"I told you the home spell I'd created for you was powerful. I was very angry, you'll recall."

"Oh, I recall."

"If it worked like I'd planned for it to work, you and everyone nearby would have been transported to their home. You came back here. Tom would have been transported to whatever rat hole he crawled out of. Nab would have gone to his parents' cottage in Langholm, and the women with him—who were they, I wonder? Servants, I suppose—to their homes.

The duke was probably dropped right in the middle of his castle, and I, of course—"

"Went to Pittsburgh. Why didn't you tell me you were from the future?"

She tucked her hair behind her ear. Turned out the Barcelonan humidity brought out the waves in it.

"The future never felt like my home. 'Twas my mother's home as a child, and she returned there after I was born and her husband left us. His last name was—well, I suppose that's not important. But she certainly wasn't going to have me use Murray, the name of the man who raped her. So we took the name Douglas, her maiden name, and lived a quiet life. When she died when I was eleven, I was going to be taken to a foster home. Do you know what that is?"

He nodded, thinking sadly about the bereft young girl.

"And I didn't want that. So I went back. She'd shown me how. She'd always been honest with me about her past. I think when she got ill, she wanted me to have a choice."

"And you went back to 1706, alone, at eleven?"

"An old spells woman in Drumburgh took me in. I cleaned for her and tended her goats. She taught me what she knew. I had a natural talent for spells. My mother—"

"Was a naiad. Yes." He grinned, hardly able to believe his luck. The lines of the Screamin' Jay Hawkins song went through Michael's love- and lust-addled head. It was hard to concentrate when he knew what dessert was going to be.

"The trouble was, when I landed in Pittsburgh this

time, I didn't know anything. I was only eleven when I left. I didn't know how to use the new phones or computers. It took me a long time to figure out where you might be, and even when I did, I had no money to get to you or papers to allow me to travel. So I had to figure out a way to earn them."

"Oh dear," he said, imagining the many things that a man might be willing to pay for where Undine was concerned.

"You have a dirty mind," she said, adding brightly, "Did I say that right? That's what the woman next to me on the plane said."

"Got it in one." He stroked her hand with his thumb. "And Bridgewater?" He was the one person Michael hadn't been able to bring himself to ask her about. He'd heard the pistol shots as he'd disappeared.

"Dead, I hope."

"Do you?" He touched her chin, so perfectly round. She shook her head. "No, not really. Michael, I need to tell you something."

His heart caught. He wasn't going to like it. "What?"

"I love you, and I never want to leave your side…"

"But?"

"But I want to go back. This," she said with a gesture that took in the rented flat, the sardines, Michael, and the deep-blue, sun-soaked sea, "is wonderful, but I need to be useful."

He pulled her into his arms. "As do I. I know where we can go."

Sixty-one

"I KNEW YOU'D BE HERE!" ABBY CRIED, SPYING UNDINE'S reflection in her bedchamber mirror. She spun like a top and threw her arms around her old friend. "I knew you wouldn't miss today!"

"Today?" Undine had expected an astonished Abby to exclaim "I thought you were dead!" Not this.

"For the *wedding*!"

"*What?*" Michael looked at Duncan, who lifted his palms happily.

"We're getting married today," Abby said, gesturing to her intricately beaded gown, though it was no more or less beautiful than the gowns she wore any other day, Undine thought. "In just a few minutes, in fact. When I woke up today, I got on my knees and prayed for you to come back."

"That doesn't sound like something you'd do," Undine said, skeptical.

"Fine," Abby said. "I drank my coffee and read the broadsheet and prayed for you to come back. But I did pray for you to come back. That is the point. Duncan thought you were dead—"

"I did *not*," Duncan said, trying to flatten the starched lace jabot that reached all the way to his freshly brushed hair. "I said I thought she was 'as good as dead,' at least to us. Why would anyone with the powers she has come back *here*?" He elbowed Michael. "You, on the other hand, I was sure were dead."

"Sorry to disappoint."

Duncan shrugged good-naturedly. "Life can be cruel to Arsenal supporters."

"I'm afraid not everyone will be as happy as I am to see your return," Abby said. "There's a warrant out for your arrest."

Undine had expected that, so the news didn't surprise her.

"I tried to talk the general out of it," Abby said, adjusting a curl that had fallen from its pin. "You know how charming I can be."

"And how much English officers enjoy the company of clan chiefs with favors to ask," Duncan put in.

"But the general wouldna be persuaded. He did mention that he would, and I quote, 'give a lot of money to be able to harness the power of that bloody woman.' He ended up in Plymouth, by the way. It seems his family also has a more southerly estate—*far* more southerly—at which he spent his youth. He was verra discommoded. It took him a week to get back here."

Oh dear.

"And Bridgewater?" Undine asked, hesitant.

Michael squeezed her hand.

Abby's smile faded. "Dead. Shot by one of the false clansmen he himself had hired. But General

Silverbridge knows everything that transpired with that blackguard and his miscreant friend Morebright."

"Bridgewater wasn't transported?"

"If you mean his soul to hell," Duncan said, "then maybe. But his body was lying in the carriage. He was buried in the Bridgewater family crypt."

"The home spell doesn't work on someone who's dead," Undine said. "He must have died the instant before the herbs took effect. Was he alone in the carriage?" she asked Duncan.

"Aye," Duncan said. "But one death will be enough to hang Tom and 'the clansmen.'"

"What about Morebright?" Michael asked. "Has he been arrested?"

Duncan snorted. "A nobleman?"

"Take care, my dear," Abby said. "You shall be the husband of a noblewoman verra soon."

"Noblewomen are quite another matter," Duncan said.

"Nab ended up somewhere safe?" Michael asked lightly, but Undine recognized the concern in the words.

"Ask him yourself," Duncan said.

Undine turned.

Nab ran in, holding a piece of cheese in front of an energetic Russian wolfhound. The lad wore a red plaid, a green velvet coat, and a gleaming short sword, and when he saw Undine and Michael, he jerked to a stop, mouth open. "You're *back*."

"We certainly weren't going to miss the big day," Michael said, tousling the boy's hair.

Undine felt the last worry slip from her heart.

"Grendel, sit." Abby smiled. "Michael, meet the newest member of Clan Kerr." She gestured to Nab.

"And my best man," Duncan said.

Nab flushed and gave them a deep bow.

"Nab's the reason we know anything about what happened that day. He's been given a citation for bravery from General Silverbridge."

"How did you get out of that carriage?" Michael asked.

"'Twas an easy matter," the boy said, rubbing Grendel's ears. "Grace—that's Eliza the cook's daughter—she was in the carriage with me, and she said she needed to take a piss—"

Duncan cleared his throat.

"Fine," Nab said. "She said she needed to use the chamber pot—in the woods." He rolled his eyes. "I think she knew they were holding me against my will. So she hid. And then they sent her mother to look for her. That left me and Harry and George. And then I escaped, partly because I wanted to eat the plum she'd given me but also because they were pissing me off."

"How did you get out?" Michael said.

"*Och*, easy. I told them I was going to puke—and I did. Just stuck my finger down my throat. I saw my uncle do it once when he'd had too much to drink. Everyone wanted out of the carriage then. Then I heard you making a stramash with that stinking arsehole Bridgewater—"

"*Ladies present*," Duncan said.

"It's nae bother," Abby said. "Nab's been offered the position of scout under the general, which, if he knows what's good for him, he won't be taking."

"*Och*, no," Nab said. "I think I'd like to stay near Kerr Castle."

"Your loyalty to the Kerr cause will be rewarded, I'm sure," Michael said.

"In this case, I think loyalty may be overshadowed by a slightly different emotion," Abby said. "Grace is going to be my new lady's maid."

"Oh," Undine said.

"Ohhh," Michael said.

Nab turned seven shades of red.

"It's a verra fulfilling quest, by the way," Duncan said, pouring four very generous glasses of whiskey and one smaller one. "May you enjoy it."

"Though I would plan on taking a good long time," Michael said. "There's a wealth of pleasure to be had in the journey."

Duncan distributed the drinks and lifted his glass. "To the journey."

"To the journey!"

"Speaking of that," Duncan said, "how did you manage your return?"

"That's an interesting story. Once Undine decided she wanted to return, we were a bit at a loss as to how to do it without her herbs. Then I remembered a fellow who knew the secret recipe, as it were. Hang on, would you?"

Michael slipped out of the room and returned a moment later with the man who'd not only showed them the patch of the magical twinflowers, but had also insisted on returning with them.

"Grandda!" Duncan's face broke into a huge smile, and he took his grandfather in a tight embrace.

"I told him you'd managed to win the hand of the smartest and most beautiful clan chief in Scotland," Michael said. "He said, '*My* Duncan? I'll have to see it to believe it.'"

Duncan's grandfather said, "Oh, lad, how I've missed ye." Then he took Abby's hands and squeezed them. "Michael was right, though. You *are* a bonny lass."

Serafina and Gerard, also in their best clothes, appeared in the doorway.

"What's all th—?" She spotted Undine and Michael, and her lip started to quiver. "You're alive!"

"There's the reaction I was expecting." Undine held out her arms, and Serafina flew into them.

Gerard thumped Michael on the back. "She just couldn't shake you, could she?"

After a long moment, Undine released Serafina and saw the shock on Duncan's grandfather's face.

"You're the…the dead spit of her," he said.

The "her" Duncan's grandfather referred to was the red-haired woman with whom he had fallen in love a score of years earlier when he had traveled into Scotland's past. Their relationship had produced Serafina, though, as Undine knew, Duncan's grandfather had returned to the twenty-first century before the pregnancy had been discovered. When Duncan had uncovered this surprising relationship, he'd told Serafina, but Duncan's grandfather hadn't known the truth—until now.

Duncan cleared his throat. "Grandda, I'd like you to meet Serafina Fallon Innes. Serafina, this is your father."

The three gingers took turns hugging and crying, while Grendel ran happily in circles around their feet and Gerard, Michael, and Nab laughed.

Undine found herself grinning like a fool. Abby elbowed her. "I haven't had this much excitement in my bedchamber since Duncan's first days here."

"We picked well, my friend."

They clinked glasses.

"Why did you come back?" Abby asked. "I was certain you'd find each other in the future."

Undine knew the one person with whom she'd shared the story of her childhood travails would not forget. "I could hardly leave you alone," Undine murmured, "not when you're with child. Does Duncan know?"

Abby nodded. "He's verra pleased."

"I'm with child too," she said, trying without success to rein in her joy.

"Pardon? What?" Michael said. "Who's with child?"

"I am no director," Abby said, "but I know a cue when I hear one." She gave Undine a kiss on the cheek and slipped away.

"Did I just hear what I thought I heard?"

Undine gazed at him imperiously. "When you are present for the laying of the groundwork, the appearance of the house shouldn't come as a surprise."

"Oh, really? Is that an old naiad saying? And if it is, shouldn't it be 'dam' or something?"

"It's so small," she said more quietly. "But the magic is quite powerful. I have no doubts."

He put his arms around her waist and kissed her. "I can't think of anything more wonderful."

Abby, who had been laughing with her guests, suddenly whooped.

"Undine," she cried, "I just realized you're a countess! On your own! And your son—Is the child a son?"

"So much for secrets," Undine said under her breath to Michael. "Aye, I believe it is."

"Your son will be Lord Bridgewater!" Abby clapped.

The guests in the room blinked for an instant. The realization that her and Michael's child would technically be considered the child of John Bridgewater was rather startling. But when Michael smiled, they cheered.

"It seems Michael's training as Orlando Brashnettle, senior wizard, paid off," Gerard said. "He's pulled a lordship for his son out of his hat."

Undine wheeled. "I *knew* you were a wizard!"

"Only in my dreams," Michael said, head spinning. "I'm hoping you can teach me a thing or two."

"I have no doubt," Abby said.

When the excitement settled, Undine pulled Michael aside.

"Is that something you could bear?" she asked under her breath. "To raise our son as John Bridgewater's? If it's not, then I shall take you to a place where none of this will matter. If it is, we must live as secret lovers for at least a year until we can marry. But I can tell you that wielding the power of one of England's oldest families will allow me to do even more to help the rebels."

"What about the warrant?"

"I have a suspicion the duke would be willing to throw that out if I offer him the chance to harness a bit of my power."

Michael's brows went up. "You'd help an English general?"

"So long as he worked for peace. So what do you say? My only priority is to be with you, so the choice has to be yours."

Michael pursed his lips. "Would we live in Bridgewater's castle?"

"Aye. Or his townhome in London or the hunting lodge in Derbyshire or the horse farm in Galway. They have money and lots of it."

"Then I believe I could bear it quite nicely. Tell me, what sort of activities would be entailed in being 'secret lovers'? Might it include stolen hours in the open fields of the borderlands? Hand-to-hand encounters in linen closets? Or perhaps something even more salacious?"

"There are certain things a noblewoman doesn't stoop to."

He pulled her into his arms. "But there are other things the secret lover of an unemployed director *does*."

"*Och*," Nab said. "They're kissing again."

"Come, come," Abby said. "I should not like to be late for my own wedding. Undine, I am eager to hear what the future holds. Tell me things that will make me long to see it."

Undine slipped her arm around Michael's waist and squeezed. "Two words, my friend. Yoga pants."

Acknowledgments

I want to thank my colleagues at Mindful Writers, especially Madhu Bazaz Wangu. Your hard work and focus provide me much-needed inspiration. Thank you as well to Meredith Mileti, Teri Coyne, Todd DePastino, Vince Raus, and Mitchell Kaplan. It's such a gift to be able to share triumphs and travails with people who understand. I owe special debts of gratitude to Trevor Swan at the Coldstream Historical Society, who supplied me with a wealth of enormously helpful information about the state of things in eighteenth-century Coldstream, and Mike Egan, stage manager extraordinaire, who provided invaluable insights into the workings of a professional theater company. Any errors in the book regarding these subjects are mine. Gene Mollica, your covers are to die for. Thank you to everyone at Sourcebooks, especially Deb Werksman. You make me look good and that ain't always easy. Claudia Cross, I am in awe of your amazing superpowers. I think you've had an opportunity to use every single one of them on my behalf in the last year. Lester, Cameron, Wyatt, and Jean, you are my great reward.

About the Author

Gwyn Cready is the author of nine romance novels. She's been called "the master of time travel romance" and is the winner of a RITA Award, the most prestigious award given in romance writing. She has two grown children and lives with her husband in Pittsburgh.

Just in Time for a Highlander
by Gwyn Cready

❧

For Duncan MacHarg, things just got real

Battle reenactor and financier Duncan MacHarg thinks he has it made—until he lands in the middle of a real Clan Kerr battle and comes face-to-face with their beautiful, spirited leader. Out of time and out of place, Duncan must use every skill he can muster to earn his position among the clansmen and in the heart of the devastatingly intriguing woman to whom he must pledge his oath.

Abby needs a hero, and she needs him now

When Abigail Ailich Kerr sees a handsome, mysterious stranger materialize in the midst of her clan's skirmish with the English, she's stunned to discover he's the strong arm she's been praying for. Instead of a tested fighter, the fierce young chieftess has been given a man with no measurable battle skills and a damnably distracting smile. And the only way to get rid of him is to turn him into a Scots warrior herself—one demanding and intimate lesson at a time.

❧

First Time with a Highlander
by Gwyn Cready

She needs a man—but only for one night

What do you get when you imbibe centuries-old whiskey—besides a hangover the size of the Highlands? If you're twenty-first-century ad exec Gerard Innes, you get swept back to eighteenth-century Edinburgh and into the bed of a gorgeous, fiery redhead. Gerard has only a foggy idea what he and the lady have been up to…but what he does remember draws him into the most dangerous and exhilarating campaign of his life.

Be careful what you wish for…

Serafina Seonag Fallon's scoundrel of a fiancé has left her with nothing, and she's determined to turn the tables. If she can come up with a ringer, she can claim the cargo he stole from her. But the dashing man she summons from the future demands more than one night, and Serafina finds it easier to command the seas under her feet than the crashing waves he unleashes in her heart.

Praise for Gwyn Cready:

"Gwyn Cready does a marvelous job of creating strong and sexy characters that stand out." —*Fresh Fiction*

For more Gwyn Cready, visit:
www.sourcebooks.com

Flirting with Forever
by Gwyn Cready

--- ❧ ---

Campbell Stratford hopes her biography of court painter Anthony van Dyck will give her the credibility she needs to land her dream job as a museum curator. One day, while doing research on Van Dyck and his successor, Peter Lely, Cam is abruptly transported to Lely's studio in 1673.

Peter is intrigued by the mysterious newcomer who is definitely more than she makes out to be—but then again, Peter has strange secrets of his own. The uneasy friends become star-crossed lovers when the centuries part them once more, forcing them to choose which they believe in: fate or true love.

--- ❧ ---

"Entertaining and lively…will leave readers breathless." —*Publishers Weekly* Starred Review

For more Gwyn Cready, visit:
www.sourcebooks.com

Timeless Desire
by Gwyn Cready

———— ✦ ————

Two years after losing her husband, librarian Panna Kennedy is reluctantly reentering the terrifying world of dating—but she accidentally enters a portal through time instead.

Flung back in time to 1705 Scotland, she finds herself in the massive library of her hero, Colonel John Bridgewater, and meets his brother Jamie, currently accused of being a Scots spy. Torn between loyalty to her hero from history, her feelings for her late husband, and her blossoming love for Jamie, Panna faces a choice that may alter the course of time forever.

———— ✦ ————